COMPASS
POINTS

COMPASS POINTS BOOK I

COMPASS POINTS

JILLIAN WITT

Published by Myth and Magic Book Club Publishing
Copyright © 2023 by Jillian Witt

Cover Artwork & Map by Holly Dunn
Developmental Editing by Rebecca Faith Editorial
Line Editing by Melissa Frain
Proofreading by Hilary Turner

ISBN (paperback): 979-8-9885603-1-9
ISBN (hardcover): 979-8-9885603-2-6
eISBN: 979-8-9885603-0-2

ALSO FROM JILLIAN WITT

Compass Points (Compass Points #1)

Tangled Power (Compass Points #2) – Coming Spring 2024

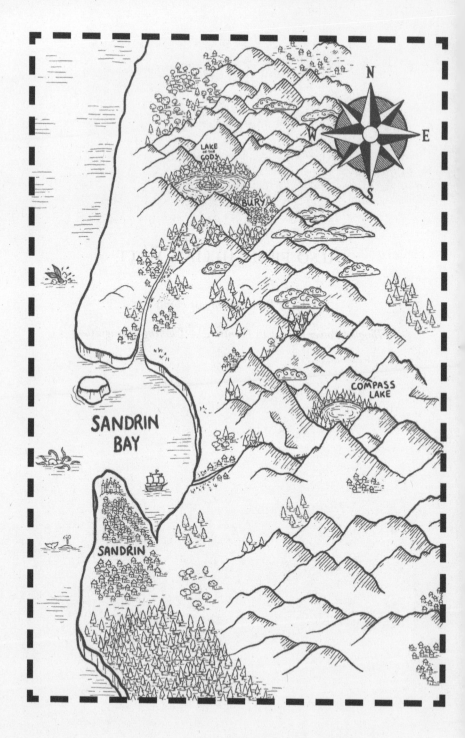

For Ian; who always wondered how he got into conversations about building worlds and sexual tension, but never left them.

CHAPTER ONE

Rose carefully tucked the cash and coin into her market belt. It sat low on her hips over her long tunic, leggings, and sturdy boots. She tucked a strand of her shoulder-length hair behind her ear as she finished the transaction with the man standing before her.

"Slow market day today?" the man asked as he once again tested the grip of his new axe.

"A little," Rose said with a noncommittal tone. She didn't want to voice what everyone was thinking: Customers were getting too scared to leave their homes. Though the stalls were filled with most of the usual villagers selling their wares, vegetables, soaps, lotions, and more, the aisles of shoppers were sparse.

"I heard the mist plague took another village, the one just north of here last week."

Rose nodded. The news had made its way up to Bury, the village atop the lake-filled mountain crater. From the conversations she'd overheard so far this morning, the villagers were definitely starting to worry. Rose supposed she was worried too; she was just uninterested in spending all her time talking about things over which she had no control. The mist plague had been slowly seeping onto the continent for years. Slow enough that most ignored it since it didn't impact their daily lives. Recently, the mist seemed to be growing in confidence, a danger that was making itself harder and harder to pretend didn't exist.

"If the Suden Point doesn't come up with some answers soon, the other Compass Points will have to do something about him."

Rose attempted to cover her laugh with a cough. If the rumors were true, the current Suden Point was one of the most powerful fae in generations. Even if he was responsible for the mist plague, which Rose doubted, she wasn't sure the other three Compass Points could do anything about it.

"I heard he's been at every village taken by the plague." The owner of the stall next to Rose stepped in to engage in the customer's conversation.

"I heard that none of the villages that claim Aterra as a patron god have been attacked either! So if you worship the Suden fae's god, you might be safe," the customer said.

She let their voices blend into the market around her. Rose had no love for the Compass Points, but claiming that the Suden Point was responsible for this mist plague seemed a stretch. She wasn't even sure that he *was* Suden Point when the first reports of the mist started. She was also pretty sure that the Compass Points had assigned him to investigate the mist plague, hence why he was at every village, but not many were interested in facts like those when they were starting to panic.

With the customer gone, Rose felt a flap of wings and a familiar weight settle on her shoulder.

"Arie, I was looking for you earlier. Why didn't you show up in your bear form to help me carry the supplies?" She spoke in a low whisper to the bird. She'd been selling at the market for years. At this point, most villagers accepted her as strange but harmless. That didn't mean she liked to emphasize that she talked to various animals regularly.

"I was busy and knew you could handle it, Rose. You're always going on about how tough you are," he said directly to her mind. She turned

her head to glare at the bird. She didn't know how to categorize Arie. He wasn't a Vesten, a shifter, in the traditional sense. He had no human form, or at least none he had ever shown her. He swapped animal forms often, though. Today's large black bird was one of his favorites.

"Is that code for not feeling up to any manual labor today? What happened to my big strong protector?" she teased.

"Like you need one." The bird's head swiveled around at her market booth and the beautiful and deadly weapons on display. He flicked his feathers at the side of her face. *"Sometimes you're too good at letting people underestimate you."*

Rose knew Arie was observant, and he'd had plenty of time to watch her interactions. He had been with her since she fled her past life ten years ago. He'd helped her then and continued to show up and help her now, whether she wanted it or not.

"So, will you tell me where you were this morning?" she asked as casually as she could. She hated to follow up on the question, hating the idea of need lacing her words, but he'd been disappearing for longer spaces of time recently.

"I was preparing us for this morning's market, checking newcomers from the surrounding villages, seeing if any were going to try and hike up the crater to Bury. As you can see, not many were willing to make the trip with the rising fear of the mist plague." He rambled on, but his words rang hollow. She knew this for the brush-off that it was.

"Fine. Keep your secrets, Arie. I have some of my own, too." There. She was happy with that reply. No clinging desperation in her tone. Hard to believe that, after initially wanting nothing to do with him or anyone else, she'd gotten so used to having him around.

He pecked at the side of her head. *"Rose, I'm not abandoning you. Just allow me to do my research. I'll let you know if it becomes important."*

She let out a small breath as she scanned the surrounding area looking for her student and friend, Tara. She must have taken longer at the temple's morning prayers than usual.

The Bury Village town square sat on the edge of a gorgeous lake. She couldn't help but laugh at herself every time she surveyed the deep blue waters. She just couldn't get away from living on a lake. The Lake of the Gods, as it was called, was a massive attraction to locals and travelers. The deep, spring-fed, clear waters were that of legends.

"You weren't trying to access the lake, were you?" She laughed. The lake itself was said to have celestial properties, channeling the powers of the gods. The problem was that no one could touch the lake to prove it.

"You know I gave up on that years ago." He ruffled his feathers. When they first arrived, Rose had watched him obsess about trying to touch the lake's water. She knew he hated the reminder that he'd failed at something.

"Whatever you say, Arie. I believe you." She shot him a wink. This was much more familiar ground between them.

She gazed at the lake-filled crater and let the morning sun fall on her white skin as a few more villagers walked by the market stall. She could easily make out the small island from here on the far side of the lake. She couldn't wait to go home. She felt like she'd been on her feet for hours.

She focused again on the villagers passing her stand and tried smiling and nodding to those who walked past. Approachable. She needed to ensure she was approachable, not daydreaming about the magical mysteries of the lake. She casually nodded to the Dawson family across the market's hastily made aisles. They sold the vegetables they grew. Next to them, the Turner family displayed their homemade soaps and lotions.

Rose let go of the thought of getting off her feet when she heard a voice in front of her booth. She knew Arie was gone before she looked. The warm weight had lifted from her shoulder. He never was one for goodbyes.

"Excuse me," came a silky-smooth voice that sent heat through her entire body. "Do you know where I can find the weapons master?"

Rose finished her scan of the active market to see if she could see Arie flying off somewhere, then took in the newcomer standing in front of her booth.

"Can I help you with something?" she replied, crossing her arms over her chest. She had little tolerance for those who assumed she couldn't be the weapons master, but it served her current purpose.

"I don't think so." He let his lip curve, easing over his initial harsh expression, drastically changing the man before her. He had olive skin, dark black hair, and a face that was all hard lines and sharp features. But the smile he presented was the real weapon. It was meant to disarm and entice, and she dug her nails into her palm behind her stall to stop the effect from taking over. "I need to speak with the weapons master. It's an urgent matter."

It was unlikely a handsome human could have this type of effect on her. She took a deep breath and tried to sort out what this meant. She couldn't panic. She'd interacted with fae before. She'd just not encountered many in Bury, even with the draw of the mythical lake. That was part of the reason she settled here. The area had a wild magic that the fae tended to avoid.

"I am sorry," she replied, her face lighting up as she leaned into the ruse of falling for his allure. "I'm the only one here. If it's urgent, you should give me some details, and I can see how I can help."

His eyes darkened, pinching in a small movement that most would have missed. He sighed as he clearly wanted something and saw no other options. "I'd like to place a custom order."

Well, that was interesting. Rose took custom orders, but few knew it, and she didn't take them from just anyone. This meant someone sought her for her ability to imbue weapons with magic—a weapon tailored to their fae court.

No one in Bury knew she could forge magical weapons.

Weapon makers like her were more sensitive to the magic around them. They could push and shape it into a weapon. Not only did these weapons make the wielders incredibly powerful, but understanding a magic's source, a fae court's element, meant a trip to Compass Lake, which she avoided like the plague of mist.

Though this at least helped explain why a fae stood before her. More curious now, she continued to survey her customer. He was tall and lean, though he didn't appear overly muscled. She could tell by how he held himself that his body was dangerously honed, a weapon to be used, just like his smile.

She stared hard into his eyes, such a dark brown they looked almost black, and made a gut decision. Not that it was hard; she never did custom orders for someone she didn't know.

"We can't take any custom orders currently," she said as a standard reply. She didn't know this person and had no intention of giving him the level of power that her custom weapons granted. A quick flash of red passed over his pupils in the sunlight. She would have missed it in a blink, but there was no mistaking what she'd seen.

"And why, may I ask, have I been so quickly dismissed?" he almost whispered through gritted teeth.

"I'm not sure who told you we do custom orders, but they are quite a time investment for us. We're a small shop and have plenty of demand for our standard wares," she replied with a courteous and logical explanation.

"I come highly recommended," he said.

"By whom?" This should cut their conversation to the chase. She knew that she had won when she caught another flash of red in his gaze, a sure indication that his anger was rising. She should be more worried. But he only stared at her like he couldn't figure out what to do with her, then gave a terse nod and left to continue through the market stalls.

She knew one thing for sure: This customer was earth fae. He was of the Suden fae court.

Chapter Two

She couldn't tell if the fae knew she had identified him during their conversation. Either way, she was in trouble. Suden fae were no joke. They were known for earth magic but were also, as most of the fae were, quite charming and seductive. Few knew that the most dangerous power wielded by earth fae was a type of mind shadow, seeping in and covering up memories with little more than a touch. Thankfully those terrifying powers hadn't been seen in generations.

Rose considered what her earlier customer had said. The current Suden Point, the earth fae leader, was the youngest in the five-hundred-year history of the fae courts to take a Compass Point position. He hadn't had to take the Suden Point position by force, either. Most said that made him all the more dangerous.

He was either very dangerous or very powerful. Probably both.

Suden fae's eyes only gave off red flares when they felt extreme emotions. Her rejection of his custom order had jolted him. Since this fae's sharp and stunning features gave nothing away, it was impossible to know whether he was aware of the flare.

He at least knew his anger was rising. That's likely why he left so abruptly. It didn't matter. She knew what she was dealing with, and knowing that she stood between a fae and his goals meant she needed to prepare.

Though experienced with fae, Rose didn't know how badly this one wanted the magical weapon. Her weapons enhanced a magic wielder's natural powers. A custom order was always both risky to take and risky to complete.

How had he found out about her in the first place? Her life had changed irrevocably before she could make a name for herself as a magical blacksmith, and in the last ten years, she'd only made magical weapons with the wild magic around Lake of the Gods.

She contemplated all the possible ways that today's interaction would blow up in her face as Tara walked up to the booth, slipping behind the counter with no invitation needed. She was already pulling her long, light brown hair back from her pale skin and securing it with a tie. The market started and ended early. It was barely midday, but at least Tara had made it to help her pack up.

"You were late today," Rose said. She bent down to lift the box of supplies she had to carry home.

"Sorry about that. I got lost in my morning meditation," Tara said.

"I figured." Rose paused, watching Tara twist the circular wave pendant, Aurora's emblem, that she wore around her neck. She seemed to have more on her mind.

"Are you worried about the mist plague?" Tara asked.

Rose hesitated over her words. "Of course, Tara. I know the mist plague is terrifying, especially since there seems to be no rhyme or reason to its attacks." Rose looked meaningfully at the younger girl. "I like how you dealt with your fear, though. When you were scared of the mist and wanted to do something, you asked me to train you. While we still don't know if that will help, learning to defend yourself is within your control and can help you in life regardless."

"And to think you tried to say no when I first asked. Listen to you now," Tara teased.

"I was being cautious," Rose replied. "Weapons training is no joke. I wanted to make sure you knew what you were getting into."

"And I've more than proved that these past months!" Tara jumped in energetically. "We train for hours with no break. I was dead on my feet in our session last night but kept pushing! I don't think I would have been capable of such effort months ago."

Tara's excitement and self-realization of her improvement brought a warmth to Rose's heart that she was unprepared to deal with. Though she cared deeply for Tara, Rose had indeed been reluctant to train her. As Arie teased her about earlier, most villagers in and around Bury underestimated her. No one knew she was the weapons master who made and wielded the swords and daggers she sold with expert skill. Yet no matter how often Rose objected to Tara's pursuit, Tara had pressed on, convinced that Rose could and would train her.

Tara had a spirit that couldn't be broken. While she held tight to her faith to defend against these uncertain times, she still wanted to do something practical. The fact that Tara was on her own with only herself to rely on was too familiar for Rose to ignore.

The plague of mist was coming. Tara was right. Even the Compass Points didn't seem to know what to do. Their efforts would have been laughable if the results weren't so devastating.

The dark mist was once such a foreign concept, but now a growing threat to their daily lives. What had seemed like a singular event in a no-name village far away on the continent was now a worry whispered by all. One day a village was fine. The next, a shadow mist crept over it and never left, sending its citizens into a seemingly endless sleep.

So far, it looked like everyone in the villages that were taken was still alive. The thick fog around the towns formed a clear perimeter that no one dared breach—not since the first time the Compass Points sent Suden fae warriors to investigate, and the first one to cross the mist boundary was also rendered unconscious. It didn't stop loved ones from watching the chests rise and fall of those close enough to the border to see. Nor did it stop others who knew victims farther inside the affected villages from holding out hope that their chests rose and fell also.

"Rose?" Tara's voice interrupted her swirling thoughts.

"Sorry, what did you say?"

"Can we train again this evening?"

Rose hesitated, only briefly. She didn't want to tire Tara out, but the whole village seemed to buzz with nervous energy. If Tara needed to train again to try and calm herself, she would help her.

When Rose was younger, she had thought one day she might be a weapons master and trainer for one of the Compass Points. Even at a young age, she was good and loved sharing her knowledge. Circumstances had made that dream impossible.

It was a risk to train Tara, to let anyone get close enough to realize the truth, but she couldn't turn down the hope in Tara's eyes as she asked for help. Rose knew what it felt like to have no one looking out for her. To have to prepare yourself for the worst.

"Yes, of course. I'll see you then," she replied.

Chapter Three

Box in hand, Rose left the perceived safety of Bury, heading out into the wild to the Lake of the Gods' mountain forest. Most at market day had quiet homes in Bury, or some lived back down the mountain path in neighboring villages.

Only Rose chose to live apart.

No one ever asked where she went or where she lived. They knew she didn't live in a village, but she'd been coming to the market days for ten years with little disruption and good wares. That seemed to be enough for the villagers to tacitly accept her.

Rose headed farther down the tree-covered crater trail. A few miles from Bury, a near-invisible track off the main path led closer to the lake. She had forged the trail when she first arrived in the area. The dense trees she'd cut through opened up to the shoreline.

Before leaving the trees' safety, she set her box down in a roughly marked circle at the end of the path and turned back toward the trail.

"You might as well come out here and talk like a civilized individual," she said. Her words were met with silence. "I can hear you," she tried again.

She felt the moment when the person following her made the exact wrong decision.

She planted her feet, sinking down slightly as bushes and branches rustled loudly. Fast, but not fast enough, a body flew from the brush onto the crudely made trail, careening toward her. She had taken away their element of surprise. Side-stepping, she threw a kick as the attacker shot past.

Her foot connected with their ribs. They grunted but caught themselves, planting both feet before hitting the bushes on the opposite side of the clearing. With feline grace, the attacker lifted his head.

The Suden fae from the market. She really should not be surprised.

He looked every inch the predator, ready to go in for the kill. Hoping it wasn't a literal kill, she decided to try and reason with him.

"Can I help you with something?"

He'd underestimated her at the market. He underestimated her still as he prepared for another attack. He thought he could scare her into leading him to the weapons master. That he could brute force his custom order request.

He'd yet to realize that she was both weapons master and fighter. His miscalculation was evident in the confidence of his stance. Seemingly sure of a quick victory, he lunged for her again.

"Guess we're doing this the hard way," she quipped as she ducked out of the way and landed another powerful kick to his side. He stumbled, catching himself quickly, and grabbed at her again, trying to overwhelm her petite frame with his mass. She surprised them both and dipped her shoulder into his grasp, rolling his weight over her back and flipping him onto his.

Enough of this. She had things to do. He was barely on his feet when she lunged, grappling him from behind. Wrapping her legs around him, she pulled him back to the ground on top of her, arm wrapped around his neck, poised to choke off his air.

He struggled. She only pulled tighter on the whole-body bind in which she held him.

"I'll try again. So what can I do for you?" she asked sweetly.

"Who are you?" was his choked-out, incredulous response.

"Shouldn't you have known that before you attacked me in the woods?" She couldn't see his face from this position, but she enjoyed the idea that multiple flashes of red were cascading across his eyes.

"I wasn't going to hurt you. I just needed to scare you into taking me to the weapons master."

She believed him. He hadn't once reached for his magic during their brief spar. He easily could have created a hole in the ground to throw her into and demand his answers. Instead, he'd opted for a brief physical confrontation. She was happy to disappoint him, but that didn't make it okay.

"Yes, that worked out quite well for you, didn't it." This was getting her nowhere, but she didn't hate it. It'd been a long time since she'd been able to really show off her skills. Though brief, their confrontation reminded her how much she enjoyed it. He stopped struggling and held up his hands in surrender.

"I just want to talk," he said.

"What happens when I don't like what you have to say again?" she asked. "You don't seem great at taking no for an answer." The bitterness of her comment seemed to ruffle him. Like he realized that she'd had to deal with too many idiots that thought what they wanted from her was more important than what she was willing to give. And that he was now one of them.

He sighed. "Hear me out. Maybe we got off on the wrong foot," he said in a smooth and seductive voice that she was more than sure was his go-to tenor for convincing others to do what he wanted. She couldn't tell if he was wielding it as a weapon or if it was as natural to him as breathing.

His voice was sin and decadence wrapped up in a cool timbre. She couldn't stop her body's automatic response to pull him tighter into her hold. She'd met plenty of fae, but she'd never heard a voice like his.

Driven by a force she did not quite understand, she dragged her tongue up the side of his face and bit his ear. He tasted of earth and wilderness, and she was unwilling to admit that she liked it. Confused by her own actions, she snorted loudly in his ear as she laughed at herself. The sound, so at odds with his mesmerizing lilt, snapped her back to reality.

"Fine," she said, releasing him. They both stood, and that stone face cracked in bewilderment. The expression was worth it.

"Luc." He shook his head and held his hand out to her.

"Rose," she offered.

"So are you going to tell me anything else about yourself?" he asked.

"I'm not the one that wants something," she pointed out. This Suden was too used to getting his way. She'd need to change that. "The one who needs something is in the weaker position. Don't they teach you that in the Suden military academy?"

That stopped him again. He must have been unaware that his Suden fae temper had shown through in their initial encounter.

Members of all four fae courts had the natural predatory ability to blend in with humans. On the surface, they could look human. In reality, they were anything but.

His glare was unamused. "It seems I'm again at a disadvantage."

He looked at her, this time really looked at her. His gaze raked over her from head to toe. It wasn't seductive. It was an assessing gaze, a general reevaluating his opponent after one too many missteps. He lingered on her strong shoulders, biceps, and the ash she could never entirely scrub from under her fingernails. His mouth turned to the faintest hint of a smile as his eyes met hers.

"Took you long enough," she jabbed, knowing he'd finally seen what he needed to make the connection.

"I'll admit, you're not quite what I expected."

"Clearly."

"So, weapons master," he purred, his eyes never leaving hers. "Is there anything I can offer you to change your mind?"

"No." She sighed. "No hard feelings, I hope, but I'm not interested in custom work."

"Even if I were to tell you this was for the Suden Point?"

She laughed at her bad luck. "You picked the one thing that could make it worse."

She realized her mistake as his eyebrows rose, his head tilting to the side to reassess her. She did not need to intrigue this fae. She just needed him to go away.

"You'd be providing weaponry to face the mist plague. Your name would be known throughout the continent. You'd have fame and fortune."

"Look at me. Look around." She gestured to the sprawling wilderness, surrounding them. "Know your audience when you're making grand promises." She couldn't help herself, adding, "I thought fae were supposed to be good at this whole charm and negotiation thing."

"Yes, I thought so too," he muttered. "It seems I wasn't quite prepared for…you." He waved his hand in her general direction as he finished.

"I'm happy to point you to a few other weapons masters I know down in Sandrin that would be more than happy to help you," she offered in a final attempt to shut this conversation down and move on with her afternoon.

Luc drew himself to his full height. "I'm here on behalf of the Suden Point, with all the privilege that affords. I've already tried all those in Sandrin; their wares didn't help." He took a breath and unclenched his fists, which had balled up with his rant. "Let's also not get modest now. We both know their work pales compared to yours, and from what I understand, your magical weapons haven't been made at the source. That is why I can't give up until I try your weapons forged at Compass Lake."

She wanted to smile at the compliment, but she knew better.

Her rebuttal faded as she felt heavy magic creeping toward them on the hidden path. It smelled faintly of peppermint. She'd think it refreshing if it wasn't so *other*.

It started to encircle them like a slow cyclone. The sun, high in the sky as Rose walked home, now only visible through a smoky haze that hadn't been there minutes before.

She dropped her cool mask as her panic rose. A glance at their feet told her the dark mist was creeping toward their ankles. Luc's eyes grew wide and wild as he surveyed their surroundings. She saw him shift from surprised to calculating in seconds.

He didn't know what this was either. That was clear. He was assessing the threat to both of them, seeking a way out. The mist continued to spill forth, taking up space in a way that Luc seemed to finally recognize.

"It's the mist plague," he whispered like he hoped it couldn't hear him. "We need to move quickly."

The village.

Rose didn't spare a thought for herself; her thoughts flashed straight to Tara. Was this mist already covering Bury? Her eyes met Luc's. "I need to get to the village," she said.

"If it's anything like the previous attacks of mist reported, we have hours or less; that's assuming it didn't start there."

"Come with me," she said, making a split-second decision as the mist moved in.

It didn't matter any longer, anyway. She could never come back to her home after this if the mist took it. He tilted his head, trying to figure out what she meant, when she stepped back into the circle carved into the path just before it opened onto the beach.

Luc didn't hesitate. Raising his eyebrow, he moved into the circle, meeting the challenge in her eyes with his own. Taking that last step over the threshold, he grabbed her hand, and they were gone.

CHAPTER FOUR

They reappeared a second later on tightly packed dirt beneath a similar canopy of trees. Rose watched Luc's face as he searched the new location, observing the similarities, lingering over the differences.

"A portal?" he asked as he dropped her hand. Rose could still feel the warmth of his touch. She wanted to shake her hand to rid herself of the sensation but didn't want to give him the satisfaction of thinking he affected her.

He glared at her, his fingers stretching and curling back into a fist, his eyes pinched as if angry that he wasn't entirely unaffected by their brief contact either.

"How far did we go?" he asked.

"Not very far," she replied.

"What? Then why bother with the portal?" She could see the wheels of his mind spinning as he scrambled to make sense of the information. "No way," he said under his breath. "This has to be impossible." The awe was evident in his voice though he tried to hide it. He took a few steps out of the clearing where they had landed. His eyes searched for visual confirmation of what everyone believed was impossible.

Acceptance seemed to hit him as his eyes fell on the hill. The unmistakable landmark of the island in the middle of the Lake of the Gods. Unfeasible since the lake was magically gated. No one should be able to get to it.

Should being the key word.

"Oh, there's a way," she said. "But let's not waste time with the difference between impossible and improbable. We've got bigger problems right now." She picked up her market box and headed quickly toward the small hill before them.

"We're on the island? I thought a magical barrier prevented anyone from touching the water. How and why did you bring us here? Can the mist still get to us?"

"That's far too many questions, well past the amount I need to answer."

He glared at her for what felt like the hundredth time in the short while they'd known each other.

"Keep moving, and I'll answer some." She shrugged as she continued her brisk pace. "First, we followed the rules, didn't we? Did we touch the water on our way down here?" She heard his footsteps stop behind her, so she checked over her shoulder to assess the holdup.

It was that bewilderment crossing his face that she enjoyed. She loved the fact that she put it there. She'd stop to enjoy it longer if they weren't in so much trouble.

The plague of mist was here. It was moving toward the villages, toward Tara. It might be at Bury already.

"How?" He pulled her out of her panic as he landed on a question, but at least they started moving again. He must have also remembered that they were on borrowed time.

"I'd rather not get into the details. A magical location was needed for some of my work, and this seemed like a reasonable solution. To answer your other question, I expect the mist to arrive eventually. It will take a little longer to seep across to the island, but I doubt the lake will stop it. And finally, I brought us here to get some weapons before we try and head the mist off at Bury."

Luc picked up the pace, and they ran the rest of the way to her hill home.

"People would know," he said. "Someone would know that this magic had been done. No amount of money could stop the fae that set up that portal from telling others about their handiwork. It isn't a standard power associated with one of the fae courts. It's too impressive of a feat to hide."

She could picture his face even though he was behind her. If she turned around, he'd be narrowing his eyes at her as he came to the natural conclusion. The only way no one would know about the portal was if the portal maker and portal user were the same.

"You did this?" he asked.

Rose shrugged and kept jogging.

"You are full of surprises."

This time she turned around, and his eyes appreciatively surveyed her face.

"Well, here's a pleasant surprise," she said, slowing to a walk as they approached the door. "We made it."

The door was built into the mountain, leading to a smooth carved-out cave structure. The entryway was narrow, with curved walls. The living space was what remained after the stone was removed and hauled away. The short entrance opened into a multi-room setting—a kitchen and dining area on the left, with living space on the right. The entire place was covered in books. Three entire walls covered with shelving, books crammed into every possible nook. It must be chaos to his eyes, but he seemed to appreciate that it was organized chaos to the mysterious owner.

The hallway continued straight to the bedrooms. She didn't have time to give him a tour. Rose was on a mission, taking him to her workshop. It was accessed through another narrow hallway that led off the living area. The workshop was the largest and most impressive room they'd walked through.

Rose led Luc into the open cavern with more tools and resources than a blacksmith would know what to do with. The walls were lined with weapons. Some were in progress, others fully finished and shining in the firelight. The centerpiece of the workspace was a considerable stone forge. The fire was blazing, ready for its weapons master to return to work.

Rose dashed to one wall and pointed him toward another. "Are you familiar with magical weaponry?"

He nodded slowly, slightly unsure for the first time since she'd known him. "The makers usually don't belong to any of the fae courts." He stopped shy of saying that they were usually half-fae.

Not many fae acknowledged the concept. They had too many rules about the fae not procreating outside of their own court to avoid mixing magics. That left no time to deal with fae–human couplings, so most pretended they didn't exist.

"They can see magic around them and shape it to their needs," he continued. "That's why the best magical weapons are made at Compass Lake, the origin of the fae and their magic."

"Very good. Remember that anything you take today is on loan. Don't get attached. We're going to Bury to see if we can head off the mist or slow it down to get the villagers out. That wall"—she pointed to the one in front of him—"has weapons tuned to the wild magic in this place. They should work fine with your earth magic. See what you think."

Grabbing her sword, she turned around to assess his progress. He held an axe and a sword, indecision apparent in his crinkled brow. She had another minute or two while he finalized his selection.

She felt like an idiot but ran back into the living room and violently whispered, "Arie! Arie! Are you there?"

He was a strange creature. He seemed able to shape-shift into anything. So she never knew when he was around or why he decided to show up when he did. She knew that having him around now would help them move faster.

"Yes, Rose....What's all the...." He stopped mid-sentence as he appeared in his usual island form, a large brown bear in the middle of her living room, as he got a look at her. *"What's going on? You look....I think deranged is the word I'm looking for?"*

"Arie, we don't have time for this. There is a Suden fae in the workshop, and he'll walk back here at any second. I assume he won't be able to hear you, but he will certainly have something to say about a giant bear in the middle of the room."

"A Suden, you say? Well, this afternoon is taking a turn. Why is he here? Did you finally follow my advice and find a nice partner? A Suden is an interesting choice...." He trailed off.

"Gods, Arie, not the time. He's here for...reasons. I don't want to get into it. The more important part is the mist plague is on its way across the lake now. We have to get to Bury. We have to see if we can stop it."

"Stop it?" was Arie's only response. *"You realize that no one has been able to stop it in any of the villages it has taken so far? No one even knows what happens in the mist! I see you holding your favorite weapon, trying to solve your problems by beating them into submission, as usual, but what can you do against the mist?"*

"Gods, Arie," she said exasperatedly. "Again, not the time. We need to try. I can't sit here and do nothing."

If a bear could shrug, he did. *"Fine. I'll meet you at the portal in five minutes."* He disappeared.

That was fine with her. She turned back to see Luc standing in the hallway, staring at the spot on the floor where the bear had just been.

"Do I even want to know?" he drawled.

"Did you find a weapon?" she challenged.

"Yes...wha—"

"No time. I need to grab one more thing from the workshop. Be ready to go when I get back." She strolled purposefully past Luc into the workshop. She went to the forge and pulled a delicate gold chain with a compass attached off the wall near her workstation. A gift from her mom, her only family heirloom. She wore it always, only taking it off when she was going to spend hours bent over the hot forge. Having stayed up too late working on a new project last night, she'd forgotten it this morning. She refused to hurtle off to the unknown without it. Carrying it felt like carrying her family's support.

Turning to leave, she felt the same weight of magic she had felt in the clearing. Searching for signs of mist and shadow, she readied to grab her weapon from her back strap as she started to turn to leave the workshop.

Nothing could prepare her as dark mist dropped down through the forge chimney.

"This cannot be good," she muttered to herself.

The mist billowed out, dowsing the fire in the forge with its thickness and covering the workshop in darkness.

CHAPTER FIVE

Rose brought up the sword that she had strapped to her back. What wishful thinking, imagining she could make it off the island before using it.

Her eyes were still adjusting to the lack of light. It was near impossible to discern the mist shadows from the smoke billowing from the interrupted forge fire.

The thick mist took over the room, permeating the peppermint scent. A cold shudder crossed everywhere it touched. She heard motion and felt a figure at her back. Risking a second to confirm, she saw Luc holding his borrowed sword behind her as she continued searching the dark room. The mist swirled around them, providing no form to strike. Back to back, their feet drew circles on the ground, mirroring the mist's movement.

More mist barreled down the chimney and onto the floor before Rose. It poured out of the forge building into a vaguely familiar shape. This was what they wanted, something solid enough to attack, but she wasn't prepared for what they saw.

It was huge. Rose had to tilt her head back to see its face. She immediately yanked Luc's arm so he knew to turn to stand beside her. The mist stacked upon itself from the ground up, legs the size of tree trunks on taloned feet, a body shaped after statues of gods. The mist thickened, crafting a warrior-like creature.

Easily two times Rose's height, and broad—so broad that if it hadn't been shaped from the mist, she wasn't sure how it would have fit down the chimney. Raising its sword of shadow, it moved toward Rose and Luc.

The only hint of color in the room was the beast's golden eyes. Their focus honed on Rose. The sword that took shape billowed like smoke but swung straight for Rose's head. She met the shadow blade with her own, and she felt the clash of their swords deep in her bones.

Solid. The shadow sword was solid.

Luc didn't hesitate. While her sword locked with the monster's, he plunged his sword into the beast's side.

The creature of shadow itself could be struck.

Releasing a piercing screech into the dark workshop, the creature finally registered that it had two opponents.

The beast reared back and attacked again. Rose and Luc responded in tandem, alternating who took the blow and who tried to strike.

She knew the moment Luc called his magic, as a new scent of pine and cinnamon burst into the workshop. His earth magic dug a pit into the ground, large enough to hold the creature. This was a classic move of the Suden people, trapping and burying their enemies and leaving them to die in the darkness below the world.

The creature took another step as it moved to strike Rose again. Sure enough, it fell into the pit that appeared beneath its foot. But as the beast fell forward, careening into the depths, shadow wings extended from its back, halting the descent.

The shadow beast could fly. This kept getting better and better.

As it placed itself back on the ground in front of Rose, she defended the next strike from the beast, teeth clenching as she held firm. If Luc's magic was useless, she had to buy him a moment to get a hit that would count.

Taking a deep breath, she considered her options. Keeping herself and her magic hidden would do her no good if she died. Maybe Luc wouldn't even notice, tied up in the battle as they were. She didn't agonize long over it, with imminent death in the form of a mist-born beast looming before her.

Decision made. She pulled on her magic.

A jolt of wind pushed her forward. Her burst of motion, farther and faster than a human could jump, forced the giant monster back just a step to defend. The single stumble was all Luc needed. He didn't hesitate as he threw himself into the air. He must have used his earth magic to push himself from the ground. This marked him as a particularly powerful Suden. His jump was like flight as he arced through the air. His borrowed blade struck true, severing the monster's head from its body.

Rose and Luc stared at the head as it hit the workshop floor. Before they could even begin to investigate it, both body and head unraveled back into a mist that hung heavy above the ground.

"Let's go! We need to get back to the village," Rose called.

Luc nodded and followed her.

Had no one else tried to defend themselves against the plague of mist? What had happened with those other magical weapons tests that Luc said he had already done? Were her weapons really the answer? She couldn't catch her breath as she thought about fighting a literal mist-born creature. The plague had a form. The form could be defeated with her weapons.

Rose strapped her blade to her back and saw Luc tuck his sword into the waist belt he'd grabbed from the workshop as they ran to the portal. Rose was still trying to wrap her head around what had happened and what it meant.

Luc had said his request for her weapons was on behalf of the Suden Point. Did the Compass Points know that her magical weapons could fight the mist? A wave of guilt crashed over her at denying Luc his request as they sprinted.

Could she refuse him now?

She hadn't been sure until the creature's blade crashed into her own if it would be solid. Maybe it wasn't? Had her blade only forced it to be so since it was magically imbued? She stopped short just before running into Luc. They'd reached the portal and saw the large brown bear sitting on its haunches.

"Took you long enough," Arie shot at Rose.

"Can he hear you?" Rose asked aloud, moving past Luc and toward the bear. It'd be nice if he could so she didn't sound like a moron while talking to him.

"No," he snorted. *"I don't want to talk to him."* Arie stiffened a little as he saw the fae stroll up behind Rose toward the portal outline.

"Why?" Rose asked. "He clearly can see that I'm talking to you." Rose gestured toward Luc, now standing next to her. "It's not like this can be a secret right now."

"I don't like Aterra. I'll help transport him since this is an emergency, but I won't speak with him. You'll have to translate."

Why was he always so difficult? "Since when are you religious? We were just attacked and fought some kind of mist monster. Whether you like the Suden's god is low on my priority list."

"You were able to fight it?" He was so predictable. He latched on to the details of the encounter without acknowledging that she had been fighting for her life.

"Yes. Hold on, let me explain this to Luc." She turned to Luc, who was smirking at her.

"Go ahead," he said, an assessing look crossing his face, "tell me you are talking to that bear."

"Well, at least you don't think I'm having a conversation with my multiple personalities."

"That's not completely ruled out yet. I have many questions, but the only one that matters now is how we get to the village."

"Finally, someone sane to work with." She huffed and took a moment to appreciate how on the nose that was when her sanity was likely very much in question by said sane individual. She and Arie had made it into the circle. Her hand on his fur, she held the other out to Luc. Shaking his head again, he stepped forward and took her offered hand.

They landed back on the hidden trail off of the crater ridge path. "This will get a little weirder before I can explain, but we'll have to ride on Arie." She turned to Luc to see if she'd broken him yet.

"And Arie is the bear?" A bemused smile crossed his face.

"Yes."

"Does he have a saddle or anything?" he asked, tilting his head slightly as if evaluating exactly how one would ride a bear.

As if I would allow you to saddle me," came Arie's arrogant reply.

"You said he can't hear you; don't bother sassing him if he can't," Rose said.

"I'm going to go ahead and guess that he doesn't like the saddle idea," said Luc.

"Just get on behind me and hold on," was all Rose could get out as she climbed up on Arie's back and held on to the fur around his neck and shoulders.

Luc seemed to assess his chances of making it to Bury without riding the bear that didn't like him. Rose saw the moment he decided he didn't have another option. Giving the bear a final distrustful glance, he swung himself up behind Rose. He paused for a second, hands hovering over Rose's hips.

"Is this okay?" he asked, his body just shy of leaning against her back—his hands inches from each side of her waist.

She held in a shiver at his breath at her ear. She could almost feel the weight of his hands on her hips, though they didn't yet touch her. Had it really been so long since someone's arms had encircled her that she was reacting so foolishly? She tucked her chin and straightened her spine.

"Just hold on," she said as the bear took off at a run.

CHAPTER SIX

"No one told me that bears were fast," Luc said after minutes of tearing through the forest. He held tight to Rose, his body pressing into hers as they continued at breakneck speed. His head in the crook of her neck sent chills down her spine as he spoke. Surely she was just anxious about the life-threatening situation they were plunging into.

"I'm glad you learned something today," she shouted over her shoulder, moving her ear away from his lips. They were already back to the village, the mist flowing like a lake of shadows before them, leading down the path to a market square entirely covered by mist. They were too late.

"Hurry up, Arie!" She urged him forward. "Tara's in there."

"You said you already fought the mist, right?" Arie asked as he seemed to calculate their odds of not being impacted if they breached the thick barrier surrounding the village.

"Yes. We did. The mist took over my workshop, and we didn't fall into an endless sleep." She chanced a glance over her shoulder at Luc as she added more softly, "I think my weapons can fight it." She tried to ignore Luc as she caught the smug upward tilt of his mouth out of the corner of her eye. "Either way, it doesn't matter. We have to get to Tara."

"Your weapons worked against it?" Arie sounded intrigued as he careened forward. *"Fine. But don't say I didn't warn you. The mist is dangerous, and I can't protect you."*

Rose didn't have time to ponder that as Arie plunged through the wall of mist.

A familiar feeling encircled her as they dove into the mist, familiar magic, she couldn't quite put her finger on.

"Who is Tara?" Luc asked from behind her. His strong arms grasped her waist, his lips still dangerously close to her ear. She thought she heard genuine concern in his voice. Her body moved of its own accord, leaning back into his strength as she started to respond.

Her mind catching up with her body, she hesitated. Didn't he try and attack her earlier?

This was a temporary truce for a likely fruitless mission if the thickness of the fog said anything about the village's chances.

She sat straight, pulling away from him as rationality found its way back in.

"She's…" Rose didn't know how to finish the sentence. Her student? Her friend? Rose still wasn't used to having them, with the exception of Arie. She responded factually. "I've been…training her. She lives in Bury, and I was supposed to meet her there this afternoon for another lesson."

The guilt squeezed her chest, leaving little room to breathe.

"I know you're spiraling. You need to stop," Arie offered her mentally.

"You can't read my thoughts," she replied.

"He can't?" asked Luc. "I'm sure this is not the right time, but that was one of my questions." She focused on Luc. Maybe answering Luc's questions would be just tedious enough to distract her as they searched the heavy mist.

"He can't. I have to talk to him out loud, but he seems to initiate some mental connection with me so that the world doesn't see a bear talking. Apparently, it's fine for them to see me talking to myself."

"What kind of magic is it? How are you bonded?" Luc asked.

"Oh, I don't think we are. I think he just finds me entertaining." Not a lie. The best she could do on short notice.

"So why doesn't he want to link with me? Do you think he can?"

The bear snorted beneath them. She hadn't even been aware bears could snort.

"I think he can. He just said he didn't want to."

"Because he doesn't like Aterra? A god I've never seen?" Luc asked.

"That seemed to be the gist of it," Rose replied.

"Hmph," Luc grunted.

Arie was unusually silent.

They'd finally reached the temple in the middle of Bury, which was as bad as she had imagined. The mist sprawled through every street, shop, and house. Anyone they passed had collapsed into the layer of shadow covering the ground.

Rose and Luc unsheathed and clutched the magical weapons from Rose's workshop. Arie slowed to a tentative trot as the mist swirled around them. Rose waited again to see if she was about to collapse like the rest of those the mist plague touched. She didn't, though she still wasn't sure why.

She took a deep breath and searched for signs of life. She pictured one of those mist monsters forming and cutting its way through each of the villagers. Maybe it wouldn't have killed her if it had been able to strike her. Perhaps it would have dropped her into the sleep-like state she saw before her.

Reaching the barn just behind the temple, she jumped off Arie and ran the rest of the way to the crumpled figure. Rose's heart cracked open in her chest as she dropped to her knees and cradled Tara's body in her arms.

She might have expected this, but she was unprepared for it.

"Tara! Tara, say something." Rose leaned in to see if her chest still rose and fell.

Logically, Rose knew the mist shouldn't have killed her. But Rose wasn't thinking logically at the moment.

"Is she still breathing?" asked Luc. He slid off Arie and took a few hesitant steps toward her, discomfort evident in the set of his jaw.

"Yes, but it's faint."

"I'm sorry," Luc said hesitantly.

Rose wondered for what. That he'd stalked her? That he'd delayed her? That he'd probably been right about her weapons and the mist?

Rose shook her head again, still cradling Tara. It was so strange. She'd just seen Tara this morning and was supposed to see her again this afternoon. Tara was so excited to learn to defend herself from something...like this. Why hadn't Rose ever left any of her weapons here for Tara? What if that really could have made a difference?

"Want me to help move her to a more comfortable location?" Luc's careful words interrupted her thoughts.

She choked down her guilt, ignoring him as she kept focused on Tara. She didn't know what to do but didn't think she could leave Tara like this.

She looked from Luc back to Tara, unable and unwilling to put all her feelings into words.

She hugged Tara's body again. Bending her forehead to the younger girl's, she whispered, "I'll fix this. I promise."

"Rose…" Arie's words cut into her guilt-ridden promise.

Just as quickly as she spiraled, Rose replaced the wealth of despair she felt at the current situation with something much easier to deal with.

Anger bubbled to rage as her gaze flicked back to Luc.

"It had to be after you," she accused.

"Rose, that's not how the mist…" Arie warned, but she cut him off.

"Why else would the mist have come here? It must have known the Compass Points had sent a Suden to find a way to stop it."

"I know you're upset, but be logical. The mist knows? Is it sentient?" Luc held up his hands, seeming ready to take a step back from her.

"Who knows anything about the mist! Maybe it is sentient!" Rose was yelling now. What did it matter? No one could hear her. The villagers around them had all been taken by the mist. "You show up today asking for custom weapons. The one thing that apparently makes a difference when fighting it. Don't tell me you overlooked that."

"Of course not. But I had no idea until today."

She carefully laid Tara down and got to her feet.

"Isn't that a little too convenient? The Compass Points wouldn't send you across the continent without knowing what they were after."

"This isn't going to help anything," Arie mentally chastised. *"What do you want from the boy?"*

"Boy." She scoffed. "He's no boy. He's fae. He's working for the Suden Point!"

"I'm unsure whether that's a compliment or an insult." Luc's smirk was back. She was beginning to hate it.

"I assume I don't have a choice to decline your offer now? Especially with what we learned today?"

A Suden, here on behalf of the Compass Points. Gods, she couldn't believe it. She hadn't adequately digested that.

She sized up the Suden fae standing across from her. Luc worked for the most powerful Suden alive, the youngest ever to take the position. And if reputation were to be believed, the most ruthless in generations. What would the Suden Point do to him if he returned with the knowledge that her weapons could protect them but without her to make them?

Luc tilted his head, eyes pinched in appraisal. "I told you that you have a choice, Rose, and you do." He held his hands out, palms up. "The magical weapons I've tried before didn't work, but then I heard rumors of the reclusive genius that made weapons up in the mountains filled with wild magic. I knew I had to try at least once more. I was desperate to prevent this." He gestured to the devastation of Bury. "Now I don't just want them; I know we need them to stand any chance at fighting this." He let out a breath, seeming to calculate his next sentence.

Rose braced herself for another threat, no matter what he said about choice.

"I've only known you for a few hours, but you don't strike me as the type that would want to horde this resource for herself." He looked down at her. His face was unexpectedly earnest. "Your first thought was not to save yourself but to get weapons to defend the village. I bet you'd choose that route ten times out of ten, no matter the risk to yourself."

She'd prepared herself for more threats, not this. Not the internal reproach she'd given herself only moments ago. She couldn't believe he'd found the argument she'd been using on herself.

"He has a point there," Arie added unhelpfully.

"Of course. I would help them," she sighed. She was exhausted and couldn't fight him and her own guilt.

"Then what's the problem?"

"What are the Compass Points' plans in all this?"

He looked startled. "They don't all know of my journey."

"What do you mean? You are here on behalf of the Suden Point, which has to be sanctioned by all four of them, right?"

Luc rubbed his palm over his face, seeming to weigh his options. "I am technically here on behalf of the Suden Point, but not in the way you think."

"What does that mean, Luc?" Knowing she'd fallen into a fae play on words, her temper rose.

He straightened his spine as if resolved, saying, "I'm here on behalf of the Suden Point because I am the Suden Point."

Well, shit. Rose tried and failed to stop her jaw from dropping.

"That was unexpectedly honest for a fae," Arie noted.

"You are the Suden Point." She parroted his words back to him, processing. "So this wasn't an official inquiry of the Compass Points, but a rogue mission of the Suden Point?" He was the strongest earth fae on the continent. He was known for his power; she must have only glimpsed it in their battle. At least it explained the way he'd pushed himself from the ground. A unique use of Suden magic, but certainly well within his renowned abilities. She was beyond screwed if he put together any pieces of her own magical display.

"Why don't the rest of the Compass Points know about the journey?"

"I'm not sure that is your business," he replied.

She agreed with Arie. His reveal was too honest. He wasn't backed into a corner. He didn't need to tell her who he was.

He sighed before continuing. "They don't know what I went searching for. They only know that I leave Compass Lake regularly for my duties and research about the plague of mist. They are uninterested in what I do so long as I'm not there." He paused, as if realizing he'd said too much. "Do you need me to make it a little more practical?" he asked, changing tactics again. "The mist is not just a theoretical problem for you any longer. It is very real. It has come into your home and taken someone that seems important to you."

That was an unexpected punch to the gut. Even if the mist didn't technically kill her, Tara was gone, lost to a state of endless sleep. Unless, of course, Rose found a cure for the plague of mist.

Bastard. Her hands clenched to fists at her side.

"I'm not going to force you. In fact, don't take the custom order now." He paused again, a slow, wicked smile crept over his face. "Come with me to Compass Lake and decide for yourself."

To make weapons for the Suden Point, she'd have to feel his power at its strongest. The Suden house on Compass Lake; his seat of power. The one place to which she swore she'd never return. Even as she thought it, she knew she'd do it. She'd return for Tara, and other villagers like her, but she'd do it on her own terms.

"Be careful, Rose, you won't be able to hide everything from this one," Arie cautioned.

She looked over her shoulder at him. They had a somewhat unspoken agreement not to talk about her power, though she knew that he knew more than he let on.

She sighed. He was right, of course, but that didn't change the path she had to take.

"I don't want anyone to know I'm a weapons master," she said.

He raised a brow as he started, "I'm not sure—"

She cut him off. "No, that's it. I'll come with you, evaluate your power at the Suden house, and decide what to do then, but no one else can know why I'm there."

He narrowed his eyes at her, calculating again. Even before the word was out, though, she knew he'd agree to it.

"Done." He nodded.

"Well, won't this be fun," Arie quipped.

CHAPTER SEVEN

20 years ago - Compass Lake

Rose loved the feeling of the warm summer breeze as it crossed Compass Lake. There was nothing better than the Summer Solstice Ceremony. Her parents enjoyed the ball at the Norden house the night before more than the actual ceremony, but Rose was sure that was some grown-up thing she didn't understand. They'd come home last night in finery, cheeks flushed, hands entangled. Her mom's hair was definitely not as tightly bound in the elegant style she'd left the house with earlier.

Rose's fake sleep didn't fool her parents for a second as Mom walked farther into her bedroom and asked, "Are you still awake, love?"

Rose opened one eye just a crack. "Maybe."

"Did you have fun with Grandpa?"

"Of course! We cleaned up and then played lots of games." Rose sat up in bed as she spoke, eager to share her evening with her parents. "How was the ball?"

"Oh, Rose. It was so lovely. We had so much fun. We missed you," Dad said as he sat at the foot of her bed. Mom had made her way to kneeling at her side.

Rose could have gone with them, but Grandpa had stayed home and asked her to keep him company. "Were there any other kids there?"

"We didn't see any, not even the Norden Point's son." Mom looked off as if trying to recollect if she'd seen him. "Which was a bit odd. I'm sure he'll be at the ceremony tomorrow."

"I'd like to meet him," Rose said more assuredly than she felt. She'd glimpsed the boy on the property so often. She didn't understand why he wouldn't come outside and play with her, especially in the summer.

"We know, Rose. Remember, different families have different rules, and while we might not understand them, we need to respect them," Dad said.

Rose wasn't sure what that meant, but she nodded along anyway as she toyed with her necklace. A gold chain with a compass pendant. Her mom had given it to her for her fifth birthday.

Mom stood up slowly, saying, "It's late. You should get back to bed."

"Will you tell me the story again?" Rose asked as she looked down at the compass pendant in her palm.

Mom's smile was soft. "Of course, dear. One story, and then you're back to bed." She tucked Rose in as she began the story of Aurora's compass. She started the tale the same way every time. Rose could probably tell this story from memory.

"Aurora, the goddess of the Norden fae, blessing us with the power of water, had an important decision to make. The gods had behaved too selfishly. They had not protected humanity, and humanity had suffered because of it." Mom glanced at her to ensure she wasn't asleep already. Rose smiled back brightly as she continued. "A plague had taken over the continent because of the gods' selfishness. Most of humanity, those they were sworn to protect, had been taken by its wrath. Aurora, Arctos, Zrak, and Aterra had met to decide what to do."

"We must do something drastic," Aurora said. She folded her arms over her chest, her skin a deep golden brown. She made deliberate eye contact with each of the other three gods in the room.

"We don't owe humanity anything," mumbled Aterra as he raked his fingers through his jet-black hair.

"In fact, we do." Zrak narrowed his eyes as he glanced at Aterra. Zrak was tall and broad, with white skin, tanned from the sun, and dark brown hair. His glare was intimidating, even to another god. "We are meant to protect humanity. Our selfishness has brought nothing but harm. We can only blame ourselves for this plague unleashed upon the continent. We must make it right."

Aterra raised his hand as if to argue.

"Agreed," Arctos said. His blonde hair fell over his warm beige skin as he lounged in the temple master's chair.

The gods had decided to meet at the first temple. A sacred place of worship. The temple was atop a great mountain, humanity traveled days just to get there and make offerings to these four gods. Aurora had felt they needed a reminder of who they were here for and what they claimed to represent.

"So what are you proposing, exactly?" Aterra growled.

"We each need to make a small sacrifice as a covenant with the people of this continent. A little of our magic needs to be used to create a balance, to create a new people that will help protect humanity on the continent. They will be our representatives in the world and hold a token of our power to keep us in check."

"A human with magic could never keep a god in check," Aterra stated.

"That's correct. That's why we will make the fae. Not humans with magic but magical beings themselves. We'll each make a fae court."

"Better. But do you really believe that will stop a god?" Aterra asked.

"It's a fair question. If the strongest among them band together, it is probable," Zrak considered. "But that's why I also think we need a bigger sacrifice. Weaken the power of the gods slightly." His patience with Aterra's objections seemed to be wearing thin.

"What do you have in mind, Zrak?" Arctos leaned forward, anticipation evident in the slight lift of his brow. The unintelligible smirk that usually crossed his face was nowhere to be seen now.

"We need a bigger sacrifice than just a bit of our magic. One of us must sacrifice ourselves to remove the plague from the continent."

Aurora, Aterra, and Arctos stared openly at Zrak as he finished his suggestion.

Aurora had anticipated it but didn't think he would state it so boldly. She'd thought she'd have to maneuver the conversation to this point. "I agree, Zrak," she said. "But how do we decide who will remove the plague?"

"I was thinking you could help with that, Aurora." Zrak's face turned bright as he looked at her. He'd always had little tolerance for Aterra, a soft spot for Arctos, and the deepest respect for Aurora. "Could you forge us a magical compass? Imbue it with an understanding of each of our magic, and we'll let it decide. Whichever of our directions the compass points to will be the one to pay the price."

"You can't be serious," Aterra said. "I will not submit to a decision of such scale based on a magic-imbued compass, even if Aurora is the most qualified to make such a thing."

"Shall we vote?" Zrak asked.

Aurora wasn't certain how Zrak was so sure of himself, but she was willing to go along with it. His plan was terrifying, but hadn't they brought this on themselves?

"I'm in favor," Aurora stated.

After a glance in her direction, Arctos said, "I am in favor as well."

Aterra caught the glance and rolled his eyes. He glared at the three of them as he turned around and walked outside the temple. He yelled over his shoulder as he went. "Let me know when this lunacy is ready."

Mom looked down at her again. "Are you still with me, sweetheart? Or do you want me to save the rest for tomorrow?"

"Please keep going. There's only a little more left."

Taking her hand, Rose's mom kissed it as she continued the story.

Aurora knew just what to do. She went to the fires at the heart of Mount Bury to forge a compass for this purpose. A tool that would point them in the right direction.

"She could forge metals with magic, just like you and I," Rose interjected. Mom's smile was patient as she nodded and continued.

Aurora pulled from the fire a beautiful compass. She called the others, feeling their magics as they neared. She pushed her water, Aterra's earth, Arctos's fire, and finally, Zrak's wind over the hot metal as she raised it from the lava-filled center of the mountain, cooling it before placing it in her palm. As she held it, she saw the needle start to spin.

"Everyone take your compass point," Aurora said as she stepped to the Northern point herself. Zrak stepped to the East, Arctos to the West, and finally, Aterra shuffled to the South.

"Ready?" Zrak asked. But his question was rhetorical, as the compass needle had already started to spin.

It spun for seconds, minutes, hours. The gods would never know as they waited with bated breath. The compass finally stopped—the needle firmly pointing East.

"Zrak," Aurora gasped. She knew it could have been anyone, but was somehow shocked to find it would be Zrak to sacrifice for all of them.

"Seems fitting," said Aterra as he crossed his arms.

"Shut up, Aterra," Arctos said. "This is serious."

"We all agreed," Aterra said. "There is no turning back now."

Zrak stopped Arctos from replying as he said, "He's right. We agreed. And I will do this."

So Zrak sacrificed himself for humanity and the gods, but not before making the Osten, the wind fae. And Aurora kept her compass and passed it into her creation, the water fae, the Norden people.

Rose didn't hear anything after that as her lids started to feel heavy over her eyes, drifting lower and lower until she was fast asleep.

Chapter Eight

Rose didn't know what to think as they walked back from Bury to the portal to her island in near silence.

The Suden Point? Compass Lake?

Arie had stayed in the mist. He said he needed to check on some things, whatever that meant. She thought she'd heard his voice, but not in her head, as she and Luc stumbled out of the village. Her mind was spinning too much to question her sanity or what he was up to. He'd proved that he wouldn't succumb to the mist for whatever reason, just like she and Luc hadn't.

Her thoughts were a jumbled mess as they walked.

She could have fled. That was always an option when the Compass Points came up. It had gotten her this far. But she couldn't leave Tara and just move on with her life. She had to see if this knowledge about her weapons could lead to any kind of cure.

Now that Rose knew her weapons could defend against the plague of mist, she didn't think she could walk away.

What if something about her magic made her magical forging different? As Luc had recited to her, most that made magical weapons didn't have elemental magic themselves.

Rose was different, of course. Did that make her weapons different?

Her gaze drifted to the Suden Point's back. Strength emanated from his body, even as he cut a path through the trees. He was the last being that needed the power boost of her magically forged weapons. And was she fool enough to believe he would just let her walk away after she made it for him? Would he pry her secrets out of her before she could?

He might not know why her weapons differed, but he knew whatever she did worked against the mist.

Taking the portal back to her island, Rose packed up a few things for their journey now that they had more time. She grabbed some favorite weapons, and the proper sheath for her sword. Her fingers toyed with the golden chain on her necklace, pulling the compass pendant from beneath her shirt, a nervous habit, as her gaze raked over the battle-ruined shop.

The spin of the needle caught her attention as she heard Luc's voice from the doorway.

"Need any help?" he asked.

She looked down. The needle stopped on south, back toward the workshop entry where Luc stood. She shook her head, thinking of a story her mom used to tell her. Unwilling to consider the implications of the direction, she slipped the compass back under her shirt.

"No," she replied. She'd keep their interactions as limited as she could. He seemed the type to ferret out secrets.

Luc took the opportunity to peruse Rose's book collection. He moved effortlessly around the room, pulling books off shelves to take a closer look and setting them back. He looked comfortable. She noticed how quickly he'd adapted to each new piece of information in their journey so far. To the island, to Arie, even meeting her requirements to get her back to Compass Lake. She didn't trust that kind of flexibility, especially from the leader of the Suden fae.

He was undeniably striking: tall, with dark hair, full lips, and that sharp, angled face. She knew many would instinctively fear him, but his features seemed only to draw her in.

She shook her head. He was a predator, gift-wrapped to distract while moving in for the kill. He was the Suden Point. She hated the Compass Points and everything they were meant to be.

Yet here she was, drooling over one of them.

One who had found her in hiding, threatened her, and maneuvered her into a situation she'd been happy to avoid for the last ten years: traveling to Compass Lake.

"Do you like to read?" he asked as she walked into the library. She hadn't made herself known, but his senses must be sharp. Her pack slung over one shoulder, her sword still strapped to her back as she readied to leave.

"You could say that," she replied. She watched him look down at the book currently in his hand.

"This one looks particularly interesting." He held up the book, which was clearly from her romance collection, *Love Eternal*, in script printed on the binding.

"You should see what they get up to in chapter fifty-five," she said before she could stop herself.

Book recommendations were clearly her weakness.

"I'm…." He blinked slowly. "Intrigued." He shook his head as he eyed her pack. "Do you need anything else?"

"No, I'm good."

"Do we have Arie?" he asked as he looked around.

"No, he tends to come and go as he pleases."

"Will he be able to find you while we're on the road?"

"He's never bothered to learn my schedule and seems to find me whenever he wants," she said flippantly. "I'm not too worried about it."

Luc's brow furrowed. She knew little about rogue shifter spirits but wondered if Luc did. Had she inadvertently given something away?

"Interesting," he said. "Mind if I bring this with us?" He held up the romance book.

"Knock yourself out." She rolled her eyes at him and headed out the door.

They made their final trip back to Bury. They reached the village border and paused. The mist still hung, creating a dark layer that few would dare enter. Bury usually held so much life. Rose couldn't help but feel its lack now as she looked in from the village edge.

She wouldn't see Tara sneak out of the temple in the late afternoon to share food scraps with Arthur, a homeless man who sat outside the tavern. She wouldn't see Tara check in on Mrs. Benton every few days since her wife died last winter. She wouldn't even see the passion-filled glances that Terence Dawson, who lived down the street, still shot at his wife of sixty years as they went about their daily routine.

The mist plague had taken these things and had left behind bodies on the ground.

She couldn't help but wonder what the point of it all was. The people were still alive, or at least she'd seen the breaths Tara still took, shallow though they may be, so what was the goal of the mist if not to kill? What was it doing?

She thought about this as she and Luc borrowed some horses that had wandered out of the village. She decided to jump right into the details as they started their journey south.

"So what's the plan? How will we explain my presence at Compass Lake? We need a cover that will ensure I have easy access to you but one that also ensures the other Compass Points have no right to question me."

She didn't know what it was about her words, but they seemed to capture Luc's full attention.

He raised his eyebrow at her.

She wanted to rip it off his face.

"What?" She sighed. "You already knew I didn't want those at Compass Lake to know my identity, or you wouldn't have gone to such great pains to manipulate me into going."

"Manipulate you?" He raised his hand to his chest as if wounded. "I'm sorry, but not even I could have orchestrated an attack by the plague of mist so perfectly timed with my request to leave you no other options. I was in the right place at the right time to offer a solution that suited all parties."

"Is that really what you tell yourself? You took advantage of a terrible situation!" She tried and failed to stop her hands from gesturing wildly at the situation around them.

"Do you not want to go?" he asked, meeting her eyes with his piercing stare.

It wasn't that she didn't want to go. She wanted to save Tara without going to Compass Lake, which she knew was impossible. She wanted to help the people of Bury and other villages like it. It was just that years of self-conditioning to run in the opposite direction of Compass Lake were not to be overcome in a single conversation.

She shook her head.

"I thought not," he said, his eyes finally leaving hers. "This whole thing would go a lot faster if you told me who you were avoiding and why so we could make the necessary arrangements."

"Oh yes, please let me share my life story with the Suden Point," she said sarcastically. "We may have established that you didn't manipulate me in this situation, but that doesn't wash away the fact that you're a Compass Point." She tapped her finger on her chin. "I'll pass on story time."

"Maybe I'm just good at finding mutually beneficial solutions? Not everything has to be some despicable scheme. Maybe I can read people and find ways to get them what they want while also getting what I want."

She shook her head again and didn't bother responding as they rode on.

She didn't know what to make of him. He was nothing and everything she expected. Not that she'd spent much time dreaming about the Suden Point. She preferred not to think of the Compass Points at all.

Chapter Nine

They made good time, even starting so late in the afternoon. After dusk, they veered off the road, to camp far enough away that no one should stumble upon them—a perimeter guarded by trees but clear enough to lay out their packs and have a fire.

Luc set to warming a meal while Rose unpacked her bedroll and blanket. It was warm in the valley. They'd be fine for the few days they traveled the main road. She worried more about when they headed up into the mountains to Compass Lake. It would get cold quickly at that elevation, though she was used to it from living on the Lake of the Gods. She'd brought a few long-sleeve tunics and a cloak.

She sat on her bedroll, watching Luc. It was time to dive in. He'd said this afternoon that he had a plan for explaining her presence to the other Compass Points, and she wouldn't like it. She'd still been sorting through her emotions about Tara, the fact that Luc was the Suden Point, and that her weapons seemed able to defend against the mist plague when no others had been able to. She cut herself a break for not pulling this particular thread at the time.

She may still be able to run if she hated it. Either way, she took a deep breath and thought it was time to learn what it was.

"So," she began. "Should we talk about your plan that I'm not going to like?"

"I thought you'd never ask." He poked at the fire. "I'd like to head this conversation off by saying I'm not trying to manipulate you. I can only think of one way the other Compass Points, and anyone else, would have no right to question you while you're at the lake."

A surefire way to know you were being manipulated was for someone to tell you they weren't manipulating you. This was off to a great start.

"And that is…?"

"The only way to ensure that they have no right to access or question you is for you and me to be together."

He let the word *"together"* hang there. She couldn't help as her gaze veered directly toward his full lips and started to imagine what they'd feel like against hers. Would they be soft as they looked? Or hard and demanding like the rest of him? An unexpected blush touched her cheeks.

The fire must be warmer than she thought.

She caught his eyes as hers darted away from his lips. A smug smile curled at the corner of that dangerous mouth. She sat up straighter.

"Be together," she repeated. "Are you going to add any clarity or definition to that?"

He couldn't possibly mean romantically.

He sighed like he couldn't believe she would make him spell it out. She definitely would.

"It means what you think it means." He wiped a hand across his face. "My people don't put fancy titles on relationships, but we would need to appear romantically involved." He sighed again. "It's the only way that I can think of to shield you from the other Compass Points the way that you asked. A romantic claim, a potential partner for the Suden Point. That is something in which they cannot interfere." He paused, letting her process.

She glared at him. "And you failed to mention this part of the plan when we made our deal back in the village? I remember something about me having choices?" She chastised herself more than him. She knew this was to be expected from the Suden Point.

Part of her wanted to believe his claims of mutual benefit, unified goals, and choice. He'd seemed so earnest in making them. But that was naive, and she knew better when dealing with a Compass Point. They thought only of power and what they could take for themselves.

"I'm sorry, Rose, truly. I take no joy in forcing us into this situation."

That hit her, "us"—like this would also be painful for him, not just her. Would he be more uncomfortable than her since he knew the people they would lie to? Her mind spun. What if he had a romantic partner that he had to cast aside for this ruse? She didn't even let her mind finish wherever that thought was going as her insides began to squirm.

"Walk me through why this is our only option. Why can't I be a specialist of some kind? Or a survivor of the plague of mist?" As she said each of these aloud, she already knew why they wouldn't work, but as if to preserve her sanity, Luc responded.

"Neither of those options will work, because there is no way that I could justify keeping you from the other Compass Points under the current circumstances. Everyone has lost someone to the mist. The Compass Points are supposed to be working together to find a solution. If I returned with a key, someone who had survived the plague, or someone who might know about helping us fight against it, I'd be required to introduce them to the others." He glanced at her for the first time since he caught her staring at his lips. His dark eyes were piercing in their focus, as if they would extract her secrets by sheer force of will. "Now, if you were willing to tell me who you're avoiding and why, I might be able to devise a different plan."

"No," she breathed, meeting his gaze. "I understand our position. I'm not thrilled about the situation we find ourselves in, but I also realize it will be worse for you to lie to your people. I'm only lying to strangers. So tell me what being with the Suden Point entails."

"No more argument?" he asked.

The barest flash of what she thought was concern crossed his face when she mentioned lying to his people, but it was gone before she could be sure. He seemed to accept her surrender and returned to his easy confidence.

"That was too easy. It's almost as if you don't mind the disguise."

Rose snorted. Was he flirting with her?

"I don't expect we will need to do much," he said. His focus dropped back to the fire, and he sounded tired. "We should be able to avoid any lake ceremonies. We'll need to be seen together in Compass Lake Village, and you'll stay with me at Suden house."

Her mind raced at that last piece of information. What was the layout of the house? What did staying together mean? She'd be damned if she appeared to break first in this standoff with more clarifying questions. If he didn't give details, she wouldn't continue to press.

"Suden aren't overly affectionate people, but we are…possessive," he finished smoothly. Her body warmed at something in his tone. "That alone should give us the protection that you require." He continued, "None of the Compass Points would dare to interfere in my relationship."

"Fine," she said.

She was exhausted mentally, emotionally, and physically. And this was just getting started.

She couldn't believe she'd been at the market this morning, as usual, selling her weapons and getting ready for another lesson with Tara.

Her heart sank, thinking of how far from that she'd come. Would she find a way to save Tara? Could the mist plague be reversed? Or could it only be prevented?

She didn't know any of the answers and found herself unwilling to ask the Suden Point any more questions.

The Suden Point may be many things—unfortunately, handsome was one—but he was not her ally. She couldn't trust him, especially not with her secrets. She could barely believe she was at the point where she thought letting him take her to Compass Lake was a good option.

She reminded herself that Tara needed this. Tara needed her, and no one else would fight for her.

Rose knew that feeling in the pit of her stomach. That feeling when you were in trouble, but the only one you could count on for help was yourself. She wanted that to be different for Tara. She didn't want the younger girl to feel the same weight Rose carried from childhood.

Rose was a part of this now, whether she wanted to be or not.

She had to use whatever means necessary to get through the interactions at Compass Lake. Whether she wanted to admit it or not, Luc's offer was good for that alone. He was right. The Compass Points would have no claim over one romantically involved with the Suden Point. She'd be protected in a way that she couldn't otherwise expect. He was offering her a lot and asking for very little in return.

Why had he chosen this path? Were the Compass Points that desperate?

It wasn't the Compass Points, though, was it? By bringing her in this way, Luc also guaranteed that her skills would only benefit the Suden if she decided to make weapons. He would be the only Compass Point who knew about her abilities and their value to fighting the mist. She didn't think highly of the Compass Points, but it was uncommon for them to operate in such secrecy from each other on such a largescale threat.

She knew they were a mess but hadn't realized it was this bad.

While many blamed the Suden Point for the plague since villages dedicated to their patron god, Aterra, seemed to be the least impacted, it made no difference when the mist crept through a village. The mist took everyone, Norden, Suden, Osten, Vesten, and human. That alone should be motivation to pool fae resources on finding a solution.

If the Suden Point operated in such isolation, something else was wrong.

Chapter Ten

"*R*ose...*Rose, wake up!*" Even as she rolled over on the hard ground, her nose chilled in the morning air. She felt victorious, knowing she'd been right; Arie would find them whether she wanted him to or not.

"What do you want, Arie? I'm not awake yet."

"*Well, let's change that, shall we?*" He sat as a large black bird on her stomach, poking at her with his wing. He had all the energy of a five-year-old on the winter solstice. There seemed to be no stopping this wake-up call.

She sat up and looked around. She'd slept later than she thought, though that made sense given everything that happened yesterday. Luc's bedroll was on the opposite side of the fire, giving her plenty of appreciated space.

Her stirring woke him, and their eyes met. She ran her gaze over his face as last night's conversation returned to her. It was simple to get lost in the depths of his dark brown eyes when they were so solely focused on her. He ran his fingers through thick hair, pushing that pesky piece back from his face as she finished her perusal.

They were to pretend to be in a romantic relationship for the foreseeable future. She could do this.

Though she had never been in a publicly scrutinized relationship before. Any relationships from the last few years had been more of a convenience. It got lonely with only Arie on the island, and sometimes she craved personal interaction and physical touch. But none of them were particularly real. She couldn't bring them to the island. She couldn't show them her work. She couldn't truly trust any of them with her whole self.

Arie continued to chatter about how he'd been able to track them down yesterday and spent time in the next village a day's ride south. Time and place never seemed to have a bearing on Arie. He could show up wherever he wanted in whatever form he wanted.

She'd lost herself in this most recent thread when she heard him say, *"They were talking all about it, that there were two survivors from this attack of the plague of mist."*

"Wait, what?" she exclaimed, getting Luc's attention.

"What is it?" he asked, glancing toward the bird perched on her stomach.

"The next village knows there were survivors of the mist attack?" she asked Arie. "How?"

Luc's eyes widened in surprise.

"They were talking about it already this morning. Some trader planning to stop at Bury saw you two stumbling out of the mist-covered village. No one has seen someone leave a village once it's been taken."

This was a problem. The last thing they needed was some rumor of her and Luc as mist survivors following them back to Compass Lake. That would ruin all their plans. Luc's romantic partner or not, the Compass Points would never leave them alone if they thought Rose was a survivor of the plague of mist. She dared a glance at Luc, a worry line forming on his brow as if he'd come to the same conclusion.

"They saw two people leaving?" he asked.

She nodded.

"We're going to have to find the trader," he said, sounding regretful.

"What are we going to do? The damage is already done. We can't make people forget what they've already heard."

Luc looked pained but said, "I can take care of it. We have to find him. There aren't any other villages between Bury and the next, so if he's still there, we should be able to make the story disappear."

Rose flinched at the callous tone. "Killing him won't stop the story from spreading. It's better to flee and pretend that we came from another direction. So we couldn't possibly be the travelers from Bury."

He rolled his eyes at her. "I'm not going to kill him. I'm not an idiot. That wouldn't change his actions, but we have other options."

"Such as?"

"Pack up," Luc said, ignoring her question. "We need to get there before the trader leaves." The black bird on her shoulder tilted his head as if he were reassessing Luc.

"What is it, Arie?" she asked. Since Luc wouldn't tell her anything, she might as well get some information from Arie as she packed her things.

"What do we know about Luc?" Arie asked.

"That he's the Suden Point. Isn't that enough?"

"I wonder…" He trailed off. *"He may be more interesting than I thought."* Arie flapped his wings and flew off to scout ahead of them.

Rose shook her head at his unhelpful responses and finished strapping her pack to the horse.

CHAPTER ELEVEN

20 years ago - Compass Lake

Rose was last to wake. She suspected Mom had let her sleep in due to staying up late to listen to the story again. She wandered into the kitchen.

"Grandpa, have you seen Mom?" she asked.

"Yes, she's out in the workshop. She wanted to get some work done before the ceremony this morning. She should be wrapping up shortly."

He was cooking breakfast, putting together a big family meal before they went to the lake's edge.

"I'm going to go watch her finish."

"Okay, tell her breakfast will be ready in twenty minutes."

Rose ran out of their small cottage and toward the workshop on the property. She hadn't seen Dad, but he had to have caretaker chores at the big house before today's event. She ran into the workshop, slowing down as she crossed the threshold. This was Mom's first rule for her being in the workshop—no running or horseplay when you're in the forge area.

"Good morning, Rose," her mom said without looking away from her project. The heat from the forge hit Rose like a thick steam the second she stepped into the room. "Did you sleep well?"

"Yes, Mom," Rose replied as she watched her smooth out the piece she was working on with repeated mallet swings. Rose's fingers went to her compass pendant as she watched.

"You want to help?" Mom asked.

This was Rose's aim in coming to the workshop. She loved when Mom asked her to help. Their training sessions were never enough. Rose always wanted to make things, to feel the magic and push it into metal.

"Yes." Rose almost ran but remembered the workshop rules and took great pains to walk over to Mom's side.

"Here you go, darling. You can take some swings." Mom pointed to the edge of the blade near the handle. "Will you work this area for me? I haven't quite got it right."

Rose's spine straightened, and her shoulders went back at her words. Mom needed her help. She preened as she went to work on the directed area. She could only manage a few swings before her arm got tired. Mom was behind her, watching closely as she started to feel the mallet's weight. Sweat dripped from her brow, but Rose didn't want to stop so quickly. Taking another swing, her arm shook as she raised the mallet. She couldn't hold on as the sweat dripped down her face and arms from the fire and her physical exertion. The hammer slipped from her grasp into the forge.

Rose didn't even think about it; she so badly wanted to be good at making magical weapons like Mom. She reached into the fire without hesitation to get the hammer back out and try again.

Mom's shriek was piercing.

Rose's hand was already in the forge's blazing heat when she realized she should feel pain. Instead, she felt a cold wind rush around her hand as she let Mom pull her back by the shoulders and inspect what should be a horrendously mangled hand.

"What?" Tears fell from Mom's face as she held up Rose's hand. She turned it this way and that, trying to make sense of what she was seeing. There was no damage. "Honey, what happened?"

"I think the wind helped me." Rose shrugged her shoulders. "It wrapped my hand and protected it from the fire."

"The wind? What do you mean?" Mom asked, her voice a whisper.

"Yeah, sometimes the wind helps me with things," Rose explained. "If I need to reach something too high, it helps knock it over so I can catch it. Or if I get a toy stuck in the tree, the wind helps bring it back down."

Mom's jaw hung open as Rose spoke. "I didn't know that, sweetie. How long has the wind been helping you?"

Rose turned her head to the side, looking to the left as she contemplated the question. "I'm not sure. I think awhile."

"Okay, honey, that's good. Can you do me a favor? Can we try and only ask the wind for help when it's just family?"

"Sure, Mom," Rose replied. "But why?"

"Rose." Mom knelt so they were face to face. "The wind is helping you because you can wield two types of magic. This is an extraordinary gift. So special that some people wouldn't know what to do with it. They might be scared of it. But me, Dad, and Grandpa, we would never be scared of it. We will protect you always."

Rose wasn't sure what that meant. People would be scared of her? Because the wind wanted to help her? She didn't mistake the severe look on Mom's face, though. It'd been the exact look that Mom had given her when she told her Grandma was sick. This was something that Rose had to do.

"Okay, Mom. I won't tell anyone else about the wind."

JILLIAN WITT

A gift from MTMC Tours

Thank you so much for joining our tour!
Happy reading!! from MTMC Tours

After breakfast, Rose and her family went down to the lake's edge. The Summer Solstice Ceremony started early, but the lake's edge was still packed, even given the hour and many Compass Lake residents' late night the evening prior.

"Come on, we won't have a good spot. I won't be able to see," Rose whined as she tugged on Dad's hand.

"It'll be fine, Rose. You know you can sneak in between people to get a better look," Grandpa reminded her.

They stopped at the back of the crowd. The Compass Points were already on the beach. The Norden Point stood tall as he called the ceremony to order.

"We're here to give thanks for the Covenant, for our creation, and the magic we were given." His voice rang loud and clear to all gathered. "In their wisdom, the gods entrusted us to keep the balance between humanity and their overwhelming power. They never wanted to unleash chaos on the continent again and installed us, the fae, to prevent it. Further, they anointed the strongest of each fae to be a Compass Point, guiding each court's actions as cardinal directions guide our travels. They trusted us to lead and to stand together to ensure the safety and happiness of all on the continent—those with magic and those without."

The Norden Point glanced to the Osten Point. She was a tall woman with light brown skin. Her dark brown hair was wrapped in a tight bun atop her head, showing off high cheekbones. Rose saw her chin lifting ever so slightly as the Norden Point said, "We thank Zrak for his sacrifice. He saved our continent, and we know the Osten miss his wisdom every day."

Rose could have sworn she saw the Osten Point roll her eyes. Rose giggled, and Grandpa shushed her.

The Norden Point started up again. Rose knew this would go on for a while longer. She was going to get a better view. She waved to Mom and pointed towards the lake as she snuck through the crowd.

Rose made it to the front. As she popped through the last line of people, she ran into a fair-skinned boy with light brown hair who seemed to have had the same idea.

"Sorry," Rose whispered as she picked herself up from their crash.

"Watch where you're going," the boy said as he righted himself. As his eyes met hers, she wasn't sure if it was a trick of the light, but she thought she saw them flash from a dark grey to piercing blue as he pointed at her. "Hey, I know you. You live in the cottage out back."

"I'm Rose." She stuck out her hand politely like her parents had taught her to do when she met new people.

The boy stared at her hand. He seemed to be talking to himself under his breath.

"Do you not want to meet? I've seen you too, and I wanted to meet you. My parents taught me this is what you do when you meet someone officially." Her gaze fell to her outstretched hand.

"That's ridiculous," he scoffed.

She shrugged and turned to go.

He stepped forward to catch her shoulder. "I'm Aiden," he said, seemingly unwilling to lose her attention just yet.

"Hi, Aiden." Her hand returned to its outstretched position.

"Fine," he grumbled as he reached his hand out for hers.

"There, that makes us officially friends," Rose said as she broke the shake. "At least, that's how I think it works."

Aiden's mouth quirked up at the corner. "How do you know? Do you have any friends?"

"Well, no." Rose paused as she thought it over. "Do you?"

Aiden thought about it. "I have one friend, but no one can see him."

Rose swore she saw his eyes flash grey again before returning to their piercing blue. "Well, I think we could be great friends. That is if you're ever not so busy."

"Where have you seen me?" Aiden asked. His back straightened at her attention.

"In the yard and in that room with the desks. But you always seem to have adults with you. Are those your parents?"

A dark look crossed his face. "No, my parents are never with me. It's probably my tutors." His eyes lit up as if he'd just had an idea. "Do you want to watch the Ceremony with me? It should be starting soon. My dad's almost finished speaking."

"The Norden Point?" she questioned. Magic started to swirl around them. The Ceremony was indeed about to begin.

"Yeah." Aiden sounded unimpressed that his father was the leader of their people. They watched together as the Norden Point, having finished his speech, loosed his water magic into the lake, pushing all the water to the center, creating a geyser-like explosion.

Chapter Twelve

The day's ride to the village left Rose's thoughts spinning again. They should be able to catch up to the trader before they moved on. That left her to wonder what they would do when they found them. Luc remained categorically unhelpful in his answers.

There couldn't have been more than twenty homes in the village as they rode in with a large black bird circling above them. The village square was already empty. Night was falling. If the trader had stayed, the tavern would be the place to find them.

"I'll do a few laps of the village, don't worry about me. Just figure out what the Suden Point is up to," Arie said to her as she and Luc stabled their horses at the lone tavern. She nodded, hoping he could see the gesture as they walked to the entrance.

"What's the play again, Luc? We're at the point where you might need to tell me the plan," Rose tried once more before they walked through the door.

"Just follow my lead." His reply was calm as he pulled open the tavern door and motioned Rose forward.

Rose sighed and walked in, following Luc to the bar.

"Why don't you go grab a seat," Luc said once they'd placed their order. The bartender behind the counter was getting a bottle of whiskey off the shelf. "I'll wait for the drinks."

Rose nodded, still unsure what they were doing, but at least she'd get a drink out of it at this point.

She sat on a stool at the end of the bar and examined the room and its inhabitants. Like the village, the tavern was small, with few tables. The stools at the bar were mostly filled with lively groups discussing the day. Rose got the sense the town didn't get that many travelers, and though the establishment also had rooms available, its main fare was the food and drink served there.

She identified three groups as her gaze roamed the room. A few men were at a table playing cards and drinking, a man and woman were having dinner at an out-of-the-way table, and she could hear the lively chatter of a group of tradespeople gathered at the opposite end of the bar, talking about the workday.

She'd bet the person they sought was in the more active group at the end of the bar. She looked back to Luc to see how much longer he'd be with the drinks. He seemed to be flirting with the bartender as she handed over the glasses.

Rose rolled her eyes.

The scent of pine and cinnamon filled her nostrils—magic. She'd smelled this before, in her island home when they'd fought the mist monster. This must be Luc's magic. She looked again as he engaged the bartender in conversation. Rose saw the moment Luc's hand slipped while reaching for the drink. She would have missed it if she hadn't been searching for it. She did not think it was an accident as Luc's hand touched the bartender's skin, and the smell of his magic strengthened.

The bartender's eyes went momentarily blank. If Rose hadn't been staring so intently, she wouldn't have seen the brief flash before the bartender leaned forward toward Luc. Finally, he took the glasses and turned away.

"What. The. Hell," Rose mumbled under her breath as Luc handed her the drink.

Luc raised an eyebrow at her. "What?"

"What did you just do?"

A slow cat-like grin crept across Luc's face as he raised his glass to hers. Clinking them together he replied, "We're definitely going to talk about this, but I need you to come with me first to talk to that group over there." He tilted his head toward the group she'd identified earlier.

"You think the trader we're looking for is among them?"

His cocky smile was infuriating as he replied, "I know the trader we're looking for is that man in the middle." Luc pointed to a large, burly man with warm beige skin in the center of the group.

"You're absolutely right; we will talk about this." She hopped off the stool, grabbed her drink, and wrapped her hand in the crook of Luc's arm. Taking a deep breath, she tried to let go of her irritation with each step towards the group.

"Successful day?" Luc asked as the circle naturally parted to allow them access.

"Oh, good enough. I spent the whole day in the square and was able to lighten my load enough to head back home," the trader said. "I'll be back on the road tomorrow."

"We haven't had much other traffic through here. What brings you two?" asked a short woman standing at the trader's side.

"Oh, we're just passing through, too, headed down to Sandrin," Luc replied before returning his attention to the trader. Reaching his hand to the man, Luc offered a handshake and an introduction. "I'm Luc; this is Rose."

The trader clasped the offered hand, and the scent of Luc's magic hit her even stronger than before.

Like the bartender, the man's face went momentarily blank before snapping back to the introduction like nothing had happened.

Luc smiled and continued around the circle. He shook each hand and discussed the day. With every touch, she saw the split-second blankness before the conversation continued.

Finishing with the group, Luc looked like he would excuse himself to the bar for another round. She wasn't quite sure what he was accomplishing, but she would find out. She reached down and wove their fingers together, saying, "One more round, darling?"

His heat-filled gaze stopped her in her tracks. She couldn't remember what she was going to do. "Yes, love, I'll join you." He nodded to the group as they excused themselves.

She tried to sort herself out as they ordered another round. What kind of magic was he using? Earth magic couldn't physically affect people like she'd been seeing, could it? She wondered about the old stories she'd heard as a child. Aterra, the patron god of the Suden, was said to wield mind shadow. There hadn't been a Suden with these powers that she could ever remember hearing about. It was just another myth of the gods, not something real.

Then again, she knew more than most that the myths of the gods could certainly be real. Her fingers went to the compass pendant around her neck as she wondered, why not this one too?

She opened her mouth to ask...what? She wasn't sure, but she was spared having to figure out what she'd say as Luc turned to her.

"We need to make one more stop, and I may need Arie's help."

"I know I'm on repeat, but again I ask, what the hell is going on, Luc?" She pushed the words out, despite her surprise at his request. She had so many questions she wasn't even sure where to start. "What are we doing at one more stop? Hell, what did we do here?" she said in a harsh whisper while working to keep a calm smile.

He leaned in close, like the fake lover he seemed already pretending to be, his mouth inches from her ear. "We're just making sure that they remember the right things."

She could hear the smile on his lips at his words. He stayed close for a breath too long, her body humming with unappreciated anticipation. Her mind started to catch up with his words, trying to ignore the feeling that his proximity was causing.

He was trying to make sure they remembered the right things with magic.

He had to be talking about Aterra's mind shadow.

Still dangerously close, he added, "I would lick your face while I'm here, but we're in public, and I don't think you want an audience." Still smiling, he pulled back.

Heat rushed through her body at the thought of what he would do with his tongue without an audience, but she shook her head free of the all too different mind haze that his presence created. She had to keep it together. He was more dangerous than she thought if he could alter memories. What else could he do?

"You being weird isn't going to stop me from questioning what we're doing," she replied as coolly as possible. She didn't think Luc bought it as his eyebrow rose. Her face must look very different than her words.

"Should I ask them about gossip from Bury?" she asked to try and change the subject.

"Great idea. Why don't you ask about that before we leave?"

They collected their refilled drinks from the bar and went back to the group.

Rose finally found a natural break in the conversation to ask, "Did you hear what happened up north in Bury?" All the eyes in the circle seemed to snap their focus to her.

"Yeah, terrible thing," replied the trader, who couldn't help but tell his story, even though she was sure everyone in the room had heard it. "I was coming past the village of Bury. It had to be right after it happened. I planned to stop there but could see something wasn't right." He paused, shuddering before he went on. "Don't have to be fae to know that the dark mist hanging over the ground is bad news."

She went for the direct approach. "Did you see anyone not affected?"

"Not affected? What do you mean? As soon as I realized it was one of those mist villages everyone has been talking about, I hightailed it out of there. I didn't see anyone else until I got here."

Rose wasn't sure what to do next. Luc had mind magic. This confirmed it. She looked at Luc, reappraising him. He was dangerous, certainly, but it was also incredibly impressive. Her magic allowed her to sense the magic of others to help tune a weapon to their specific strengths. She'd known he was powerful when she met him, but it'd been so long since she'd been around fae she didn't have a good comparison of how powerful he truly was.

Luc held her gaze for a second too long before picking up her dropped conversation thread with the group. "Well, ladies and gentlemen, we've had a long day of travel and, unfortunately, more tomorrow. I think we'll take our leave for the night. Thank you all for the welcoming conversation."

The trader laughed behind them as they turned to walk away. "No way is that couple going to their room to sleep, if you get my meaning."

The group laughed as Luc led Rose back to the bar, where they got a meal and a room. Apparently, they had already started their fake relationship, and their audience believed it. She wasn't sure what to make of that since they hadn't really been trying.

She couldn't think too long about their fake couple status as they entered their room. Rose barely took in her new surroundings as she swung around to face Luc. "Explain yourself. No more deflecting."

He gave her his patented half smile, indicating that he had as many questions to ask as she did. "How did you know I did something to the bartender?"

She tilted her head. She was caught off guard by his question, and she replied far too honestly. "I can smell your pine and cinnamon magic, and what you did down there was very different than the earth magic you threw around yesterday. So start talking."

His smile turned predatory as he stalked forward to her.

She closed her eyes, disbelieving her own stupidity. Still cursing herself, she inadvertently stepped back as he moved, finding the door at her back.

"You must have misspoken. Magical weapons makers can feel magic, but I've never heard of them smelling it," he crooned as he caged her with an arm on each side of her body. He inhaled deeply, leaning in as close as she'd allow.

"Ugh." She pushed him back with both arms on his shoulders. "Don't smell me. You know that's not how this works."

"Can you blame me?" He seemed pensive.

"I'm not using magic. You won't get a scent."

He rubbed his hand down his face. "I missed even more about you than I thought yesterday." Shaking his head mostly to himself, he said, "You can be quite distracting."

She didn't know what to make of that. "You're right. I misspoke." She didn't think he'd buy it, but she'd been an idiot and was out of options.

Ever the predator evaluating his prey, he tipped his head, respecting her personal space since she pushed him.

"Oh no, Rose, I'm not letting this go. You're fae. I just don't know how I missed it."

CHAPTER THIRTEEN

R ose froze.

She knew she'd made a terrible mistake but hadn't been prepared to hear it stated so boldly. No one had called her fae in ten years. Not even Arie acknowledged it, though she was sure he knew.

Luc's gaze hadn't left her face at his declaration. He watched her every move. Her eyes shifted around the room. She was blocking the door; a window directly behind him was the only other way out.

What was she thinking? She wasn't going to run. She'd known this was a risk of coming with him. Arie had even warned her. They'd guessed Luc would figure it out, but she'd decided it was better than drowning in her own guilt.

He'd just figured it out sooner than she hoped, thanks to her own stupidity.

She rolled her shoulders back, straightening her spine. "So?"

"You're not going to tell me how I missed it? Do we need to worry about others at Compass Lake realizing it?"

She sighed heavily. "You know as well as I do that it takes time to learn a fae's magical scent."

Luc tilted his head. "And yet you just described mine quite succinctly."

Her cheeks colored slightly. "You've used magic multiple times since I met you. I'm pretty good at recognizing the smell, given my weapon-making senses," she replied.

"But those abilities are traditionally aligned with"—he stumbled over the phrasing—"half-fae parentage."

"They are."

"But you are not half-fae. They can't smell magic."

"They cannot."

He took another step back, sitting on the edge of the bed, his hands resting on his knees. "I thought I was done underestimating you."

"Well, if it makes you feel better, I underestimated your magic too."

"It does not, but what do you mean?" A smirk tugged at the curve of his lip.

"Mind magic, Luc? I didn't even think that was real. I thought it was a bedtime story."

The smirk turned to a small smile as he replied, "I used it to make them forget they saw anyone leaving Bury."

She guessed they were being honest with each other now. At least, sort of. He still hadn't asked what kind of fae she was.

"When you touched them?" she asked.

"Yes."

"And you were somehow able to tell who all had been told the story?"

"Yes."

"And so you know that there is one more person in the village that we need to track down, and you need to touch?"

A nod this time. He'd given up on verbal responses as his eyes locked on hers. She had a feeling that, as Suden Point, there were few he was completely honest with about his magic.

"Have you ever used that magic on me?"

A pause and another head tilt. "No, Rose. I want you to remember every one of our interactions." His mounting concern at sharing information about his magic seemed to melt into a seductive smile before her eyes.

"Even the interaction where you attacked me?" she asked pointedly.

"Ah, but that fight was our proper introduction. Never underestimate the power of first impressions. You liked me so much you licked me."

Gods, would she never live that one down? Impulse control. She needed to learn impulse control. "Keep telling yourself that." She said, her hand coming to rest on her cocked hip. "But you can take memories about others, not just yourself? You were able to remove their memories of me?"

"No one remembers that two people were coming out of the village. Well, almost no one. Let's wrap this up. Can you call Arie?"

She opened the window and didn't have to look far before the familiar black bird flew into the room.

"Took you two long enough. What were you doing in here? It smells weird." Arie looked at Rose's face. It must have shown the weight of her revealed secret. *"What happened? What did he do?"* The bird's head snapped towards Luc.

"Nothing—well, I messed up, and he caught me." Luc's gaze darted to her, trying to pick up the thread of the conversation with only her side of it. "He knows I'm fae."

"Want me to kill him?" Arie said as he ruffled his feathers.

Rose raised an eyebrow at the bird. "Could you do that? He has a lot of power. Mind shadow, if you believe it."

"I wondered," Arie said. *"Offer still stands. I can take care of him if you'd like."*

Rose laughed. She was never sure how seriously to take Arie. Did he really think he could fight the Suden Point?

"I'm good. I still need him at the moment to see if there is a way to save Tara." That brought back the reality of the situation. She had known this was a risk. She hadn't been near another fae for over ten years. While very good at not using her magic, she was bound to slip up.

"I'm glad I still have some value to you," Luc cut in, looking at her. He arched an eyebrow. "Who knows, if you tell me more about yourself, maybe I can help you in another way. I am the Suden Point."

"Pass."

He shrugged. "I appreciate what you told me tonight, even if your companion isn't thrilled with it."

Arie seemed to ignore Luc and looked around, taking in the small room. Rose hadn't even had time to evaluate her settings, but she saw Arie's eyes lock and stay on the one bed that Luc sat on. *"This keeps getting better and better."* His voice held a smile that the bird's face couldn't replicate.

"Grow up, Arie." Rose tried to brush it off but couldn't help a glance at Luc. His eyes bounced between the bird and Rose, and finally settled on the bed as their source of conversation as a half smile appeared.

"I've been a perfect gentleman, Arie."

"Stop it." She wasn't sure who she was snapping at, but they both stopped. "Don't we have a person to find? What do you know about them?"

"A person?" Arie focused on the task.

"Yes, the seamstress purchased goods from the trader today and heard his story. We need to visit her."

"It's getting late. What exactly are you thinking will get her to open the door? And while I'm asking, do we even know where she lives?"

"Yes, and that's where Arie comes in. Arie, can you take any shape? I think we need an adorable, unassuming, lost dog."

"I think I missed something, but I want to know what this boy is up to, Rose. Tell him I'm in."

CHAPTER FOURTEEN

Luc didn't take long to walk them over a street to the house he deemed "the one." It was a modest house like the other dozen in the village. It was late enough that most families were having their evening meal, though hopefully not late enough that one would be too scared or nervous to open the door to a stranger.

Arie transformed into a small dog and chased them down the cobblestones. Luc picked Arie up as they headed for the front door.

They didn't have to wait long for a middle-aged woman to answer their knock. She had a discerning look about her as she appraised the two strangers and a dog on her doorstep. Not opening the door fully, she could still slam it in their face if necessary.

"What can I do for you?" She was polite but showed a hard edge that said they would only get a few moments of courtesy before the door closed.

"We're travelers, staying at the inn for the night en route to Sandrin. This dog followed us as we were taking an evening stroll. He stopped here, and honestly, I know this is a little strange, but we wanted to see if he was yours. We don't want to leave him outside all alone."

"I'm insulted by this storyline. I can, of course, take care of myself," Arie remarked mentally to Rose. She struggled to contain her eye roll.

"Not mine," the woman said as she reached to pet Arie's head.

"Oh, no! We were sure this was his home. Do you mind holding him for a second?" Luc lightly brushed her bare wrist as he placed the dog in her arms.

That glazed look overtook the woman's eyes as she held and mindlessly stroked Arie for less than a second. Luc faked a sneeze into his elbow, and then reached to take Arie back.

Arie, however, had different plans. He wiggled out of their grasp, falling to the floor. He took off at a run into the woman's house.

"Oh, I'm so sorry," Luc murmured. He must have realized Arie's fall was intentional and was trying to make sense of what Arie was doing.

"Tell him I'm just checking for others in here. What if she's told someone else since she saw the trader?"

Rose lifted her hand to her mouth to cover a laugh. She, of course, couldn't tell Luc that with the woman standing before them, but she appreciated Arie's commitment to his role.

"Well, I'll be," the woman said as she turned to yell after the dog, but she didn't move from the door. She still used it as a partial shield, clearly not wanting to give the strangers an opening to get in. Rose guessed from her behavior that she was likely alone.

"Do you want me to try and collect him?" Luc offered.

"No. Stay there. I'll be back in a minute. Don't leave without this dog. He's not mine." The woman closed the door on them and went in after Arie.

"Arie's looking for anyone else in the house," Rose whispered to Luc now that they were alone.

"He's not very good at following directions, is he?" Luc commented.

"Definitely not."

The woman reappeared moments later with Arie in her arms. This time she set him down outside the door instead of trying to hand him back to Luc. "There you go, out where you belong." She spoke primarily to Arie at this point.

Luc must have realized as much as he said, "Well, thanks anyway. Sorry to disturb your evening."

They turned and headed back down the road, Arie trotting along behind them, still committed to his role, sniffing out other houses as they went.

"There was no one else there and only one place setting at the dinner table. I think we're safe," Arie said to Rose.

"Luc thanks you for your dedication. However, he didn't appreciate your improvisation. He seems like a planner."

Luc turned to glare at her as they continued to walk down the street. "I'm just saying I had it covered. When I touched her, I could tell she hadn't told anyone else."

"Ahh, I must have forgotten to share that part of the explanation on how your powers work with Arie." Rose laughed a little. She wondered if she was having some kind of stress reaction to her secret being out.

Luc's lips pursed. "Hmph." He sighed, his hand rubbing his temple. He stopped walking and fixed his gaze on Rose, seeming to come to a conclusion; the preceding deciding points she was unaware of. "I can take memories, and I can also show memories. As you noted, it's a very rare gift in the Suden people. I haven't met any others that have it."

Rose let out a breath. "And why are you telling me this?"

"Because I want you to know." He leaned forward a little, his intense focus making their prolonged eye contact feel intimate. "I thought I finished underestimating you back in Bury, but then you surprised me again tonight."

She mentally cringed at her inexcusable slip-up. She'd just have to wait and see what it would cost her.

"You obviously carry a great deal of past pain with you. So much so that you hide your very nature. And yet you still have this unbelievable determination to take care of people. I've never met anyone like you. I want to know more about you, Rose, and the only way I can think to earn that is by giving a little of myself."

Rose felt her cheeks warm.

What was this? Was this more of the Suden-perfected charm? Or was he being serious? Her traitorous body seemed to hope for the latter as she relished someone seeing her, even if they also saw her pain.

"Can you show me a memory?" she asked.

"Hmmm," he hummed, tapping his finger to his chin. "Not tonight," he said as he looked around. "Tonight, I can give you a quick taste of some emotions." He extended his hand toward her, and she took it unquestioningly. "Feelings and emotions are an inseparable part of memories. When I show someone my memories, they feel them with me. For this, I will let you experience the feelings without the visual memory."

She nodded. She had asked for this, after all. He interlaced their fingers, a chill traveling up Rose's spine at the contact.

"Ready?" he asked.

Rose nodded as she fell into a dizzying mix of emotions: determination, attraction, amusement, and admiration flashed through their connection.

As he went to untwine their hands, she caught a single image before he pulled away—her standing at the door to her island workshop.

Her cheeks heated further, but thankfully it was dark enough now that she hoped Luc wouldn't notice. She stepped back from him, her heart pounding faster than she'd like, and said, "Thanks for that."

He surveyed her face; she wasn't quite sure what he was looking for. He looked like he might ask something as pup Arie burst into the space between them.

"Come on. Let's get back to the inn."

Rose looked down at Arie as he wandered ahead, nose to the ground, sniffing everything in sight. The only thing that Rose could smell was the perfect mix of pine and cinnamon permeating the air around them.

CHAPTER FIFTEEN

R ose was in a room with two people she didn't trust.

"You've done a remarkable job on the magical test. Some of
the strongest magic we've seen," said the first man. He had gentle eyes
and looked the same age as Dad, but she knew he was much older.
Fae age wasn't an easy thing to guess.

The second man looked much like his son, Aiden. He glared at
the first man.

She watched as the first man brought another item from the cupboard
closet and held it before her. She knew instinctively she had to touch it.

Holding it in her hands, both men staring, horrific new magic
assaulting her nostrils.

Frozen in terror, she dropped the item.

She had to go.

She tore out of the room to the surprised shouts of both men.

No matter how quickly she arrived, she knew it would be too late.
Faster, she ran, pushing herself harder than she'd ever gone. Finally,
coming upon the cottage, she knew that something was wrong.

The air was thick with the magic she'd sensed. Nothing could
have prepared her for the chaos and devastation in front of her when
she opened the door.

Mangled bodies, limbs in places and at angles they didn't belong,
far too much death for her sixteen-year-old mind to process.

She dropped to her knees and started screaming.

"Rose. Rose...wake up." A rough hand on her bare shoulder. She flinched away from the contact as her brain wiped away the fog of the terrible nightmare.

"Rose?"

She sat up, and Luc backed away from the bed, back to his mess of blankets on the floor before the door. When they returned last night, he hadn't even asked about sharing the bed. He'd mumbled a few things about when they would leave in the morning and then said he was going for a walk. She'd wanted the space and time to think, so she hadn't questioned it and must have been asleep when he returned.

"I'm awake. It was just a dream. I'm fine." She didn't bother looking at him. Her lie was more than evident in both her voice and actions.

"That's doubtful," he said. "At least everyone knows we're awake now."

She appreciated that he tried adding some levity to the morning's heavy start. The morning that they would make it one step closer to Compass Lake.

"Let's just get going."

If she just kept focused on the next step, she wouldn't think about what she was actually doing—returning to the place of her nightmares with the Suden Point, who now knew she was fae.

Luc gave her a slow and assessing look as he seemed to think through his next words.

"We still have another day and a half of travel. Is there anything I can tell you about what to expect at Compass Lake that will ease your worry?"

This was a dangerous line of questioning. Rose still didn't know if he was aware of her element. He knew she was fae, but at Compass Lake, it was more important to know which court she belonged to.

He hadn't asked, and she wouldn't offer. Not when the answer might be more dangerous than knowing she was fae.

"I'll think about it and let you know," Rose replied. It was too early, and she was still too frazzled from her nightmare, from this journey, to choose her words correctly. "Let's just hit the road."

Rose remained stuck in her thoughts for the morning ride. She was re-evaluating everything that had led her on this journey and where she had gone wrong.

She was heading to Compass Lake.

She was heading to Compass Lake with the Suden Point.

She would laugh at herself if she weren't worried that her life was in danger.

Would the Suden Point's plan for their fake relationship be enough to protect her? Would the Suden Point learn too much from their proximity? He'd learned so much, but she still had plenty that it'd be dangerous for him to know.

For a ruthless leader, he'd shown more contemplation than anger at learning another one of her secrets. She knew she was getting some measure of grace from him because he needed something from her.

He needed her to make magical weapons. But he also wanted to know her? He saw the pain she carried? Those words didn't seem necessary for a fake relationship. They were confusing. She'd disregard them, but the emotions he showed her seemed to match, and magic was much harder to fake than words.

Her thoughts were interrupted by the twang of an arrow released from a bow. She turned to see a bolt flying directly toward her. She didn't think as her whole body twitched slightly, and her wind magic, reacting on instinct, pushed the arrow off course.

After not even a moment's contemplation of what had just happened, Rose was faced with another sound. Screams no less alarming but infinitely more terrifying wrenched her ears. Rose searched the scene, trying to piece together what was happening.

Someone had shot at her.

They'd missed with a bit of help from her magic.

Her gaze turned behind her to Luc. Was he hurt? Was he the one now screaming? His eyes met hers, red-rimmed and fierce.

He was unharmed but certainly not unaffected.

Her mind kept spinning as the screaming continued, but muffled. If he wasn't screaming, who was? She watched Luc's eyes leave hers and return to the ground beneath a tree just off the main path. He hopped off his horse and walked toward it. The dirt was disturbed, as if it'd been recently moved. The screams quieted as she noticed the earth continued to push itself down, flattening the area.

"Luc," Rose called, her eyes following him as he moved, her mind catching up with what happened as she picked up the telltale scent of cinnamon and pine—Luc's magic.

"Luc," she said, still disbelieving. She hopped off her horse and followed him over to the mound of dirt. She grabbed Luc's arm as the screams started to quiet, but she couldn't break through whatever rage he was in. His eyes still boring into the mound, the red ring around his irises unwilling to recede.

"Luc, we need to question him," she said as she put herself in front of Luc. His eyes had to look at her instead of his target. The sounds from the pile of dirt had quieted. She hoped she wasn't too late. She risked her wind power again to send some likely needed air underground as she saw Luc's eyes turn from red back to dark brown.

"Shit," Luc cursed under his breath. "I'm not sure they survived that, but I'll dig them back up."

Rose nodded as Luc started to unearth the archer. She sighed in relief when she realized the archer's chest was still rising and falling.

"Who sent you? What were you after?" Luc pressed as he lifted the archer from the pit with his magic. His hood fell back to reveal a grey-haired man.

"I was just after your money." The man coughed and sputtered as he likely tried to readjust to breathing normally.

"Money?" Luc wondered aloud. Rose watched his eyes roll in an exaggerated fashion. "Why were you trying to take it?"

"I was a farmer, but my village was taken by the mist plague a few months ago. I was out of the village for the day when it came." The man looked off into the distance. His eyes filled with tears as he continued to cough. "I just don't know what else to do. I can't go back to my village, to my family."

Rose saw a frown flicker across Luc's face as he rolled his neck slightly.

"Go to the village just north of here. They have a temple that should be able to help you. If I hear any reports of thieves on this road, I will come back myself."

The man swallowed loudly as he nodded, turning almost immediately to walk in the direction from which Luc and Rose had come.

Rose snapped her mouth shut as she evaluated what she was witnessing. She'd seen the terrifying Suden Point in action, willing to destroy someone who had shot at her. She knew he would have killed the man if she hadn't stepped in.

She'd returned to her horse, deep in thought, when Luc interrupted them.

"That arrow should have hit you." His words were unassuming, his tone was anything but.

She remembered the smooth timbre of his voice from their first meeting at the market stall.

"That man should have also been dead when I dug him up. You were right to stop me, I lost control, but I wasn't just burying him. I crushed the earth down on top of him too." Luc shook his head as his eyes locked on Rose's. "He definitely shouldn't have had enough air to survive."

Rose didn't know if he told her this to try and scare her, but he stated it as if it were simply a fact. She couldn't bring herself to fear his magic. She might fear what he'd do with her secrets, but she didn't fear his power.

She knew what it was to carry more power than those around you.

"Are you asking me something, Luc?"

Luc gave her a catlike grin.

"Rose, why are you stopped?" Arie arrived in bird form again, landing on her shoulder.

She wondered if he knew how excellent his timing was. She tried to pat his head, but Arie shook her off with the brush of his wing.

"We ran into a thief on the road. We handled it." Her eyes tracked the archer's receding shape as he walked away from them. "Though it was a somber reminder about the impacts of the mist plague on more than just those lost to the endless sleep."

Luc's eyes shifted to the black bird. He'd seen Arie in bird form enough to recognize him, especially when he landed so casually on

Rose's shoulder. The fae didn't seem happy to see him. She was sure he'd been moments away from taking a guess at her magic line.

"Let's get back on the road. We've still got a lot of ground to cover," Luc said as he gave Rose a meaningful look.

She couldn't help but smile to herself. He thought he knew what type of fae she was, did he? If only the answer were so straightforward.

Chapter Sixteen

15 years ago - Compass Lake

"On the count of three, Aiden," Rose yelled from the lake's edge. "One," Aiden yelled as he sprinted down the hill toward the beach and Rose.

"Two," Rose shouted back at him as she called on her magic.

"Three!" they yelled in tandem as Aiden leapt into the air, on a collision course with Rose and the hard ground if she didn't change his trajectory.

She reached for her magic as Aiden's frame came barreling towards her, calling the water from Compass Lake. She didn't want it to burst through the ground like last time. She worked to picture it creating a slide that caught Aiden in mid-flight and shot him out into the deeper part of the lake.

She heard him laughing with glee and then a splash.

She let go of her magic and turned to look as Aiden's head burst above the surface.

"Nice!" Aiden yelled from the water as he grinned.

"Your turn," Rose said as she ran back to the bottom of the hill to get a running start. She turned back toward the lake as Aiden emerged and moved to take the position she'd been in at the water's edge.

"When I say go!" Aiden skipped the countdown. "Go!"

Rose didn't hesitate as she rushed forward. Bare feet connected with grass and then sand as she gained speed. She watched Aiden concentrate as she moved. She readied herself to lunge, just as he had. Rose felt the second that Aiden started to call the water around him. She hurled herself into the air, with no fear that she wouldn't slide gracefully into the lake just as he had.

She was already in midair when her eyes locked on Aiden's. They widened in panic and flashed grey. He flailed his arms as he tried to pull his magic to create the slide just as she had. Not so much as waves rippled from the motions. She was running out of airtime as he tried to call the water to shoot directly from the ground instead of pulling it out of the lake. It would at least stop her from crashing, even if it wasn't as elegant.

Nothing happened.

Rose was out of time. She was no longer leaping; she was falling, about to land face first on the sandy beach. She didn't want to take Aiden's turn from him but knew she had to act fast. She called the water to her as she headed for a crash landing, using it to push her body off its current trajectory, catching her inches from the ground and sending her splashing into the lake.

Pushing her head above the surface, she looked toward Aiden.

His head hung, drooped between his shoulders. His eyes were closed, and his hands balled into fists at his side. She understood he'd be disappointed, but she'd landed fine. It wasn't until she turned back to look at the shore that she saw the real reason for his disappointment.

Aiden's parents stood at the bottom of the hill, his father's brow furrowed and his mother's arms folded across her chest as they both studied their son.

"Want to try again?" Rose asked Aiden. He lifted his head, his blue eyes shining with unshed tears.

"You alright, Rose?" he asked. "I'm so sorry. I'm not sure what happened."

"No worries, Aiden. Want to try again?" she echoed.

His parents had unfortunately moved closer. His mother stepped cautiously as she twisted her hands together. His father's eyes searched the lakeshore as if assessing if anyone else saw his son's failure.

"Aiden, haven't you been practicing?" his father asked as he moved onto the beach.

"Good afternoon," Rose called as she paddled back to shore, pulling herself out of the lake.

"Rose," Aiden's mother replied.

Aiden's father's eyes flicked over her as if she weren't even there before landing back on Aiden. "Aiden, I asked you a question."

"Yes, Father. I have been. Rose and I were practicing now." He hung his head again, unable to make eye contact with his father after his poor showing.

"It didn't look like it. We will ask Mrs. Winter to increase your lessons on the movement of water. I can't believe you couldn't call anything to soften the girl's fall."

Aiden's cheeks flush, but he still didn't raise his head.

"Yes, Father."

"You should go in now. You have more theory work to study before your next practical lesson." His parents turned and retreated, assuming that Aiden would follow without question.

He did, only stopping to look briefly at Rose as he passed. His bright blue eyes bore into hers. "Are you sure you're okay?"

"Of course, Aiden. I caught myself. It was just practice."

He nodded as he turned away, chasing his parents up the hill.

Rose dried off and trekked into Mom's workshop.

"Mom, can I work for a bit?" Rose called over her shoulder. Mom was working on her own project in the corner of the shop. But since the accident when she was young, Mom never liked to be far while Rose worked.

"Go for it, baby," Mom called.

She picked up an axe blade that needed some evening out and set it to heating. She started working the metal well before it was fully ready, but she had some feelings to work through. She really didn't like the way that Aiden's parents treated him. Let alone the way they mostly ignored her.

She'd been working longer than she thought when she felt Mom at her shoulder, watching as she worked the blade into submission, smoothing out the rough edges.

"I can't figure out what to do with this part." Rose pointed to the top edge of the blade. There was a unique swirl in the metal, breaking the uniform shine of her work.

"Leave it," Mom said. "It makes it unique, just like its maker."

Rose smiled at that. She put her work aside to cool, pushing her wind over the weapon to speed it along.

"Be careful, Rose." She looked toward the door. "Aiden could walk in."

Rose paused her cooling wind and looked up at her Mom. "He won't. His parents called him away." She paused and asked the real question. "Why can't I tell Aiden, Mom? I tell him everything."

"I know, Rose," Mom said, kneeling to get to eye level with her and carefully reaching out to grasp her shoulders. "I know it's hard not to share our whole selves with our friends. The thing is, you're Norden, and everyone knows you to be Norden because that's what

Dad and I are. The Compass Points still have"—she stumbled over her words a little—"outdated ideas about families. They think that Norden should only be with other Norden."

"But you and Dad are Norden," Rose said, still not entirely understanding. "We are a Norden family." Rose tilted her head to the side as she finished the sentence. "Wait, am I not Norden because I have wind magic?" She started speaking faster, panic evident in her lack of breath. "I have water magic too. Water magic stronger than Aiden's."

Rose's hand lifted to cover her mouth at her last statement. Voicing that she thought she was stronger than Aiden, the Norden Point's son, wasn't kind.

It was also dangerous.

"You are unquestionably Norden, Rose." Mom stopped there to let that statement sink in. "You are right, though I hope you know you shouldn't say it to anyone but family. Your water magic is stronger than Aiden's. You two may be playing now, but it hasn't gone unnoticed by his family. You know Aiden's parents and the very high hopes they have for him."

"Why does that matter? We're still years away from the test."

Each fae had a way for young adults to test the strength of their magic. They were used to help guide a fae to where their power could be most well-suited in society. Rose was old enough to know that the test also told you who you could marry if you were trying to create a powerful fae line. She knew what Mom wasn't saying about Aiden. His parents weren't in love the way Mom and Dad were. They had married as a result of their tests. They had matched specifically to make a powerful Norden family, to have a child that could be the next Norden Point.

Of course, they wouldn't know for sure until Aiden turned sixteen and took the test.

"You know why it matters, Rose, even if you don't want to say it."

Rose nodded to Mom. She didn't like that Aiden's parents expected so much from him. She just wanted to be able to play with him like normal kids. Instead, he was always getting whisked away to special tutors or practices.

She didn't pity Aiden, though. No one liked pity. She was just angry at his parents on his behalf. Sure, his father was the Norden Point, but she often saw other Compass Points with their children. The Vesten and Suden Points were both quite old, though they didn't look it. They were never seen without their children and grandchildren around them. The Osten Point seemed to appreciate her solitude, but she also didn't have children, so it worked out.

Even if Aiden's parents married solely to try and raise the next Norden Point, it was never a guarantee. The Norden trials weren't solely about magical power, though it was a significant factor. If her magic remained stronger than Aiden's, there was a chance she, the groundskeeper and weapons master's daughter, might have more of a claim to the next Norden Point title than he did.

His parents were never particularly happy, but she thought they'd be especially displeased with that information.

CHAPTER SEVENTEEN

Though a heavily trafficked road due to its proximity to Compass Lake, the turnoff up to the mountains didn't have a town or village. Most travelers ventured between Compass Lake and Sandrin, and Sandrin was just another half-day ride west.

Rose had awoken on the hard ground, screaming from another version of the same nightmare. She could still feel the Norden Point and the elder's stare as she fled the room. She knew she would never be able to rid her mind of the images of her family. They had haunted her for ten years, but she had never had constant nightmares reliving them.

She could only blame her growing proximity to Compass Lake.

Her mood grew foul as she readied her horse to make their way up the mountain. They would make it to Suden house today. Compass Lake was just over the pass, nested high in the mountains. Something on her face must have given away her mood as they started the ride, the sun not yet visible over the horizon.

"We're just here to make an appearance and use Suden Point resources to see if we can learn anything useful." Luc's words, interrupting her thoughts, held an uncharacteristic hesitation.

She still couldn't look at him, especially after waking up screaming again. Would she see pity on his calculating face? Or something deeper, something she couldn't name, but that she caught in his glance each time she woke from the nightmare?

She didn't think she could handle either option.

"Don't tell me you're chickening out now, Luc," Rose cut him off before he could say something stupid. "We're nearly there. The plan will work. Our relationship will give me the cover to make you a weapon tuned to your magic. Then we can decide what to do about the mist."

She could feel his gaze on her as they rode. It was the first time she'd acknowledged that she intended to make him a weapon. Though he'd told her not to take the custom order, just to come and evaluate for herself how much it would help, she knew he'd still need something. She didn't believe that she could walk away and leave the continent defenseless, even if it turned out there was no way to help Tara.

It might be better to make him a weapon and leave. That would stop him from learning more about her powers and stop anyone from taking too much notice of the Suden Point's current romantic partner.

"Do you know what to expect at the lake?" Luc asked.

She didn't know at this point if it was even worth pretending. He knew she was hiding from someone. He was also, thankfully, unwilling to press her on it and jeopardize her weapon-making expertise.

"I'll be fine," she replied. She decided the best defense was a good offense. "How many Compass Points do you expect to run into today?"

She was right, and Luc switched from something that had started to look like concern to business and agendas.

"They should all be on the lake. The Compass Points have been sticking close to the power seats with the mist attacks. However, per our agreement, I don't expect you to have to interact with any of them. My plan is for us to be seen stabling the horses and crossing the lake to Suden house. From there, we'll rely on the nature of gossip to fill in the blanks."

She nodded along. This should be easy enough. She'd have to stick by Luc's side in public and follow him behind a closed bedroom door tonight.

Who was in Luc's bed was a big deal. It could mean a lot for the Suden court. People cared if he would try to sire another Suden fae strong enough to be the next Suden Point.

Her mind swirled with the variations of the Suden Point she had seen. Luc, who wanted to know her and shared parts of himself and his magic? The man who had buried a thief alive without hesitation?

Rose bit her lip as she tried to remind herself why she hated the Suden Point.

She hated all Compass Points on principle. It was the Compass Point power and position that had led to her greatest loss.

Yet, just as she'd mentally chastised her customer for blaming the Suden Point for the mist plague, she chided herself for putting all of the Compass Points' failings on him. Her logic about why she hated him was looking flimsy, at best. She needed to get ahold of herself.

Whether she was ready or not, Compass Lake would believe she was sharing a bed with him before the day was out.

She felt they'd been climbing back and forth along switchbacks for hours when they finally crested the ridge. She looked down and saw a sight she'd hoped never to see again.

Compass Lake.

A perfectly circular lake. It was indeed a marvel that it was naturally occurring. Though, "naturally occurring" was questionable if one believed in the rumored godly intervention in its creation.

Four beautiful houses stood at each point as if on a compass. Norden, Suden, Osten, and Vesten, each a spacious manor, large enough for the Compass Point, their family, guests, and formal event rooms. They were the leader's residences and the official spaces for governing each fae court.

Beyond each house, away from the lake, were smaller subsets of homes for court officials. From the point cresting the ridge, they could see three of the four houses and none of the village. Suden, Osten, and Vesten houses jutted right up to the lake. Each house's door led out directly to beach and water.

Only Norden was hidden away. Well, not exactly hidden. It was still a large estate like the others. Once you were on the lake, it was plain to see along with the rest, but from the ridge, only the path headed up a small hill was visible. Norden house sat on top of a hill. The extra tree cover added a layer of protection and mystery, like that which had always shrouded the house itself.

Rose didn't need conversation as she drank in the sights long forgotten. She spent most of the way down trying to sneak peeks of Norden house between the canopy of trees. As they made their way to the communal stables on the Northwestern bank, she registered that Luc was riding much closer to her than he had been their entire trip.

He was close enough to reach out and touch. Their horses fell into step next to each other, and his eyes raked over her. She guessed he was silently observing the wonder and terror crossing her face as she began to re-experience Compass Lake.

Magic, Norden magic, reached out and wrapped around Rose as if it would never let her go again. She felt warm and safe momentarily before opening her eyes and remembering where she was.

She had run from here without a second thought when her world shattered at sixteen. She never thought she'd be back.

"I knew we'd be back," Arie spoke to her as his bird form landed on her shoulder.

"That makes one of us. Have I told you I've got a bad feeling about this?" she replied. "I want that on the record when this all goes to hell."

"Of course you do, but as your beautiful and dangerous Luc has pointed out multiple times, you seem to have been backed into a corner by your morals."

"He's not my Luc," she whispered.

Luc turned at his name from her lips, noticing the bird on her shoulder. His half-smile tilted dangerously as he realized they were talking about him.

"I'd take that wager," Arie replied as they rode into town.

CHAPTER EIGHTEEN

Compass Lake Village sat at the end of the mountain path they traveled, the northwestern bank of the lake. It held the communal stables, market, town square, and other necessities.

Just past the square were some boats pulled up on the shore, which were considered the only public entry to the lake, aside from the Compass houses. The most natural path to each of the houses was by boat.

Luc offered Rose his arm as they left their horses with the Suden grooms and made to follow the path through the village leading to the lake. Cautiously accepting, she reminded herself why she was there.

For Tara. For others like her that had succumbed to the mist plague. To stop more people from losing their friends and family.

Whispers and stares followed Rose and Luc through the streets, though no one dared to meet the Suden Point's eye or question him directly.

They stopped for bread for dinner. The baker didn't look familiar to her, though she was sure the shop had been there when she was younger. The baker barely made eye contact as he passed back the change to Luc.

"Good to see you again, sir. Glad you made it back safely."

Luc's face gave nothing away as he responded as if he were speaking about the weather. "Has the news reached here of the last mist attack?"

"Yes, sir, multiple small villages up north by Lake of the Gods fell." He hesitated. "Did you have a productive trip?" he mumbled as he passed the bagged bread to Luc.

"I suppose that depends on the definition of productive," he replied, and he pulled Rose closer, sliding his arm around her waist. The baker's eyes locked on the motion, Luc's touch seeming to confirm his suspicions about the nature of their relationship.

Rose was amazed by the baker's bold stare as his gaze moved from the Suden Point's arm to Rose, then quickly back to his notes and tallies behind the counter. The Suden Point certainly hadn't answered his questions about the mist, but he gave him something more exciting: confirmed gossip.

When they found themselves at the boats, she did not doubt that Luc's plan for her cover would succeed. Not only had every eye in the village been on them and their proximity to each other, but none of the other Compass Points had appeared.

She felt confident that word would spread that she was romantically involved with the Suden Point without talking to any courtiers. Things were going just as Luc had anticipated.

As they got into the boat, Luc took up the oars and started them in a clockwise loop around the lake. Though it was a relatively small lake, just over a mile in circumference, they were headed from the Northwestern corner to the Suden house at the southern point. This little boat ride would take them most of the way around—an obvious promenade to solidify their story.

The Suden Point was at home, and he had company.

"How's this going?" she asked when they were finally far enough away from shore.

"They seem very interested in you, don't they?" he drawled, and actually smiled at her as he paddled them forward.

"I am fascinating," she shot back. "Though hopefully only fascinating as the Suden Point's current passing fancy."

Luc coughed. "I certainly agree that you're fascinating, Rose, and don't worry, these villagers don't know half of it. They underestimate you, just like I did." He looked out over the lake as he paddled them forward. "They see someone on the Suden Point's arm as interesting. I doubt they see the merits of the woman herself."

Rose wasn't sure what to make of that statement. She appreciated the acknowledgment of his initial misjudgments. It was certainly part of the plan to make sure people saw her but weren't looking at her too closely. Her appearance was quite different from the sixteen-year-old who had run from here, but not so different that no one would recognize her if they had known her then. Her only saving grace was that everyone assumed the girl she had been was dead.

She shook herself free of her past at Compass Lake. "Will the gossip get back to the Compass Points?"

"Oh yes, don't worry about that. Even if we hadn't spoken with anyone in the village, the news still would have gotten back to them." He paused as if debating how to continue. He was saved from explaining further as Arie landed on her shoulder.

With barely contained glee, Arie launched into his announcement. *"The gossip behind us is saying he's never brought a lover to the Suden house."*

She looked up and glared at Luc, knowing that this was what he'd been debating whether to tell her. She immediately understood now why he was so confident the gossip would get back to the other Compass Points. Rose on Luc's arm was no casual occurrence. It was a bigger deal than she initially thought.

"Don't you think that's the kind of information you might have shared before we proceeded?"

"You forget that I can't hear what your bird is saying to you," he gracefully evaded the confrontation for another moment.

She fumed, as she was sure he was aware of the topic of discussion.

"You've never brought a romantic partner here, Luc? I know that you know that's what he just told me. Don't you think this will bring us more attention than we need?"

The bird on her shoulder made a sound like it was choking. Rose assumed Arie was trying to giggle in delight at the drama he'd caused but found it hard to do in his bird form.

Luc glared at the bird before continuing, "Don't worry. The other Compass Points tend to keep their distance from me. I rarely agree with them, but I have too powerful a reputation to directly confront. They tend to only deal with me in official Compass Point capacities." He shrugged. "Sometimes the Vesten Point will get close on our western border, but it's usually just when he's shifted and running through the trees on that part of the property."

Like Luc, the Vesten Point had only come to power since Rose left Compass Lake. And from what she'd heard, he'd been raised in Sandrin, the city on the bay on the westernmost side of the continent. He wouldn't know who she was anyway.

"You don't get it, do you? It's one thing if I'm one of the many on the Suden Point's arm. It gives me the protection we sought but no expectation. Everyone will assume you'll move on soon enough. But if I'm the first partner in…" She paused. "How long have you been Suden Point?"

"Eight years."

"The first partner you've brought here in eight years!" she whisper-yelled at him so her voice didn't carry across the lake. "The first partner you bring here will get more attention than may be beneficial. People will want to know how we met, your intentions, and my loyalties."

"I'm aware."

"Since you're so aware of it, what are we doing about it?"

"We're leaning into the fact that most here are too scared of me to ask questions. I know that comes as a shock to you since you seem to have no fear of me." He raised an eyebrow at her. "I promise, most do. So while everyone will undoubtedly have the questions you listed, they won't ask them of me directly, and there is no one else to give them the answers."

She pondered this. He might be correct if the conversation with the baker was any indication. She took a deep breath.

"You still should have told me."

Sensing the tension was over, Arie said, *"While this was fun to watch, I'm going to do some laps around the lake and see what else I can learn."* Then he flew away.

Luc watched Arie take off, still not making eye contact with Rose. He said, "Telling a woman that I've been unable to share enough of myself to have a public romantic partner in eight years doesn't sound like the information you lead with for a relationship."

Her gaze narrowed at him. "This is a fake relationship, Luc. My judgment of you doesn't matter."

"Funny, isn't it, that I find that it does," Luc replied.

Rose hesitated before continuing. He caught her off guard with his unexpected honesty. "For what it's worth, I certainly wouldn't judge you for not being able to share enough of yourself to make a real relationship work. I lived on a magical island with a talking shapeshifter. You can guess how many partners I've trusted enough to bring there."

He gave her a soft smile at that. One she didn't think she had seen on him yet. He wore it well.

"At least you have Tara." Immediately he shifted in his seat and started, "I'm sorry, Rose, I didn't mean to…"

"It's fine, Luc. You're right. I have Tara." She looked off after Arie's bird shape in the distance. "I have Arie too. They may not be life partners, but they're like family. Do you have family here, or are they still back…Where are you from again?"

"My brother Aaron and his partner Andrew will be at the house with their kids. They moved here from where we grew up in the south a few years ago after our mother passed away."

"I'm sorry to hear that." She wanted to ask about his father, but the pain was evident on his face as he spoke of his mother. He nodded at her condolence as he seemed to push down a wealth of emotion.

"The first few years of being Suden Point, I didn't have anyone I trusted. I was already an outlier, taking the position at such a young age. So I didn't turn him down when my brother offered to move here. They have rooms in Suden house, though they also have their own house off the lake. They tend to bounce between both during the day. I sent notice ahead that we're coming, so they'll prepare enough for us to join their evening meal." He held up the bread. "We're even contributing."

"That sounds like a nice way to spend the rest of the day." She could use the rest after the last few days of hard riding and camping to keep to their schedule.

They were well past Norden house now, though she couldn't take her eyes off it. As they followed the smooth curve of the lake's edge in the boat, her eyes darted up through the thick trees to the front porch. From the lake, one could easily see up the hill to the majestic house through the natural tree barrier. It was only from above that the house was truly sheltered from view.

A figure on the porch watched their progress. Though too far away to make out the details, she had no doubt who stood on that porch. She could sense his power from the lake.

This was the Norden Point.

She glanced down at Luc, who registered the weight of her gaze and looked back to what she'd seen. Noticing the figure on the porch, he gave the briefest nod to the Norden Point. He turned to look at her as if he'd ask her a question.

"What is your family like?" she asked him first. He shook his head at her, seeming to acknowledge her diversion. He looked thoughtful for a moment as he considered a response. She couldn't help but notice how good he looked on the sunlit lake, his shirtsleeves rolled up and his forearms flexing as he paddled.

His casual power radiated through this everyday activity. No one watching him would mistake him for ordinary. No matter how at rest he seemed, he was a threat—capable of violence at a moment's notice. Especially here, at his seat of power, on Compass Lake. His otherness increased with every stroke.

She felt his magic building around them as they passed Osten house and were on the final turn to Suden house. The smell of pine and cinnamon grew stronger. He seemed less able to hide his power the closer they got to his lake shore.

"I was always close with my brother and his family. He found a partner when he was quite young and started a family. My nephews are delightful terrors, three boys between the ages of five and eight. They give Aaron and Andrew new adventures every day." He smiled to himself, another genuine one.

He must also be more relaxed at his seat of power, or maybe he was just more relaxed with his family.

He sighed and continued, "It feels more like their house than mine, but I'm fine with that. I spend a lot of time in Sandrin with our soldiers, so it all evens out." He shrugged before concluding his thought.

It was out of character, even with her limited exposure to him. He was always annoyingly assured.

"When I'm here, it feels like a true family home, as opposed to some stodgy and lifeless seat of power."

There it was. A subtle hint that he might not fit in with the rest of the Compass Points. The Compass Points she knew craved power and the prestige it brought. Luc didn't thrive in a cold and austere Suden house. He didn't like the secrecy and isolation of power. He'd rather make it a home with those he loved.

He was definitely in the wrong position for that. Though he hid this fact about him well with his scary, external persona.

It was also something she understood. In her time at Compass Lake, the Norden house had always seemed only like a seat of power. It was a thing to be revered, not a home in which to live. The cottage on the property, well, that was different. That was home, and it, too, was once filled with love and family.

"So, will they have questions about me? It doesn't sound like you'll be comfortable lying to them." From the warmth in his brief description, she wondered if he was capable.

"I won't enjoy lying to them, and I'll try not to do it outright." He sounded like he was convincing himself more than her. "It's true enough that you are with me, and we are spending time at the house together. I won't bother to correct any other assumptions they make."

The fake relationship seemed so simple. She'd barely fought him on it, but the stakes seemed to rise with each moment they got closer to Suden house.

CHAPTER NINETEEN

Rose saw the transformation overtake Luc the moment he stepped out of the boat. His eyes flashed red, and his spine straightened as the power of his home rolled through him. He stretched out his fingers and rolled his shoulders as he took a deep breath. She wasn't even sure he realized how much he was luxuriating in returning to his seat of power.

Pine and cinnamon encircled her as he offered her a hand. She took it without thought, wanting nothing more at that moment than to lean into the power he was radiating.

What was wrong with her? They were in a fake relationship. She needed to keep focusing on the "fake" part.

He took her hand and wrapped it again in the crook of his arm as they made their way across the beach to the front door of Suden house. It was nowhere near as imposing as the Norden house, but Rose knew more than most how appearances could be deceiving.

The pathway from the beach to the front door was lined with shrubs and flowers. Someone spent a lot of time carefully pruning and caring for them. Not in a perfectly manicured way, but someone clearly had a love for the house and property that they poured into taking care of the land. It made her think of Dad as they walked through the deep brown double doors that opened warmly into a family room. She was sure this was an imposing receiving room to past owners, but Rose felt the family Luc had described in every feature of this home.

Luc led them right in. The place was his, after all. He may let his relatives stay here, but the power that radiated from him showed that this was unmistakably *his* house. Rose took it all in. A staircase by the front door led up to a second story with a hallway overlooking the family room and additional hallways on each side. A tall, thin man with white skin exited one of the rooms, chasing three little boys with similar features as they came barreling down the staircase.

"Uncle Luc, Uncle Luc," came the chaotic chatter of a family welcoming one of their own. She hadn't thought it possible, but Luc's face softened as three boys hurtled down the stairs, throwing themselves off the final step. She took a quick breath as the small bodies careened toward Luc. He had no chance of catching them all at once. Nearly stepping in to catch one of them herself, since they seemed to have so little regard for their safety, she halted as Luc gently touched her forearm.

From the corner of his eye, Luc caught her gaze and shook his head. She stayed put and watched while he casually slipped his hands into his pockets instead of reaching out his arms to grab them.

The boys flew toward them, but instead of the crashing and crying she expected, she saw them floating in the air as if frozen in place. Slowly, they started rotating around like they were each a ball to be juggled. Wild laughter, pointing, and shrieking at Luc told her this was not the first time such an event had occurred.

"Uncle Luuuuuc!"

"We would have landed fiiiiine," one whined.

"You can't keep us here forever!" another giggled.

Only then did it occur to her that Luc was doing this. Rose had spent too much time hiding her magic to think of it as a first response. Luc had led a different life. He was able not just to use his magic but to play with it. Without lifting a hand, he was levitating three little boys in the air and tossing them like they were no more than circus balls.

She didn't know many earth fae, but from what she did know, this was an uncanny display of power. More, even than she'd glimpsed in their first battle with the mist monster. Most Suden could move the earth, using the ability to dig holes and build mountains, but what Luc was doing was different. He was pushing the boys off the dirt beneath the building to create the concept of floating.

It was a show of his strength, yet he did it in such a casual way.

She watched delight dance in his eyes as the boys begged to come down, though they would undoubtedly scream for more as soon as he let them.

Appreciating the easy family love, Rose missed the man coming down the stairs and giving Luc a hug. His boys were still bouncing in the air as he turned and introduced himself.

"I'm Andrew—I'm Aaron's partner—and you must be Rose."

She gave an easy nod. "Thanks for having me."

"Oh, it's his house," Andrew demurred. "Either way, Luc is so busy these days. We're thrilled when he can spend some time with us."

Luc had finally let the boys down; as predicted, they were clamoring for more. Andrew took charge. "Let your uncle make it past the family room, boys. They've just walked in. He'll have plenty more time for treating you each as his personal juggling balls later."

Luc smiled in acknowledgment to Andrew.

"I'm sure Uncle Luc will want to give Rose a tour of the house and grounds before dinner," Andrew finished as he started to lead the boys away.

It was then the boys realized there was someone they didn't recognize in the room. Six eyes darted to Rose, and the chaos once again sprang forward.

"Who are you?"

"Are you Uncle Luc's wife?"

"Do you have any cool powers?"

"Want to play?"

It was an endless stream. Luc moved closer, putting a hand on the small of her back as he made introductions. "David, Thomas, Joseph, this is Rose. She's my friend and will be staying with us."

Andrew's knowing eyes seemed to try and pierce through Luc's simple words. Clearly deciding to save his questions for later, he said, "Okay, boys, let's finish those lessons for today so we can be ready for dinner with Uncle Luc and Rose in a few hours." He gave one final glance between Luc and Rose as he swept the storm of energy and curiosity back out of the room.

CHAPTER TWENTY

L uc took them out a side door that led to the back of the property. "Your family seems nice. How often do you all get to stay here together?"

"We see each other most days when I'm here, though they usually stay at their cottage. I think they like using the house as a school for the kids while Aaron works in the library, so they can all leave the cottage together during the day but have different activities. I'm here as much as possible—I prefer this place—but that probably turns out to be three weeks per month?"

"And the rest?" She decided that she needed a better picture of him. How did Luc spend his time, and who did he spend it with?

"Mostly in Sandrin or other areas with large Suden fae populations. Trying to ensure my people have easy access to me without coming out here, though they rarely take advantage of it."

"Or off on rogue missions to find secret weapons?" She meant to tease, but even she could hear the sarcasm dripping from her voice.

"Yes, secret missions where I get my ass kicked by the target I intended to win to my side are a regular part of my duties as the Suden Point." He paused and tilted his head, continuing with a slow smile. "Though referring to yourself as a secret weapon might be a bit much, even for you." She laughed out loud at that, her lingering anger evaporating for the moment at his self-deprecation.

She had kicked his ass, and she'd enjoyed it.

They'd kept strolling as they talked, passing by a few outbuildings. Her steps slowed as they passed one that could only be the forge. The smells of a forge would never get old to her. She loved having one in her home in the Lake of the Gods. The fire, the hot tang of iron, and even the smell of sweat dripping down her skin as she worked.

The fire was hot, and a man stood close to it. She couldn't see what he was working on but saw his arm rise and lower with a mallet. She heard the telltale clang of metal being worked. She saw the muscles in his upper back and arms ripple as he swung. She must have watched the man longer than was appropriate as she heard Luc's cough behind her.

"Should I leave you two alone?" He had sidled up closer to her, whispering in her ear. Though she could feel the heat from the forge where she stood, a shiver ran up her body unbidden at Luc's nearness. She jumped at his voice, knocking on one of the swords hanging on the wall, making enough noise to gain the blacksmith's attention.

"Sir." He stopped his work and stood stiff and formal as he gave a short bow to Luc.

"Jonathan," Luc acknowledged, with no anger but also no warmth in his tone.

"Do you need the forge, sir?" he asked hesitantly, his eyes shifting between Rose and Luc.

"Yes, Jonathan, that would be helpful. Do you mind giving us just a few minutes?"

Jonathan cleared the room faster than Rose thought possible. He left his work to sit on the anvil.

She turned to Luc. "He'll have to start that again. There was no need to make him leave." She was still off balance from the effect of his proximity. She needed to get used to it. They were in a relationship for all everyone here knew. She should enjoy his touch.

That could be the problem. Her body seemed to enjoy his closeness too much.

She glared at him as she walked toward the forge, examining the workshop and tools. She was getting herself some much-needed distance from the Suden Point.

"What do you think of it?" he asked without acknowledging her reprimand.

"The Suden are warriors. I expect you to have the best forge and armory on the continent." She let out a breath as she said more softly, "It's beautiful. I always wanted to work here."

She covered her mouth as the last slipped out. She didn't mean to say that. She didn't want to talk about it. Luc crossed the room, closing the distance between them.

"It's yours. You can work here anytime," he said.

She shook her head. He wouldn't understand the import of what she said without fully understanding her fae court affiliation. She stepped toward the discarded item the blacksmith had been working on—an axe. Moving herself to the forge, she restarted work on it. It had almost been finished. She took a few swings as her muscles warmed to the familiar motion.

The swings were a habit. Once, they had been their own kind of communion with the goddess of her people. Now, a soothing ritual as she wondered where the gods were and why they continued to let the mist plague spread. She wasn't sure how long passed as she lost herself in it.

After a time, she looked over her shoulder, remembering Luc was in the room. She regretted her decision immediately as she saw only heat in his gaze. A heat that had nothing to do with the forge fire in front of her. One she was much more eager to see than she should have been.

She tried to shake herself free of the effect of his desire. Turning from his gaze, she resumed her work. She used the forge's flame to sharpen the axe blade the blacksmith had worked. As a child, she remembered wanting so badly to work at the most revered forge of Compass Lake. That was undoubtedly the Suden Point's.

She was young, though, and had never voiced her desire. Even her loving family would have seen it as a betrayal of her people. A Norden would never work for a Suden. The fae, though living in close proximity at Compass Lake, learned at a young age not to spend time with those outside of their own court. Each fae people had too many secrets they guarded from the others. Only the most powerful among them, the Compass Points, had to work together by order of the gods.

She finished the axe and set it to cool. She turned to meet Luc standing much closer than he had been. The desire in his eyes was still unabashedly apparent.

"I could watch that all day," he said. "You seem to fall into a rhythm with your work, even in the little while we were here. I can't imagine what happens when there is magic involved."

Rose had to shake herself a little, thinking about evaluating Luc's magic while working. He was right. Her work was soothing in its repetition, but all bets were off when she evaluated someone's magic. It was an intimate thing to know someone on the level that a weapon's master needed.

She didn't think she was ready for what that would mean between her and Luc. The fire burning between them was already much hotter than she'd like. She knew this was supposed to be a fake relationship, but his admiration and desire seemed to request a different definition.

She breathed, "How about the rest of that tour?" Her voice was embarrassingly rough, and Luc seemed to notice as a slow smile crept over his features.

"Of course." He held out his arm to her, and she took it. His shirt sleeves were still rolled from their ride around the lake. Her eyes closed briefly at the feel of her hand sliding across his forearm, resting at the crook of his elbow. Her mind wandered to her hand sliding across the more hidden planes of his body. Opening her eyes, she tried to slowly blink away the image.

She was in so much trouble.

Chapter Twenty-One

The setting sun's rays danced across the smooth surface of the lake as they strolled the grounds. It was such a calm lake. The only waves created were by those paddling it. As they approached the property's eastern edge, a figure moved toward them.

Luc stiffened at her side, tension evident, he placed his body in front of hers—a half-hearted attempt to block her from view. She looked around, trying to assess the threat as the smell of pine and cinnamon met her nose. Luc seemed to quickly give up on trying to shield her—they were too exposed, and a figure was moving toward them from the east. It was clear they had already been seen.

Luc linked their hands together. He squeezed hers with some meaning hidden from her as he gave a solemn nod to a breathtaking woman who came into view before them.

She was tall with light brown skin and generous curves. Her dark hair fell in wild curls down her back. Her bright, emerald-green eyes perfectly matched her sweeping green day dress. She smiled warmly at Rose as she approached.

Rose's heart rate escalated as recognition caught up with her—recognition and understanding of Luc's desperate attempt to keep her hidden.

The Osten Point stood before them.

Luc believed Rose to be Osten from the incident with the archer.

Of course he'd assume it was the Osten Point she hid from.

"And who might this be, Luc?" the woman purred.

Every instinct Rose had told her that the Osten Point was not to be underestimated. She was beautiful, yes, but she was a Compass Point. Only the most powerful made it to that position, and this woman had held hers for a long time. She had come upon them when they had no chance to disengage politely. Rose was sure that she was here on a mission. While Rose held no illusion that the Osten Point would know who she was, a lowly daughter of the Norden house groundskeeper and a swordmaster, she had been Osten Point when Rose last lived at Compass Lake. She may not be the Compass Point that Rose hid from, as she was sure Luc supposed, but she was still a danger to their current plans.

Luc seemed to be still waging an internal war. His magic swirled around them as if he were readying himself for a battle. Rose put her hand on his arm as she briefly shook her head, hoping to signal that this was not cause for attack.

She knew Luc had promised to keep her from the other Compass Points, but she was still more than a little baffled that he was preparing to fight the Osten Point on her behalf.

Luc acknowledged her touch, at least putting off an outright attack for the moment. He slid his arm gently around the small of her back.

It was showtime for their fake relationship.

Making introductions, Luc said, "Juliette, may I introduce Rose? Rose, Juliette is the Osten Point."

Rose could feel Juliette's gaze raking over her from head to toe. Her appraisal seemed quick, but her eyes lingered.

"Pleasure. You must be the one Luc brought across the lake today. It caused quite the stir through the village." Her smile lacked warmth. "I'm not sure Luc has ever promenaded on the lake in such a fashion."

Rose felt Luc's magic start to stir again. At Juliette's lingering gaze on her? He was in his seat of power. Not even the Osten Point on her side of the property could touch them here. That didn't seem to calm Luc as his body went more rigid with every second that Juliette's gaze was locked on Rose.

Rose decided to feign ignorance on the import of the gesture. "It was such a peaceful ride. Easy enough to forget how on display we were." She didn't like how Juliette looked at her either, but she wasn't sure why Luc was so unsettled.

"If you were mine to promenade with," cooed Juliette, "we would have put on a much more lascivious display." She winked.

Rose couldn't hold back a genuine laugh at the boldness of Juliette's words, cutting the tension building around Luc and his magic.

Luc—she was here as Luc's partner. She found herself becoming a little defensive on Luc's behalf. If he hadn't brought anyone to the Lake before, he certainly didn't need this beautiful wind fae to ogle and flirt with his choice. She instinctively reached her hand down to place it on top of his where he held her. She pulled his body forward to meet hers.

She could feel his magic pulsing around them, building and swirling, as she pulled them flush together. Their connection seemed enough to bring him from his staring contest with Juliette.

"Don't mind Juliette," Luc muttered, putting both arms entirely around her waist and resting his head on her shoulder. His lips were close to her ear as he spoke. "She can come on a little strong before you get to know her." He nodded again at Juliette, not in greeting this time, but in some unspoken acknowledgment.

"And once you get to know her?" Rose asked. She worked to control the shaking in her voice, not at the danger that Juliette, a

Compass Point, represented, but at the sensation that Luc's nearness caused.

"Oh, still strong, but it's much more expected." He shrugged.

Juliette laughed, her eyes dancing as she looked between them. As if she was delighted with today's proceedings. As if this had been a test. The way her eyes glowed as she watched Luc's fingers start to glide casually up and down Rose's side told Rose that they had passed her test.

Did she believe that their relationship was genuine? Or had something else transpired between the Osten and Suden Points here?

Rose did not believe the Osten Point's joy was because she was happy for Luc to have found a partner. No, Juliette was already making plans, and Rose and Luc's relationship appeared to fit nicely into them from her expression.

"Rose, I'd be honored to have you over for coffee or tea during your stay. Nothing stirs gossip like the newcomer jumping between Compass Point houses."

Luc stiffened but was decidedly unwilling to speak for Rose. She wondered at that but instinctively knew it was bad form for a Suden guest to visit the Osten. Even though she'd lived in an area with few fae for the last ten years, she knew this hadn't changed. The fae didn't intermingle.

Rose decided to let her down gently, just in case. "That's very thoughtful. We've got quite a bit to do the next couple of days with our arrival."

"Consider it an open invitation." Juliette's smile was still shy of genuine, but her gaze was much more casual now. "I do hope you stay long enough for the Summer Solstice Ceremony. It's coming up, and I'm quite sure that Luc has managed to miss the ball every year since he's been Suden Point." Her smile turned self-satisfied as she said, "Well, I just wanted to say hi and see what all the gossip was about. I can see that they held back. I'm not sure the rumor mill knows quite what they've got here." She glanced again to where Rose and Luc's bodies connected and the casual intimacy of the posture before waving a hand and turning away. "Have a lovely evening."

They both nodded, and Luc took Rose's hand, entwining their fingers again as he moved them away from the border and towards the lake shore.

Chapter Twenty-Two

Waiting until she thought they were far enough away, even for fae hearing, Rose asked, "What was that, Luc?"

Luc let out a deep sigh as he wiped his hand across his face. "I'm sorry, Rose, I promised you one thing, and I didn't even make it a day."

"What?"

"I didn't even keep the Osten Point away from you for a full day."

"That wasn't what I was asking about. What was with your magic flaring?" Rose asked.

Luc raised an eyebrow at her as if his actions had been for obvious reasons. "I thought she'd recognize you and that I would need to move quickly."

Rose almost laughed. She had been right. He was planning to fight the Osten Point for her. She couldn't help but smile as she replied, "She doesn't know me."

His head tilted ever so slightly as he tried to process her words against what he thought to be true about her being Osten herself.

"I wouldn't be so sure about that," Luc said. "Though I find myself curious why the Osten Point wouldn't know you. She was Osten Point when you were last here, right?"

"What do you mean?"

"Taking the easier question first, I see." Luc seemed…Was it disappointed? She couldn't be sure. "I mean that there was a calculation in her eyes and a recognition that had my magic standing on end."

"I noticed the magic part." Rose sighed again. "But what do you mean recognition?"

"As I said on the boat ride, I notice how people react to you. The people in town were intrigued by you just because you were with me, but they didn't see you." He gestured to the eastern border. "I'd bet anything that Juliette saw you. I don't know what she saw, but I know she recognized you as a much more important piece to the puzzle than simply a pretty face on the Suden Point's arm."

She felt a warmth bloom in her chest at Luc's words. But it was instantly cooled with the consideration of fear. Had Juliette recognized her? Rose couldn't think of why the Osten Point would have known who she was. She had rarely been seen playing with Aiden, given his demanding schedule. It wasn't like the Osten and Norden Point were so close anyway. She'd only been to Norden house for meetings and celebrations.

"Wasn't Juliette the Osten Point when you were here last?" Luc interrupted her thoughts to re-ask his question.

"Yes." She didn't see much point in lying about this.

"May I ask why you're so sure she doesn't know you from your time here? Wouldn't you have met with her?"

Rose laughed. There Luc was still assuming she was Osten and that, as an Osten fae, she would have at least had a test of her magical abilities with the Osten Point.

"That's a no, then." Luc couldn't help but smile as he shook his head. "I still can't quite work out how I can be so wrong on that," he mumbled, mostly to himself.

Was she now a mystery to be solved as well as a tool to be used against the mist? If she was honest with herself, she didn't want to believe that. She wanted to believe that their fake relationship had some real, unexplored feelings. She wasn't entirely sure why she was still hiding it from him. She'd already proven that it wasn't Juliette she was hiding from. That only left two other options. For too long, she'd been used to making sure no one knew.

"Luc…" She let his name hang there, unsure how she would continue. Was she ready to tell him more about herself? About her past here? About what it could mean for her future? Was she prepared to let the reality of who they each were interrupt the trust they were building?

"Rose, I've been looking all over for you." Arie, in bird form, flew down to meet them on the lake shore.

"What's going on, Arie?" Rose said aloud, smiling apologetically to Luc at the interruption. He nodded as she started a conversation that he could only half hear.

"Did I see you with the Osten Point? Did she recognize you?"

Rose glanced at Luc before responding, "We were just discussing that. I don't know why she would, but Luc seems to think she knew something."

"His instincts about you are good. You're so used to people underestimating you. I fear sometimes you actually expect them to."

"Tough love, Arie."

"Just…" He sighed. *"Maybe listen to the boy on this one. He seems to keep an eye on you."*

"Hmph," Rose grunted. "Anything else?"

Arie looked out over the lake. *"It seems so peaceful, doesn't it? Even with all the magic here?"*

Rose wasn't sure what Arie was getting at, but she nodded. The lake was peaceful.

"Compass Lake is where the Covenant was made. It's where the Flood waters receded, and the gods created the fae."

"That's just legend, Arie," Rose said. "It's convenient so that things like the Refilling Ceremony make sense."

"I assure you, it's quite true," Arie said. *"By setting up the Compass Points here, at the origin point, the gods promised no further acts of destruction as long as the Compass Points helped preserve the balance. It seems we might be teetering away from that promise."* He flapped a wing out toward the water. *"Makes it seem a little more deadly and a little less beautiful, doesn't it?"*

She shook her head at the topic change. "It makes you wonder how long we have before the gods decide that we've failed at keeping the balance and have to enact more destruction."

"Is he talking about the Lake?" Luc asked.

Rose nodded. "The Covenant. The promise it represents, the balance it seeks to keep."

"I'm not sure about the balance if the Osten god, Zrak, had to sacrifice himself," Luc commented.

"That's debatable," Arie answered, even though he wouldn't speak to Luc directly.

"Arie, if you're going to respond to Luc, you should make sure he can hear you."

Arie ruffled his feathers.

"Fine. He says that's debatable," Rose translated.

"Many believe that the gods had driven the continent so far off balance with their greed that it wasn't enough for them to give part of their power to create the fae courts. They also had to make a sacrifice, one of themselves," Arie said to Rose.

Luc considered this as Rose repeated it to him.

"If that were the case, I'd be angry if I were Zrak now." Luc looked around. "He sacrificed himself, and yet we still end up back in the same situation."

Rose couldn't help but laugh, thinking of the story her parents used to tell her as a child. "You know, Luc, you've got a point." She started pacing the lake shore as a thread twisted in her head. Trying to organize her thoughts, she began. "Everyone wants to blame you for the current plague of mists." Rose gestured to Luc. "The natural one to blame, though, would be the Osten."

Luc raised an eyebrow and asked, "Why do you say that?"

"The mist moves and feels like the Osten's wind magic."

His eyes narrowed like he didn't quite know what to make of this.

"It's also particularly focused on calling out the Suden Point." Rose was on dangerous territory now, but she knew there was something here, and she needed to try and think it through out loud. Trusting Luc had to start somewhere, maybe she could test this theory and see how much he pressed.

"Didn't Zrak hate Aterra?" Rose asked no one in particular.

"Yes."

"*Yes.*"

The resounding affirmative came from both Luc and Arie.

"Is your theory that the mist is somehow related to the Osten power?"

Rose shrugged. "Related to the Osten power, possibly is the Osten power?" She returned her gaze to Luc's as she spoke the words she hadn't entirely known how to say. "What's to say that the lost god isn't quite as lost as we think?"

"What do you mean?" Luc asked.

"I mean, Zrak sacrificed himself, but can a god really die? Do we even know what him sacrificing himself meant?"

"It's been hundreds of years since the Flood, and we've never seen anything like this. Why now?" Luc challenged.

"You walked yourself into that one, Rose."

Rose glared at Arie as he flew away, leaving her alone with the response. It was uncharacteristic of Arie to even allude to what he knew about her past, but his comment indicated he might know more than she even realized.

Something had changed. And what had happened to her ten years ago…as much as she didn't want to think about it, the coincidence was too great to be ignored.

"Rose?" Luc asked a little softer, watching Arie fly away.

"I don't know," Rose said. The picture still didn't make sense in her head. She needed more.

Luc stepped toward her. She met his gaze.

"Come on," Rose said, interrupting his forward progress. She wasn't sure what she would do if he got closer to her now. She didn't trust her body's reaction to him. "We'll accomplish nothing with this staring contest, lovely though your eyes may be." She smiled coquettishly at him.

He blinked, pulling himself from wherever his mind had wandered to and breaking their stare. He pointed his finger back towards himself.

"My eyes are lovely? You mean these?" He batted his long lashes intentionally this time, leaning even closer to her face. Mere inches separated them, their breath intermingling as the sun set over Suden beach.

"You know the ones," she whispered into the inches between them. "The dark eyes with endless depth. The ones that make you think twice about all your rational decisions and offer reckless ones instead."

She inadvertently leaned in closer as Luc replied, "Why, Rose, I had no idea."

She laughed in his face, forcing distance back between them. "You had every idea and use it to your advantage at every turn. But in the spirit of this partnership, I'll pretend to believe you if you take me back to the house and feed me."

"Your wish is my command, my lady. As a point of clarification, for those keeping score, does this constitute a rational or reckless decision?"

She shook her head at him again, an increasingly familiar gesture as they walked back to the house.

Chapter Twenty-Three

"Given what I saw of your home, I figured you'd appreciate this," he said as he gently put his hand on the small of her back and guided her into the library. Dinner would have to wait a little longer.

It was beautiful, more beautiful than anything that she could imagine. With dark bookcases built into all four walls, the only breaks in the line of spines were the doorway and windows looking out to the lake. Every shelf was filled with beautiful leather-bound books.

The room was inordinately tall, reaching higher than she thought possible, with a ladder sitting on one side that was not a standard library size. The room had to be magically supported in some way. The curtains and seats of rich, plush materials made the room a place you'd want to get lost in for hours.

A man with warm brown skin and short dark hair sat in an oversized velvet wingback chair, book in lap, feet up on a matching rest. Though his skin color differed, Rose could see the resemblance to Luc in the set of his features; this had to be Luc's brother Aaron. He was tall, too. She could tell even with him sitting down. Where Luc had that lean, coiled strength, Aaron had brawn. His shoulders were broad, and he had a more traditionally handsome face, square jaw, with a touch of stubble. Looking at him, it was hard to believe that this was the librarian of the Suden. He looked like he spent hours doing manual labor, not perusing books. She knew better than to judge a book by its cover, though.

The table next to him held a steaming mug that smelled of vanilla and cinnamon. Rose couldn't remember the last time she'd seen such a peaceful repose. It reminded her of evenings in her family room reading, with Arie curled up as a black cat at her side. It reminded her of evenings with her family in the cottage, even if those memories were tinged with sadness.

She looked up to find Luc observing the flutter of emotions that had just crashed over her face. He gave her a sad smile like he knew she was remembering something painful. He just wasn't sure what.

Undisturbed by the silent conversation, Aaron continued, unaware of their presence as he flipped a page in his book. Luc laughed as they moved closer.

"Even as a child, Aaron had this unique ability to read in any setting. No matter what chaos erupts around him—screaming, crying, laughing—he doesn't hear it when in the company of a good book."

"Hilarious, Luc." Aaron finally looked up. He stood and reached out to hug his brother. His gaze quickly lifted to Rose over Luc's shoulder.

"And you must be Rose." He smiled warmly and shook her hand.

"And you must be Aaron," she replied, sharing a genuine smile of her own as she surveyed the room. "You have a beautiful library. I'm envious of every moment you get to spend in here."

"Oh, it is comfortable enough, and if you get past the dull histories, you'll even find some fiction in there. I'm sure Luc already said this, but help yourself to anything you find." He held up his hand and stage whispered to her, "Though Luc keeps the best fiction in his room." He winked.

"I hate to interrupt," cut in Luc, who didn't sound like he hated it at all. His voice turned serious as he continued. "Rose and I want to speak to you about the shadow we fought a few days ago. It's a formation of the mist, stronger than anything we've yet seen."

"You fought something in the mist? You were in the mist and didn't succumb to it?"

Rose tried to cover her curiosity with her hand at her chin, her fingers moving across her jaw. How much would Luc tell his brother?

"Yes, well." Luc nodded stiffly. "How about we describe it to you and see what you decide to call it." They tucked into the couch just to the left where Aaron had been reading and told him their story.

"Well…" Aaron seemed to hesitate. "While 'mist monster' is certainly fitting, I think I came across something relevant to this story just last week." He stood up and grabbed a volume off the shelf behind the chair. He flipped to the index, found what he was looking for, and opened the book to a specific page as he set it on the table before the couch.

Before them was an image of a terrifying figure, tall and broad, skeletal looking. The illustrator captured that the figure was not quite solid and wreathed in shadow. Though a black and white illustration, it was clear that there was a gleam in the beast's eye. Above the illustration was a name, Nebulus.

Rose read the definition on the accompanying page. The Nebulus was described as shadow and mist taking physical form. And to her utter triumph and horror, it was listed as an agent or affiliation of the god Zrak.

Too shocked to speak, Rose nodded as her hand touched the image in the book. She couldn't believe how like the monster from the island it was. She couldn't comprehend that there was knowledge about it in this Suden library. She looked at Luc, who seemed to be processing better than her, but not much.

"The Nebulus are the harbingers of the mist? I guess I'd assumed they were responsible, but…" Luc stopped his sentence as his eyes locked on Rose, concern rising as his thoughts seemed to switch tracks.

"So if they would have struck you if your sword hadn't stopped its swing…." Luc didn't finish a sentence, but she understood, and agreed. If she hadn't been able to defend herself against its sword swing, if the sword had struck a blow to her body, she believed she would have fallen like the rest of the living dead in Bury.

Rose had collected herself as Luc seemed to be losing it. "Are we going to say nothing about the fact that the Nebulus is listed as an agent of Zrak?"

"We were getting there," Luc choked out. She caught him fighting to suppress the red rim of his irises as he considered how close Rose had been to succumbing to the mist plague.

"Do you two need a minute?" Aaron asked. His gaze flicked from Rose to his brother. Rose was unsure what he saw in either of their faces.

"No, sorry. This is just a little shocking," Rose tried to explain.

"Probably about as shocking as you two saying that you were in the mist and didn't succumb to its endless sleep," he replied dryly, giving Luc the time he needed to calm himself.

"Touché," Rose replied.

Aaron looked to Luc. "You didn't tell the other Compass Points that you were in the mist, did you?"

"Not yet," Luc hedged.

Aaron laughed loudly. "Do you plan to, then?"

Rose noted Aaron's eyebrow raise as Luc's gaze darted toward her. "I don't know."

"What does the mist being an agent of Zrak mean?" Aaron asked.

"Aaron…" Luc didn't seem to know what to say as he let his brother's name hang there.

"Fine, fine," Aaron said as he got up from his chair. "I'll leave you two to it." Disapproval hung heavy in his gaze as he looked at Rose for another moment.

"It's not her fault," Luc said.

Rose had no clue what was going on.

"I didn't say anything was anyone's fault." Aaron lifted his hands as he walked away. "I am glad you're both okay. But Luc, if what you're saying is true, it's probably time to talk to the other Compass Points. I know you don't trust them, but this is literally what the Compass Points are for. They uphold balance. That means both balance between human and fae"—he gave Luc a meaningful look—"and the balance between the gods and the continent. If you suspect this mist to be related to Zrak, you can't keep them in the dark." Aaron seemed to catch his own wordplay, rolling his eyes at himself. "No pun intended."

Luc sighed deeply, putting his forehead in his hands and running his fingers through his hair.

"Aaron, wait," Rose said as she stood to bring him back into the conversation.

This couldn't be good. Would Luc have told the Compass Points about his mist plague survival without their deal? She hadn't thought of that. Since he'd been on a mission without their knowledge, she assumed that his findings would also be a secret.

Luc interrupted her thoughts. "The balance on the continent has been steadily declining as long as I've been the Suden Point." Aaron turned back toward them as Luc continued. "Simple decisions by the

Compass Points require far too much discussion and ultimately come down to votes instead of a natural best-course solution." Luc shrugged.

She pondered this. It was common enough to vote selfishly regarding matters between the Compass Points, but not on issues involving the entire continent and humans. The Compass Points had historically taken the mandate to protect humans very seriously. Any decision that seemed to take land or power away from humans to benefit the fae courts was shut down quickly. The fae were happy to take control or land from each other but not from those unable to defend against their magic.

Based on Luc's solo mission to find her, she'd expected the Compass Points' internal politics to be a mess, but she couldn't believe it had gone this far.

"So you're saying it's not just the gods. The Compass Points have made moves to upset the balance between humans and fae too?" This made more sense to her. The imbalance wasn't because of her. It was because the Compass Points were showing exactly how selfish they were, just as she expected. "You're saying that we have no one to blame for the infestation of Nebulus but the Compass Points themselves?" Rose's voice had started quiet, but elevated with each passing word. This was why she hated the Compass Points. That much power, and they couldn't be trusted to act in the best interest of the continent. She really shouldn't be surprised. But she found fury building inside her all the same.

She saw the pages of the open book start to flip and the drink in Aaron's mug start to splash.

"And you, Luc, what did you do to stop this?" She stood, and she was yelling now. She felt her anger and power swirling around her. Luc was supposed to be better than her low expectation of Compass Points.

Luc looked at her as if he didn't know her. The Suden Point appeared; Luc's face hardened as he stood from the couch, placing himself between Rose and his brother.

"Aaron, why don't you go downstairs? Thanks for your help with this." Luc's words came out calm, but his eyes never left Rose's as he directed his brother to go. She saw the telling red glow flash across his irises; the power he pulled from his seat made the flash much stronger.

The lack of hesitation as Aaron left the room spoke of many years of obedience to his Suden Point.

The library door clicked shut behind Aaron while Rose and Luc stared at one another.

Luc's steely voice filled the room as soon as they were alone. "Come at me all you want, Rose," he whispered, rage filling every word as he spoke calmly and precisely. "I know I have failed this continent, but if you ever threaten my family with your power like that again, I won't hesitate to defend them."

Rose freed herself from the rage that had overcome her, locking her magic back up to focus on his confusing words. "I…" She paused. "I didn't threaten Aaron." She looked around. She'd been so focused in her rage against Luc, against the Compass Points.

"I know you don't realize that you did. That is the only reason we are talking about this rationally instead of tearing apart the library, and not quite in the pleasant way I had previously imagined." His power pulsed through the room as his voice found a way to threaten and tease her in perfect balance. His power pounded strong and seductive, reminding her that this was his domain. The mix of emotions was the distraction she needed to rein herself back in. She sat up straight.

"What'd you see?" she asked Luc.

"What I saw doesn't matter, Rose. Honestly, it still confuses me, so don't worry about your secrets." He shook his head as he pushed his fingers through his hair.

"So you brought me back? With talk of a pleasant way to tear apart the library?" Her mind was going in a million directions, but a picture of Luc took precedence: pressing her against the bookshelves, his arms caging her body, his head pressed into the crook of her neck, nipping and licking its way across exposed skin. The books were strewn around them as they knocked the smaller shelves over on their way to the wall.

She needed to get a hold of herself. She shook herself free from the heated thoughts that his words conjured.

"Among other things." His confident smile was back, though his whole body was still trained on her every movement, waiting to ensure she was defused, that his family was safe.

She coughed, straightening herself in her seat. "Will you tell me more, if I promise to react rationally?"

"As if you're capable of that when my eyes are involved."

Rose let out a snort at Luc's reply. His posture softened, relaxing.

"Tell me, what have the Compass Points done?"

Chapter Twenty-Four

Settling back in her seat, she watched him ready himself for a confession. She wanted to break this new tension between them. It was heavy and messy, she aimed to lighten the mood. "I know I've been living in the wilderness, but I think I would have heard of the Compass Points doing something to upset the balance."

"It was small at first. I started seeing it in one of the first meetings after I became the Suden Point." He paused again, weighing a decision she wasn't yet privy to. "It might be easier if I show you," he said, holding his hand out to her, asking her to take it. She sat up a little bit more at that.

"Show me—as in more than just a sample of feelings?"

His lips twitched up at the corner. "Yes, though I think you got more than I bargained for with that last taste."

She smiled thinking of the final image of her face that had snuck in. "It's possible," she replied, and leaned forward. Her hand poised over his, teasing closer but not yet touching. "Do many people get to experience these extra gifts of yours?"

He gave a shake of his head. Her fingers slid over the open palm of his hand, a spark that had nothing to do with magic igniting between them.

"Why have you decided to trust me with them?"

His eyes remained locked on her fingers trailing up and down the length of his palm. His posture loosened as her fingers moved. A comfort eased over him, even as he was about to perform magic. Pine and cinnamon started to swirl around them as Luc replied, "You know why."

She stopped tracing his palm and grabbed his hand, intertwining their fingers.

His lip turned up at the corner as their hands locked, and she plunged into his memory.

She fell into an overly plush library. One that she happened to know well. She looked around to orient herself on the outskirts of the filled circular Compass Point table. She was sitting in the Suden Point seat. The face sitting directly across from her was also one she knew too well. His fair skin and light brown hair a consistent part of her childhood memories. It was Aiden, the Norden Point.

She felt a swell of her own emotions rise up at the sight of him. He shuffled the papers before him, raising his blue eyes to meet those at the table. He didn't yell about an intruder in the group, so she assumed in the memory all others saw the Suden Point in her stead.

"We need to confirm the allocation of the joint tax resources for the year. In the last meeting, we discussed funding a new fae training program focusing on magical weaponry."

Her hand rose, and she flipped through Luc's folder automatically. She must be mirroring Luc's actions in the memory. He said this was his first meeting, and she wondered if he was nervous. Her gaze shifted between the Osten and Vesten Points to see if they objected to this declaration. Neither moved.

"I thought the funding was supposed to support training and education in fae farming techniques for humans." Her voice was Luc's, his tone even. The Norden Point barely lifted his eyes as he replied.

"Yes, but as there has always been some fae training program offered with the allocation, we didn't see the harm in offering a new focus this year. Shake things up a little bit. Shall we vote?" the Norden Point casually suggested, as if this was an insignificant decision.

She replied as Luc again, "Though a fae training, yes, magical agricultural techniques are heavily used by human farmers. Humans rely on that program and the learnings and improvements it provides for their crops. It also fosters continued collaboration between human farmers and fae of all courts."

Rose, as Luc, looked around again at the Osten and Vesten Points for support.

The Osten Point met his gaze with pity in her heavily coaled eyes. She'd been a Compass Point the longest among them. He must seem like a young pup to her, too eager and energetic to understand the demands and decisions of this position. The Vesten Point looked less sure. His shaggy brown hair fell into his eyes as he looked down at his notes. He was heavily tanned due to all the time that the shifter leader spent outside. His appearance made him look like he had not a care in the world, but his body language told another story altogether. His shoulders seemed to hunch up to his ears as he continued to ignore Luc's attempt at eye contact. When his gaze found the Norden Point's, his posture changed, straightening, regaining its focus.

"I think we can vote," the Vesten Point announced. "We can't remain stagnant. We can reassess the program's success next year and return to the agricultural offering."

The vote proceeded—three to one.

Rose shook herself free of the surge of feelings that seeing Aiden, even in memory brought forth. She turned her attention back to Luc, and the event he'd just shown her. "So the Compass Points let the funds be diverted to training that had no current benefit for humans? And by doing so, took away resources that did."

"Yes," Luc said, his eyes not meeting hers. He held her hand tightly as if willing her to understand. "I voted against it; I even worked on a rebuttal after that, proving the need for the magic education for our current agricultural practices to persevere, but the others barely reviewed it. They said my earth magic was biasing me." He finally met her eyes. "The Norden Point holds too much sway. After that initial decision, I started trying to figure out what he had on each of the Compass Points and how he could hold such influence. Still, there is a legacy of distrust between us, so no one is very welcoming with information."

He wiped his hand down his face. "But since then, it's been more of the same, small changes in a few places. The changes could be seen as an investment in experimentation for the future, but done with no consideration or thought for how to replace what's been reinvested." Every inch of his body begged her to understand that he'd been fighting this death by a thousand cuts without declaring an all-out war within the Compass Points. All the changes were passed legally, even with his dissent.

"Funnily enough, investing in things like research for magically imbued weapons seems to have led us to a need for magically imbued weapons. As you may be able to guess, based on my attempts to persuade you to help, they haven't made much progress."

She thought about that. It'd been eight years since that first change, and he'd still come looking for her. Not just looking, but threatening, to get her help.

"They've come up with nothing from that program in the last eight years?" she voiced aloud.

"Not a thing." He sighed. "I've met with multiple researchers after the first year of too-optimistic progress reports. They don't seem to know where to start. They've got half-fae from all four courts running tests with different materials, but the most they've accomplished is a blade that doesn't require sharpening."

Rose made a grunting sound of acknowledgment.

"So when I came across a rumor in my travels of a weapons master at the Lake of the Gods that could make custom magical weapons, I had to see at least if it was true. Little did I know that I'd find you or that you'd be exactly what I needed." His cool demeanor slipped as he tripped over the last word. Realizing what he'd just said, he coughed as he continued, "What the Compass Points needed, I mean."

Apparently, he decided that the conversation was over, standing and straightening himself again. "Unless you'd like to tell me why your magical weapons are so different?"

She wasn't even sure she knew the answer. She knew her magic was different, but was that the missing piece? She shook her head at him.

"Then I suggest we head down to dinner."

She took his offered hand, letting him pull her up from the cozy seat she'd sunk into. She gave the library one last, longing glance before she let the door fall shut.

Chapter Twenty-Five

10 years ago - Compass Lake

She stared around the scattered and destroyed room. Chairs and tables flipped, lamps broken, the dinner table settings strewn and cracked across the floor. That wasn't even close to the worst of it.

Her family.

Her heart.

Mom and Dad were in the kitchen on the floor, throats slit and limbs at incorrect angles. Mom, always the defender, was closer to the door, as if she'd noticed the threat a moment too late. Not able to get in front of Dad to stop it.

In the family room, Grandpa must have been sitting with his knitting. A knife was still stuck in his heart as if someone had thrown it on their way by, not bothering to stop and collect it.

The tears started without a thought. She was kneeling in the kitchen, crawling through her parents' blood, trying to make sense of the carnage. Who would have done this? Why? Then she heard it—voices outside the cottage.

"I just saw her go in. Let's do it now and get this over with." The voice was too familiar. She couldn't process the implications of hearing it outside, of it saying those words.

She smelled smoke from the front of the house as she heard something bulky sliding across the ground. Something was being pushed in front of the door, blocking her in. A fire began to crackle. The evidence of her family's fate, and hers momentarily, would be ashes soon enough.

Still, she couldn't move to save herself. Covered in her parents' blood, she held Mom's body in her lap as she rocked back and forth on the floor. Tears continued to stream down her face.

She looked at the family that she loved. They were gone to her now. She knew, more than anything, they would want her to get out. To get away.

The voice outside struck her ears again.

Aiden.

How could Aiden's voice be outside? How could Aiden be any part of this?

Rose moved to the front window as smoke began to fill the room. As if her brain needed visual confirmation of what she already knew to be true, she sought the owner of the voice. Aiden stood feet from the cottage with two of his father's lackeys.

His eyes were a dark grey.

She'd seen the grey more and more, but nothing could have prepared her for this. Sure, he was different when his eyes flashed grey.

Grey-eyed Aiden cared only for himself.

But even grey-eyed Aiden couldn't do this. She looked back at her family, tears still spilling down her face. She looked out the window again. Aiden's eyes remained grey, no return to their usual blue. She didn't have time to think about this as the heat set in around her, as the fire burned hotter and faster. It began to consume the cottage, moving towards her spot of chaos, confusion, and devastation in the kitchen.

She'd mourn later. She'd think about what this all meant later. Right now, she just had to survive.

Mom had taught her perseverance. She wouldn't give up when a dagger wouldn't bend to her will nor when her only friend betrayed her and her family.

She pulled Mom to her one more time, kissing her forehead. She gently set her back on the floor and rolled to her knees.

She was sure both exits were blocked, and Aiden and some thugs were out front. That made the back door, with the covered porch, her best chance for escape. Her water magic felt far away, and Aiden would undoubtedly be ready for that.

No, she'd need to do something he didn't expect to get out of here alive. She was glad now that Mom had made her keep her secret.

She crawled through the cottage to the back door. The covered porch was its own kind of garden. It was surrounded by bushes too thick and high to fight through and framed by a wood fence that allowed air to blow in on hot days. No windows were in the back, but the covered porch door wouldn't budge when she pushed. As expected, something was blocking the way.

Though this was the farthest from where the fire had started, she still felt the heat following her through the halls. The smoke preceding it began to fill the room. She coughed as she crouched, trying to figure out what was outside the door and how she could move it.

She closed her eyes and thought of the time in the workshop with Mom and all the times they'd secretly practiced after.

She knew she could use her wind magic. There was little chance that Aiden would understand what she'd done. It was this or perish along with her family. Mom would forgive her for using her wind freely now.

The fire creeping ever closer, smoke filling her lungs, she closed her eyes and reached for the hidden strength. She pulled a gust forth, smothering the flame, so she had more time to think.

She checked again through the glass, trying to see what was in front of the door. It was no use. It didn't matter anyway. She was sure it was something she shouldn't be able to move. But with the help of her wind, maybe she could.

She didn't think of the summer breeze crossing the lake on the hottest day this time. That was happiness to her. Instead, she thought of the coldest winter night, a bone-chilling wind ripping through the forest as she rushed to finish collecting sticks for the fire. This wind sank into her skin, freezing everything it touched, propelling her to pick up sticks faster and return to the cottage, her family, and the warm fire.

At the thought of her family around the fire, she nearly crumpled. Survive. She just needed to survive. They needed her to survive.

She pushed those thoughts of desperation and the frosty wind toward the object before the door. She pushed harder. She drove the winter wind faster and with more force in her mind. She pushed until she heard the thing in front of the door shake. It teetered as the wind hit it with a final shove.

Then she heard it. The object in front of the door rocked far enough and fell to the side.

Part of the object was still in front of the door, but barely. She used her strength to open the door wide enough for her small frame to slip through. She clambered over the fallen object—Mom's sizeable wooden tool chest from the workshop.

Mom's hammer had spilled from the box as it fell over. Rose had no time to wonder why no one came to check out the noise. Taking this small mercy she'd been given, she grabbed the hammer, if only to have its reassuring weight in her hand as she ran.

The fire was still raging and crackling in the cottage. It may have made enough noise to cover her movement. She turned away from the fire and stifled a scream. As if things couldn't get any worse, a giant brown bear appeared on the scene. The image didn't make any sense, but nothing tonight had made any sense. Then the bear charged after her attackers.

Bewildered, she thanked the gods for small favors amid this terror as the bear gave her a brief moment to dash for the tree line. She ran as fast as her legs could carry her to the forest: her favorite adventure, now her only escape.

She knew it like the back of her hand. She realized that tonight, she would have to go farther into the woods than ever before. She'd need to run until she recognized nothing, until she was lost.

She was no longer safe here.

She'd lost her family, her home, and her friend. Tears pricked again as she ran faster through the woods, avoiding any main trails, unsure if anyone was following her. She kept running until she was beyond exhausted.

But even exhausted, she knew she had to keep moving. When she couldn't run anymore, she walked. She kept putting one foot in front of the other, listening for any unexpected noise that could signal being followed.

Her heart sank when she heard something barreling through the woods.

She was being chased.

She focused on her family and how much they would want her to escape. With a deep breath she pulled the winter wind back to mind, aiming it at her back as she was mentally preparing to run. The bone-chilling wind of her creation moved her forward. It pushed her faster as she lifted her feet and let it carry her farther than her fastest sprint.

It was still not enough.

The barreling noise grew closer. She peeked over her shoulder to see who was pursuing her. A new kind of fear took over when she saw it was a bear.

It would catch her shortly. She closed her eyes as she rushed to stay ahead of it, thinking of Mom.

As she scrunched her shoulders with her next length, knowing the bear closed in, she braced for impact. Attempting to turn her head while not slowing down, she found the bear keeping pace beside her.

This was too much for her. She stopped running and turned to stare at it in bewilderment. The bear stopped too.

"Hello there. If you don't mind me saying, you look like you could use a little help."

Was this shock? She was losing it. "Did you say something?" was all she could reply in her bewilderment.

"Yes, I said you looked like you could use some help." There it was again. The voice spoke directly into her mind.

"And you want to help me? I thought you were chasing me because you wanted to eat me." She guessed it didn't matter if she told him. He seemed uninterested in tearing her apart for food. His voice felt like the forest in her mind. It felt like tree roots straining into the dirt and like life springing up around her.

He chuckled at her comment. *"No, I don't want to eat you. I'd like to help you. My name is Arie, and you can climb on my back. I'll get you far away from here."*

She did not doubt that he could help her. He'd been moving much faster than she, but she had to ask why.

"Why do you want to help me? That is the opposite of what people want to do right now."

The bear's deep black eyes stared into hers. *"I know, and I'm sorry, you've been through a lot tonight. I don't think it will get easier for some time, but you're stronger than you know."*

Something inside told her this wasn't an answer, but she was past caring. She climbed onto his back, and Arie took off so fast she couldn't help but shriek. He barreled through the woods, taking her farther from home than she'd ever been.

Chapter Twenty-Six

Dinner was delicious, and spending time with Luc and his family left her feeling a warmth she hadn't felt in ten years.

"Oh, I didn't realize they hadn't put this in my room," Luc said as they passed the front door, noticing her bag in the entryway.

She found it funny that her bag was sitting in the hallway, and Luc's was nowhere in sight. The caretaker hadn't known where to put hers. With all the gossip they'd left behind in the village, they must have wondered if her things belonged in a guest room or Luc's room. She felt a flush rise to her cheeks at the thought of people she hadn't met making assumptions about her sleeping arrangements.

Luc led her back towards the library but passed it, heading for his room. It was large and spacious with a beautifully carved, dark wood, four-poster bed as the centerpiece. It was flanked on each side, not by end tables but by bookshelves, each filled beyond capacity, similar to her own.

The room had matching dark wood floors like the rest of the house, with a large fireplace next to the door. Suddenly unable to look at Luc, she wandered away from him and found an attached bathroom and a closet. It wasn't overly extravagant but elegant in its clean simplicity. In front of the fire were two reading chairs with a table between them. She briefly wondered if this cozy scene saw any actual use. An image of herself wrapped up in a blanket reading there helped itself to the forefront of her thoughts.

Luc set her bag down next to the chair and looked back at her with an expression she couldn't parse. Was he interested in her reaction to his most private space? He'd said he cared about her opinions this afternoon, what she thought about him, about his past romantic life.

Her eyes continued to scan the room, lingering longer on the bed. She knew that there would only be one. They'd already slept in the same room together on their trip here, but sharing his bed in his personal space was an intimacy nonetheless. One for which she wasn't entirely sure she was prepared, especially when his gaze threatened to set her aflame.

Warmth pooled low in her stomach. She rolled her neck, reminding herself this was only day one of their fake relationship. No matter how real it felt at times, she needed to get a grip.

She looked around. There wasn't anyone here to pretend for.

Did he want her?

She'd felt their relationship growing more real by the hour, but to what end? It couldn't be real once he knew who she was.

Before she could think too hard about it, she spoke. "Luc, we need to talk."

He gave her a pointed but reassuring glance. "You have my undivided attention, I assure you."

Her cheeks warmed. Had she been staring at the bed that whole time?

"I want to tell you something about me."

He raised an eyebrow. "I want to hear it." He gestured for her to continue.

"I'm not Osten like you think I am."

"Believe it or not, I figured that out this afternoon." His gaze roamed her features, seeming to prepare for what she might be trying to say.

"The thing is, you're not wrong." She stumbled over her words. She'd never said this to anyone but her family. Arie knew. She wasn't sure how, but he'd always seemed to know. "You're not wrong about me being wind fae.... Well, it's just that Osten is not my only court."

A slow smile crept across his face as he crossed the room toward her. "Ahhh, why hadn't I considered? Well, it's so rare."

She held her hands up, stopping his progress before he got too close. She had trouble thinking clearly when he got that close. "I've never told anyone." She lifted her chin, daring him to judge her, to judge what mixed fae lineage meant about her family.

"Rose, you have to know." He faltered. "I hope you know I don't care what kind of fae you are, or how many courts you belong to."

"How could you not? You're the Suden Point."

His eyes narrowed at her words. "I'm the Suden Point, yes, but I'm also an earth fae who doesn't know anything about his father. The village where I grew up believed him to be Suden, but with some of the uniqueness of my magic, I"—he weighed his words—"can't be sure, I guess."

"You didn't know him at all?"

"No. He and my mother weren't together. They weren't even in a relationship. In fact, some believe she was already in a relationship with Aaron's father at the time." He paused again. "Anyway, I'm very confident that my father doesn't even know I exist." He shook his head. "Sorry, this isn't about me. This is about you. I tell you about my father so you know we have more similarities than you realize, but even if I were sure my father was Suden, I still wouldn't care. You are amazing, Rose. You, as you are."

Her body felt ablaze at the weight of his full attention. He was staring at her, his eyes sparkling with the light from the fire.

"Arie knows too," she blurted out, unsure where she was going with it, but knowing she needed to get him to stop looking at her like that.

"I assumed." He tapped his chin with his finger. "How did you and Arie meet?"

Somehow this was a much safer topic for Rose. He hadn't pressed her on what her other fae magic was. Instead, he asked her for a little more of her story. She wanted to give it to him.

"Arie saved me," she breathed.

She didn't expect it to feel like such a confession, but it did. She'd never had to tell anyone about how she and Arie met.

"My family was attacked and killed when I was a teenager. I miraculously got away, but it was terrible. I was running, stumbling through the woods, when a giant brown bear found me, and"—she remembered the terror of that moment—"I honestly thought it was over. I survived the attack on my family only to be eaten in the woods by a bear. Very fitting," she said dryly. "But then he spoke to me instead and told me to hop on."

Her hands inadvertently shook as she relived the night. "I was so scared, and my limbs were on fire from my escape."

Luc took her hand, and she let him, leaning into the solid reassurance as she continued.

"He helped me find and build a new home. A new life. The one you saw in the Lake of the Gods." She hesitated again. "He's not here every second. But he always shows up when it counts. And he asks for nothing in return. We bicker, and he teases me always, but he and Tara are the only family I've got now." She smiled halfheartedly. "He's the only one that knows me well enough to tease me so accurately."

Luc's thumb continued its gentle path from her thumb to her wrist as she spoke. She couldn't believe a simple touch could be so soothing.

"He sounds like a great friend," Luc said, reluctantly dropping her hand. She felt the warmth of his touch leave her.

"That's it?" she asked. "No follow-up questions on"—she fumbled with her words—"on anything I've told you?"

She gave him a side eye, and Luc sighed dramatically.

"Rose, of course I have follow-up questions. I want to know everything about you. Who were your family? Why were they attacked? Who did this to you?" He wiped his hand down his face. It was becoming her favorite gesture to draw from him. "I don't think asking you will get me the answers. I'll happily continue to prove my friendship to you since Arie proves it can be done successfully. Then maybe someday you'll trust me with those stories too." He returned to running his fingers through his hair as he finished.

He nodded at her, almost to assure himself more than her. Then he headed to the closet and pulled out a pile of blankets. She didn't know what she wanted from him, but she wanted him near her, and sharing some things about herself tonight had gone better than she could have hoped.

Any evaluation of her desires would require her to remind herself what a bad idea they were. He was the Suden Point. She did not want to be at Compass Lake any longer than necessary. His life was at Compass Lake. She processed this list and realized she wanted him in arm's reach anyway, especially after all they'd shared today.

"It's fine, Luc. We can share the bed." She looked from him to the giant bed again. "It's plenty big enough."

"I have no problem sleeping in the chair by the fire. It's quite cozy," he replied, not stopping his work gathering blankets and pillows.

"Suit yourself." She decided to try another tactic. "I certainly don't want to make you uncomfortable." She glanced at him, and his eyes snapped to hers with barely restrained response to the challenge in her words.

"I would not be uncomfortable sharing a bed with you, Rose." She could tell he struggled to keep his voice even. "I want to ensure you have your own space while you're here."

"To be clear, I mean two people lying beside each other in the bed. This is not a seduction tactic," she stated.

He stopped trying to appear indifferent; his predatory smile was back.

"Oh, I know. I am confident I will be able to tell when you decide to seduce me." He shook his head and pulled his hand across his face again, another point for Rose in their little game. "If you're sure it's fine…" He trailed off.

"I'm sure, Luc, or I wouldn't have offered."

She headed into the bathroom to get ready for bed herself. When she returned, she triumphantly saw that he'd put the extra blankets away.

Chapter Twenty-Seven

With a jolt, Rose flailed her arms and hit something solid. Not the forest floor, so she hadn't fallen off the bear she'd been riding. Soft sheets, she was in the Suden Point's bedroom.

Her cheeks felt wet, like she'd been crying. That solid object was radiating warmth around her. Not the heat of the inferno she'd been remembering, but a comforting heat to combat the cold and dark memories she'd been reliving in her dream.

Rolling the side of her head slightly on his thigh, her eyes found Luc's as he lifted his hands in surrender. He sat on the shared bed, legs folded, and she was sprawled across his lap.

She held his gaze. The corners of his mouth were downturned, like he knew she had been experiencing pain, but he didn't know how to help. He'd offered the only comfort he could, his arms around her as her dreams replayed her most significant loss.

"I tried to wake you. You were yelling. You wouldn't wake, no matter what I tried. Then something happened, and you reached for me."

He wanted to help. She could see it in his eyes.

"I'm sorry if I overstepped, Rose. I didn't know what to do."

She closed her eyes again, reopening them to see his gaze steadfastly fixed on her.

"Thanks, Luc."

She counted to ten, still sprawled across his lap. She became hyperaware of everywhere they touched. Skin touched skin as her slightly raised shirt exposed her hip to his leg. The side of her chest draped across him, and one arm stretched past his knee. His hands were still lifted in the air. She couldn't help but want them back in place. She felt their absence on her shoulder and side, where he must have cradled her as she rocked in her sleep. She wanted him to hold her close again and use his delicious warmth to chase away the bone-chilling wind from her horrible memories.

She tried to devise some quick reply to deescalate the intimacy of the situation but came up blank. Rose took a deep breath and sat up, pulling herself completely from his lap.

"Sorry if I accosted you. I promised to stay on my side, but it seems I failed." She tried a smile. It was small but genuine, and he returned it warmly.

"It's not a problem," he reassured her. "Want to see about some breakfast?"

She nodded, more grateful than he could know for his attempt at normalcy when she felt the situation was anything but.

With Rose no longer sprawled on his lap, Luc got up and headed to the closet.

"Let's go into Compass Lake Village. The baker makes the best chocolate pastries you've ever had."

Rose couldn't help but laugh. She knew precisely which pastries he was referring to, and they were better than he claimed. The door closed to the bathroom as she mentally went through the menu and decided which delicious items she would order. She was wondering how many she could eat without making herself sick when the door opened again.

He'd bathed. Though a clean pair of pants hung low on his hips, he walked out shirtless. His torso gleamed with remnant drops of water still meandering down the ridges of muscle. He was stunning. He must have felt her appraising gaze raking over his abdomen, chest, and shoulders. He had the audacity to wink at her as he grabbed a shirt from the closet and pulled it over his head.

"I can't tell if the look on your face is for me or the promise of chocolate pastries." His smile was devious. "But given my fragile ego, I'm going to choose to believe it's for me."

Rose still had difficulty formulating words. She coughed and started, "I..it…it's the pastries. I've had them before, and they are very satisfying." She cringed, her word choice reflecting the multiple thought paths her brain was currently proceeding down. There was no way that Luc would let such an easy target pass.

On cue, he responded, "I assure you that I could be every bit as satisfying as the pastry." His smile held a laugh now as he made his way toward her.

She rolled her eyes. "How can you be so sure?" Now she was holding back a laugh too. "Do you count repeat business like the baker? Or do you collect comment cards from any lucky enough to sample your offering?"

Luc continued to close the distance between them, arching an eyebrow at her last comment. "You'll just have to wait and see," he said, offering her his hand.

Taking the walking paths around the lake instead of promenading on the boats was a nice change of pace. It gave Rose time to clear her head. She'd woken up in such a state this morning, and Luc had been so safe and reassuring. He flirted shamelessly with her to pull her mind from her pain, and she liked it.

He was the Suden Point. She somehow kept forgetting that part. She should be scared of him or, at the very least, wary of the fact that they could have no real future together once he knew everything.

That didn't do much to douse her building desire. Even in their short time together, she saw that the Suden Point persona was one he wore as needed. There was a side to him that wasn't quite soft but also wasn't the hardened exterior he showed the world.

She'd think of this side of him as Luc, just Luc. The Suden Point was a brother, a doting uncle, and a fierce protector of those he cared for. She knew because, in their short time together, he seemed to treat her like she might be on that list.

She knew that the way he looked at her, like she was a gravitational force holding his undivided attention, was more than their fake relationship required. He saw her, he saw her strength and her pain, and he seemed to want to understand it all.

She believed that she was more than just a tool to him. She'd still evaluate his power and make him a weapon. She knew enough to know he'd use it to stop the mist plague. To prevent more like Tara from succumbing to endless sleep.

She'd shared more with him yesterday than she had with anyone in ten years. She chewed on her lip as they walked, knowing she still hadn't shared enough.

If only her biggest secret were her mixed fae heritage.

Rose's mind wandered as they walked, still holding fast to the crook of Luc's elbow. She heard a familiar caw seconds before a large black bird dropped onto her shoulder.

"Good morning, Arie," she said.

Luc turned, also nodding at Arie.

"Well, isn't this quaint," Arie spoke to Rose alone. *"You two make quite the handsome pair."*

Rose turned her head to glare at Arie as he continued.

"I came by the room this morning, but it sounded like you were having a nightmare."

Rose warmed again at the memory of waking up with Luc's arms around her. Her body had been cradled in his lap.

"I just want to know if you are ok. I can't imagine being here is doing anything for the countless memories you've spent years repressing."

The hard line of Rose's mouth slipped up into a smile. Only Arie could phrase something so terrible so eloquently.

"I haven't slept well since we decided to return." Rose shrugged. "I knew that would be the case when I agreed to come. We have bigger things to worry about than my repressed memories."

The bird on her shoulder tipped his head as he appraised her. She knew if he had a human face, he'd show a little pity and a lot of concern. Thankfully, those emotions were difficult to display with a beak.

Still sitting on her shoulder, Arie replied, *"Unfortunately, there is much more for you to worry about while you're here than the tragedy that happened to your family. You are still stronger than you know, dear. I'm going to go ahead and scout the market for us."* Arie took off, flying ahead of them.

Chapter Twenty-Eight

Any lingering gloom from the morning was whisked away as she stared in disbelief at the display of pastries before her. There were more than she remembered, and it took her adult self-restraint not to push her face up against the front window to get a better look. A broad smile crossed her face as she imagined how good they would taste. Luc followed her inside the shop.

"Good morning," came a call from somewhere in the back. The baker made his way out to the front counter, taking in his guests. Rose saw the exact moment he realized that the Suden Point was in his shop again. His whole body straightened and he gave a half bow over the counter.

"You honor us, sir. Please, tell me what I can get for you. Would you care to sample anything?" Rose looked back at Luc, her smile still wide as she realized that people in town would respond differently to him. Had it only been a day since they walked through the market together? She was so comfortable with him that others' discomfort still surprised her.

During her first interaction with the Suden Point, with his brisk and arrogant attitude, she certainly hadn't known who he was, but she'd been able to tell he was used to getting his way. But these people? Those who lived and breathed Compass Lake and its politics couldn't help but know the faces of the Compass Points. She could tell by the slight rise of his shoulders that he was not a fan of these deferential interactions, no matter how expected, and it made her smile just a little wider to watch him try to hide his embarrassment.

He caught her enjoying his discomfort and narrowed his eyes at her, before responding to the baker, "Thank you, sir, no need to sample. I think we already know and love your pastries. Can you give us a dozen, a little of everything? And can you wrap it up for us?"

The baker made quick work of the task. He seemed to select each item carefully before adding it to the box he was putting together. He was serving the most powerful Suden on the continent. He clearly revered the power of Luc's position.

She wondered how many Compass Points stopped in the village for breakfast like this. That thought set off a string of anxieties she hadn't even considered. What if they ran into another Compass Point while here? She couldn't believe she'd been so careless. She'd been too distracted by her nightmare this morning to think about it.

Eager now to be on their way, they paid for their breakfast and headed back to the market square. Rose had taken the box when the baker offered it. Luc only laughed and decided not to get between her and her pack of sweets. She let the warmth and fresh smell of the goods comfort her as she focused on getting out of the market without running into anyone unexpectedly.

Taking a quick turn around the small square looking for Arie, Rose tried to gently rush their progress.

Chills broke along her spine as she felt it—the moment she dreaded. A pair of eyes rested on her back. She could feel it in the icy tingle that crept down her neck and the excited bubbling that came over the previously tame market crowd. A buzz of energy filled the air as the one man she'd been trying to avoid entered the market.

The Norden Point was here.

Her grip on Luc's arm inadvertently tightened, her stress seeping into everything she touched. Luc was instantly at attention, assessing the threat.

It didn't take a genius to narrow the targets based on the new arrival. Rose didn't have time to appreciate Luc wiping his hand across his face, usually a sign that she'd gotten under his skin. This time, the display showed his exasperation.

His process of elimination about who she was avoiding and what her unnamed second fae heritage was must be complete.

He quickly took her hand and pulled her down the closest alley. She couldn't think. All of her energy was spent on pushing breath in and out of her lungs. She was in no state to put a plan together. She knew she had to get out of there before he recognized her.

And Aiden *would* recognize her.

The alley was a dead end. Luc must be panicking too.

"Luc, we need to get away from the market."

As if he didn't already know. As if he couldn't already tell the severity of the situation by the clamminess of her skin or the raw panic in her eyes.

"The Norden Point, Rose? I know I shouldn't be that surprised, and I realize that now is not the correct time to discuss this." That fact didn't stop him as he whisper-yelled, "But *the* Norden Point, Rose?"

He moved his body entirely in front of hers. Anyone looking down the alley would see only his back.

"Not the best time, Luc," she snapped. His sharp tone undoubtedly helped raise her temper, freeing her from her frozen panic. Anger instead of fear; she could work with that. She looked down the alley, back to the main square. She could see the Norden Point strolling toward their side of the market. She dragged her eyes away from him and met Luc's deep brown eyes staring at her, taking in every inch of her panic.

"We have to wait for him to pass," Rose mumbled. "He's headed our way now, but I doubt he'll come down this alley. Once he's passed, we can slip out behind him and leave the market the way he came in. We should be able to blend into the crowd." She was thinking out loud, but as she finished the last sentence, she looked at Luc and remembered that they would not be "blending into the crowd" as long as she was on the arm of the Suden Point.

"We can do it, Rose. Let's wait for him to pass, and then we can go. No one stopped us in the street on our way to the market. This will be no different."

She relaxed slightly, a tiny bit of the stress seeping from her shoulders. But when she looked over Luc's shoulder, the Norden Point had already gotten closer. He looked around, eyes lingering down other alleys as he passed them.

Rose made a split-second decision. She'd never really know how much of it was born from believing she had a solid plan to blend in or simply the urge to do something she desired. Either way, she looked at Luc, eyes locking on his.

"I need you to kiss me," she whispered.

His face flashed a complex and rapid set of emotions. She could only pick up one or two, seeing a glimpse of his desire and doubt. He didn't think she knew what she was doing. He thought she was panicking.

"I know what I'm doing, Luc. He's glancing down each alley as he passes. He's looking for someone. It honestly could be you. We should make sure he doesn't give us more than a passing glance. We need to be occupied. Please, Luc."

"You certainly don't need to beg, Rose," he murmured as his strong frame closed the space between them. His shoulders further blocked her from the view of anyone looking down the alley. His eyes met hers again, seeking something. Reassurance? Her desire to match his? She wasn't sure, but she didn't have time to figure it out. She nodded once more, closing her eyes, leaning forward into him.

"Ah ah ah," he whispered, his smooth and taunting voice only for her. "You asked me to kiss you." His hand moved slowly up her arm, and her grip on the pastry box loosened. It was evidence of the impact of his touch that she didn't spare a thought for her breakfast when she heard it fall to the ground.

She could barely hold herself still as she marked the path of his hand and the delicious warmth it left in its wake. Her heart was racing so fast she thought it'd escape from her chest. Already a disaster of emotion from this place and the Norden Point's appearance, she thought she would explode as his hand slid higher, crossing her shoulder, finally finding the nape of her neck. She gasped at the heat of the skin-to-skin contact.

A satisfied smile crossed his face as he guided her gently back a few steps, his body following hers like a magnet. Her back found the brick wall behind her, leaving her nowhere to go. She wouldn't dream of being anywhere else. A flame built low in her belly from the way his eyes devoured her. His attention finally settled on her mouth.

She sucked in a breath as his hand at her nape guided her head forward, and his lips met hers. They were surprisingly soft and warm, erasing any lingering doubt that his Suden Point exterior was a facade. She felt wrapped in the pine and cinnamon scent that was his and only his as she sank into his kiss.

She knew there was a logical reason they were doing this. Wasn't kissing part of the plan?

She lost the thread of thought the moment his lips moved against hers. Her hands snaked up to Luc's chest, wrapping themselves in fabric as they grasped his shirt. They seemed to have a mind of their own, their one goal to get him closer to her. She tugged him in for a deeper kiss.

He needed no further encouragement as his mouth covered hers, his tongue teasing as she opened for him. Fingers still clutching the fabric of his shirt, she smiled as his body came stumbling forward against hers, his weight pushing her further against the wall. She kissed him back, relishing the contact, thrilled to have caught him off guard with her advance.

His tongue intertwined with hers, he worked his hand into her hair and then sucked her lip. Rose couldn't stop a small moan as she focused on eradicating all distance between them. Hours, minutes, seconds later, their lips parted. Breathing heavily, Rose broke eye contact first, her gaze darting over his shoulder. The Norden Point must have passed. She could no longer see him. She met Luc's eyes again, still unable to form words, and nodded.

He took her hand, his face mirroring her surprise at the intensity of their kiss. He worked to even out his expression as he led them back up the alley. They were taking their chances heading in the opposite direction of the Norden Point. Both of them paused when a black bird landed on Rose's shoulder.

"You thought now was the best time for that little interlude?"

"We had a plan," she said back to him, measuring what words Luc would hear as she replied.

"Of course, you did. He just went into one of the shops down there on the right." Arie gestured with his beak in the direction opposite of

where they were headed. *"So you should be clear to scamper off. I'll see what he's up to and meet you at the Suden house later."*

"Thanks, Arie," she said, nodding at him as he took off, soaring over the market. She turned to Luc, working to control her emotions even as her eyes distractedly darted toward his lips.

"Arie says we're clear. Let's go."

She tried to maintain the same calm with which they'd entered the market. It had been a close call with the Norden Point, but Rose feared that she'd crossed a far more precarious line with the Suden Point with that kiss.

Chapter Twenty-Nine

Quickly and quietly, they made their way back down the path. Rose's heart was still racing. She couldn't be sure if it was from the danger or the kiss, and she didn't want to analyze it too closely. She snuck a glance at Luc, as if that would help. Unfortunately, he was staring right back at her.

"So how much closer did we just get to the Suden Point," came Arie's singsong voice.

Her cheeks warmed as she thought about the multiple implications. She'd given away a little more of her past and spent quality time getting acquainted with his tongue. Judging by his stare, he was affected by at least one, if not both events.

She'd say that closer was an understatement.

Pushing the kiss momentarily from her mind, she focused on the knowledge he'd gained. He already knew she had two fae lines. Knowing the second was Norden wasn't that big of a deal. No, the problem now was the enormity of her reaction to the Norden Point. Luc was observant. It wasn't just fear of recognition he would have seen. It was fear of the man himself, though she hated to admit it. Luc deserved an explanation.

Her eyes never left Luc's as she responded, "A lot."

"What's he asking?" Luc finally broke the silence between them. "Wait, don't answer that. That is in no way how I want to use my first question."

"What do you want to use your first question on?" She found it easy to tease him. This was familiar when everything else for them seemed to be changing by the second. She knew he was in a tight spot in the market, but if he wanted to leave her to the Norden Point once he'd realized that's who she was hiding from, he could have.

He hadn't.

If Arie was curious, he didn't share. He continued to fly above them. Close enough to hear, as clearly the drama in this conversation was too good to pass up, but also high enough to see if they were being followed out of the market.

"Why are you hiding from the Norden Point?" he asked. He was going in for the kill.

She swallowed. "Really? No working our way up to that question? You're just jumping right in?"

"I think it's time." His face gave nothing away—well, almost nothing. She swore she could see the concern. Was the concern for her, or himself and what he'd inadvertently stumbled into?

"If I tell you, you won't be able to pretend you didn't know. You and your family could be in danger for knowing. People have been killed for my secret."

Luc appraised her again, taking a good look before nodding.

"You seem to forget, Rose, that I am the Suden Point. Like the Norden Point, it is not an insignificant position. I can help you. If you'll let me."

"I am all too aware that you're the Suden Point." Rose sighed as they continued down the path. They were almost to the Suden property. Luc gently tugged her to a halt, but she heard Arie start talking before he could get a word out. She held up her finger to stop him from saying something simultaneously.

"Because of your ruse, everyone will assume he knows your secrets, Rose," said Arie. *"You do him more disservice by not telling him now."*

"He's no innocent in this, Arie!" She forgot herself and yelled at him as he circled. "He tried to kidnap me, force me to work for him, or whatever he had planned." Luc's head snapped back at that as if he'd been slapped.

"Rose." He looked at her and took her hands in his. "If I haven't before, I apologize for my initial"—he had the good grace to look sheepish as he finished—"attempts to work with you. They were wrong, and I was desperate. I'm not sorry for trying anything within my power to find a cure to the mist plague, but I am sorry that I didn't try and explain myself better." He took a final breath. "I, like you, am not used to having someone on my side."

She looked at him and up at Arie, wondering if Arie had intentionally provoked her anger to force this conversation. It didn't matter. They were having it. She'd deal with Arie later.

Shaking her head, she replied, "I know. I'm just making more excuses for myself. Arie is right because of our supposed relationship." His soft smile briefly started to curve into one much more seductive at the mention. She reined in her incomprehensible desire to close the distance between them like he had in the market and continued, "Others will assume you already know my secrets. Whether or not I tell them to you. I don't want to leave you in the dark if I have to run."

"Rose, you won't have to run." He pointed a finger to his chest. "Me. Suden Point. Remember? It means something. Why is it such a problem for you?"

She couldn't help but laugh. In any normal circumstance, it would mean a lot.

She took his hand and pulled him along behind her. They weren't to the Suden property yet and were still exposed. He may be willing to overlook the fact that he was the Suden Point, and she was, well, whatever she was. But the rest of the world wouldn't, especially with the missing information she was about to tell him.

Her mind spun as it had on the walk to the village. Whatever happened or didn't happen between the two of them, he deserved to know. If Aiden really was the reason there was an imbalance with the Compass Points, she was the only one who could do something about it.

So she took a deep breath and readied herself to utter the words she'd never said aloud. As they took the final step across the Suden property line, she whispered, "I'm the rightful heir to the Norden Point seat."

This time, it wasn't a snap as his head gracefully turned to her. Something like relief flashed on his face.

"Finally," he breathed.

CHAPTER THIRTY

"Finally? What do you mean, finally?" she nearly screeched at him as they continued walking toward the house. "You could not have possibly expected that." She all but flipped her hair over her shoulder in assurance.

"No, I couldn't, but the pieces became clearer the more you decided to share with me." His words were soft, but his statement held confidence. "You don't seem afraid of much, but even from the first day we met in Bury, you had a visceral fear of someone or something here."

Her cheeks warmed, though she wasn't sure why. She told herself it was anger. She didn't like to acknowledge the fear. But it was perfectly reasonable to fear the man who tried to kill you. Who killed your entire family.

"Based on your magic, I assumed that it was Juliette, the Osten Point. But when it wasn't her, that only left one other guess."

"That should have left two guesses," Rose interjected.

Luc waved his hand as if to brush off the idea. "Have you met the Vesten Point?"

"No, I would have met their predecessor."

"You'd get it if you had. He's a powerful shifter, but sometimes he seems afraid of his own tail. I couldn't imagine him instilling the kind of fear you have."

"So what does this mean?" she asked, a little harsher than she meant to, bringing them back to the heart of the problem.

His hand brushed hers as they continued their walk. "What I don't understand is what about the Norden Point instills that fear? He's a bastard, to be sure." Luc stopped them both, gently pulling her shoulder so they faced each other. "How do you know him? He couldn't have been Norden Point when you were here." Luc looked up, like he was trying to do some rough math about their ages.

She took a deep breath. He hadn't pieced the whole thing together yet. "The story I told you about the night I met Arie? That night, the Norden Point—Aiden then—killed my family and tried to kill me as well."

Luc sucked in a breath as his fists balled at his side. Rose smelled the scent of pine and cinnamon start to work its way around them as Luc worked to control his building anger.

"How could he do that, Rose? People would know. How did he become Norden Point?" Luc said through gritted teeth, barely leashing his rage.

"We were friends." She weighed her words. "He was my only friend, really. My father was the Norden house caretaker, and we were the only two children on the property. I don't know if you've met Aiden's parents, but they are…" She fumbled for the right words. "Not the most nurturing."

"You will likely be unsurprised to hear that his father is no longer alive."

Rose wasn't surprised. Though the current Norden Point didn't have to die for the next to take over, Aiden's father would have still been in his prime. He would have been unlikely to have stepped down for Aiden so soon.

"Did Aiden kill him?" Rose asked.

"If he did, it hasn't been proven. Though I'm not sure if anyone thought to investigate it. You know how the fae are; anything that happens to a different court isn't our problem. We just assumed the Norden would take care of it."

"I think the Norden elders have turned a lot of blind eyes." Rose felt her words almost a betrayal of her people, but she was sick of covering for them. The Suden Point cared more for her well-being than the Norden elders. The elders had failed her.

"Forgive me, Rose, but I have to ask. The fae courts are so secretive. I'm not prying for intel when I ask, how do you know you're the rightful Norden Point?"

Rose gave him a half smile. She trusted him enough to tell him the entire Norden testing ritual, but that wasn't what he was asking. "I had just finished my test. The elder told me: Aiden's father was still hemming and hawing about it not being sure, but before we could settle it, my body was gripped with a fear I'll never forget. I ran to the cottage to check on my family, but it was too late. Needless to say, I never returned to confirm my status."

Luc bowed his head for a moment, acknowledging her loss. He took her hand as they stood facing each other. "I'm so sorry that this happened to you, Rose."

"Even at his worst, I didn't think him capable of what he did. I still think…" She choked off her words but knew she had to get this out. "I hate him. I hate him completely but will forever wonder if he was himself that day."

Luc stared, shock apparent on his face as he waited for her to continue.

"His eyes. It was always his eyes. Sometimes…I know this sounds ridiculous, but sometimes they would flash grey. The longer they held grey, the less he seemed like the Aiden I knew."

"His eyes change color?" Luc asked quietly.

"I know it sounds unbelievable. Have you never seen it?"

"I think I saw it once. In that first meeting. But I haven't seen it since."

Luc reached for her hand. His thumb softly moved up and down where it rested above hers. He paused the motion when she asked, "Is he doing something with the Norden power?" She looked up into his eyes.

"I honestly don't know. The secrecy of each fae court makes it challenging to tell when they change things."

"How can you take this so calmly?" Rose asked.

"You saw my memory. You know the sense of wrongness I felt even at that first meeting. I assure you, it's only gotten worse over the last eight years." Luc wiped his hand down his face, but this time Rose took no joy in it. "I didn't know why, but this…" He gestured to Rose. "This makes sense."

"What do you mean?"

"It was never supposed to be him. It was always supposed to be you. Whatever the gods started, the imbalance has only worsened with the wrong Norden Point in the seat. The plague of mist, whether it's Zrak or not, it's all connected. You have to know that."

Arie circled above, not providing any entertaining commentary for once. Rose wished he would. She'd suspected that the imbalance had to do with her on some level, but she'd also thoroughly convinced herself that that couldn't be the case. That if something were wrong with the Norden Point, others would know.

Well, here Luc was, telling her that others had noticed. And now she had to decide if she would keep pushing her past away.

She'd paused too long. He continued to fill the silence. "I don't think you came here with me to take your rightful place as the Norden Point, but I think you should. You came here to find a way to stop the mist, to save Tara. Your magical blades will help, should you choose to make them, but I think the only way to stop the mist permanently is to have the rightful Norden Point in the seat."

"I never wanted to believe that this was the cause—that I could be the cause."

He put his hands on her shoulders, forcing her to meet his gaze. "This is not your fault. No one would blame a sixteen-year-old kid for running after your experience. This is Aiden's wrong. I'm just asking you to help right it. If you still don't believe I want what's best for you, at least believe I want what's best for the continent, for my people. I want to stop the spread of the mist plague, and I believe you are the key to that."

"Are you sure your people would agree with you? Or will they assume that your judgment has been clouded by my…" She took a second to wave her hand up and down the length of her body. "Charms."

"For the record…" His smile turned sinful. "I am taken with your, as you say, charms." He gave her a pointed look, refreshing the memory of their recent kiss.

She met his gaze, seeing the desire that matched his bold words.

"I don't think that means I would take on the Norden Point with you without reason." His full lips turned up at the side in what was becoming her favorite smirk. "No one would believe I was that selfless, no matter your charms."

"Truly?" She couldn't help but arch an eyebrow back. Their fake relationship ruse had been a wild success. The entire lake would *know* that they were together.

"Think about what you knew about me before our travels. What did you know of the Suden Point?"

"He was the most powerful Suden Point in generations. He was cold, calculating." She stopped herself as she continued to rattle off the other ruthless attributes in her head.

"Yes, and that was from someone relatively unconnected with Compass Lake since I came to power. I assure you the people who interact with me regularly think I'm much worse."

"Why is that? I've only known you for a week, but I can tell that while you would cross lines for what you believe in, there is much more behind it than a cold and cruel calculation."

"Why not let my enemies think the worst of me? Those I work with closely tend to see a little more, but it's proven to be in my best interest to let the general public fear me."

This was something she understood more than she wished she did. Hadn't she done the same in Bury with everyone except Tara? It was better to let the common folk fear her and leave her alone than have too many friends and people wanting to get into her business. It made sense, in a sad and lonely sort of way.

CHAPTER THIRTY-ONE

Morning came sooner than expected and Rose stretched languidly as her hand grazed a familiar hard surface. She peeked open her eye to find herself lying in a sea of warm, down blankets and her hand firmly placed on Luc's chest. His eyes held nothing but wicked delight when she met them.

She quickly pulled her hand back as she tried to orient herself, but not before Luc grabbed it and pulled it back to his chest.

"I don't mind, really," he dared her playfully.

She rolled her eyes at him. He'd spent the rest of the afternoon and evening alternating between planning with her and avoiding the topic of her rightful position. He was giving her time and space to decide if she'd make her claim to the Norden Point known. It had been a long time since she'd felt so supported.

She couldn't argue with the fact that Aiden, as the Norden Point, was causing imbalance. Whether it was because he wasn't supposed to be there at all or because he was making terrible decisions with his power, she didn't know. She supposed it didn't matter.

She still wasn't sure she believed that the mist plague, the wrath of the lost god, was solely focused on the correct Norden Point being in place. But she felt that fixing one thing usually helped point her toward the next item that needed fixing.

The problem here was that fixing this would change her life drastically. She'd planned to leave Compass Lake as soon as she could. As soon as she'd decided whether or not she'd make weapons for the Suden Point. Of course, she knew that she would make them for him now. She could start today and leave Compass Lake in a few weeks, wishing everyone well. Would that be enough? Would she be able to run away and start a new life without seeing this fix through? Without seeing what a balanced Compass Points could do about the mist plague?

She knew the answer to all of these questions was a resounding no. Now she just needed to do something about it.

"There is some food over on your nightstand. I didn't think we'd want to risk the market this morning, so I brought up some things from the kitchen."

He dropped her hand, finally releasing it from his chest, as her stomach gurgled. She rolled over to survey her food options. He'd put together a plate of fruits, nuts, and some bread that looked delicious. After grabbing one of the pieces of bread, she rolled on her back to chew it without getting up. She looked over at him as she heard a pointed coughing sound.

"I know you're not going to eat that in bed." He eyed her suspiciously.

"What good is breakfast in bed if you can't eat it in bed?"

"You'll get crumbs everywhere!"

"I have a solution for that, Luc." She gave him her most suggestive smile as she shimmied herself closer to him. It was a large bed, and he'd given her space each night they'd shared it. Yet there was no disguising the want in his eyes now as she made her way firmly towards his side.

She leaned in close as first her legs tangled with his and, using the leverage, she slid the rest of herself over, inches away from him. She lay on her side, staring at him as he hungrily gazed at her.

"And just what is that solution?" he asked.

She moved her hand with the piece of forgotten bread back between their mouths. She took a big bite right in front of him. He couldn't mask the shock, seeming to have forgotten about the crumb argument when she started inching her body toward him.

"I'll just eat on your side of the bed so we can consider that side the crumb side."

His gaze narrowed as he said, "I guess that means we'll have to share your side. It seems only fair."

She couldn't help but laugh at the antagonized admiration she saw on his face.

"Thank you, Luc." She'd mentally changed topics, and she could tell he realized it as his features softened, turning more contemplative. He nodded.

"Have you decided what you want to do?" he asked.

"I think I've got a pretty good idea, but we should probably talk about it while I finish this." She held his gaze as she took another big bite of the bread, crumbs falling to the sheets that she didn't even try to catch.

"How does going to the ball accompanying the Compass Lake Solstice Ceremony, which I've successfully avoided every year since I've become Suden Point, necessitate a trip to the Sandrin?" Luc asked in exasperation as he packed some necessities from the kitchen for their trip. She had come to understand that his exasperation meant he already knew the answer. He just wanted to be difficult.

"We're making a statement. I'm going to need the right tools to make it." She looked at him meaningfully, reminding him of the plan she'd laid out that morning. "We can't find everything we need in the market. Even if we could, we don't seem to have the best luck there." She grabbed a bedroll and her backpack to head outside.

"Agree to disagree," he murmured as his smile went from playful to predatory. As if he remembered their bodies pressed against each other in the market alley yesterday just as clearly as she did. The smolder in his eyes told her he'd be only too happy to repeat it.

Luc had offered her quite a bit yesterday—an ally in treason, a haven from which to plan and strategize as she decided whether to make this move. And that only covered the political aspects of their relationship. He looked at her increasingly with something like reverence. He'd kissed her as if he needed her, as if his life was colorless and dull without her, as if she was the answer to his prayer to the gods.

She wasn't sure she hated it.

It was unsustainable, though. If they were successful in their first endeavor, making her Norden Point, they would still find themselves on opposite sides of the Compass table, literally and figuratively.

The Compass Points barely trusted each other, let alone built romantic relationships. The distrust between the fae courts was too strong. She still recalled the fear in Mom's eyes when she realized that Rose could wield two elements. The fae did not take well to those of mixed lineage. She was convinced that if not for the gods' creation of the Compass Points and their responsibilities, the four fae courts would never interact with each other.

She had always been told that it came down to no one wanting to see powerful fae magic dilute or converge. No one wanted to think about the offspring of such a union. Would they even be able to have children? Would a child have both magics? Which fae court would claim them if they did? Rose had gone through her own identity crisis about all of that. Thankfully, she'd had her mom's unwavering support, but she could imagine someone like Aiden's parents disowning him if he didn't fit the specific mold of their expectations.

She wasn't surprised that it always came back to power. She wanted to laugh off the idea that any Compass Point would have a child killed for power, but her own history punched her in the gut. It was the first time she thought about the worst night of her life and laughed a little. Not a happy laugh, of course, but even an ironic laugh was better than tears. She shrugged to herself. Luc was staring at her.

"What?"

"Nothing, let's go," she said as she grabbed his arm. They headed back around the lake to the stables. He let her lead him as they took the back roads again.

They made it through the village without incident. Gear and horses in tow, they set off for the few days' ride to Sandrin. It wasn't that far away on a map, but part of Compass Lake's charm was the barrier to accessing it. The mountains meant that trips to and from the lake weren't simple. They had a full day's ride to get out of the mountains before another day and a half to Sandrin.

They had not gone far when a large black raven landed on her shoulder.

"Good morning, future Mrs. Suden Point. Or are we going with future Mrs. Norden-Suden? Hyphenated? Or will he be Mr. Norden Point?"

She glared daggers at Arie. "I'm not dignifying that with a response."

"Aren't you even going to wish me a good morning?" he teased.

"That depends entirely on how the rest of this conversation goes. It's trending towards no, for your reference."

"I did a check from here to Bury again," he said, as if her threat was irrelevant. *"The plague of mist is making its way south. A few outposts and small villages between here and there have been taken by it already."*

"Do you think it's headed to Compass Lake?" she asked.

"I can't tell," Arie responded. *"It's hard to determine since the lake is so far off the traditional path south. We won't know until the mist either hits the first outpost past Compass Lake or ends up on our doorstep."*

"Has the imbalance gotten that bad? That the mist plague would attack the seats of power?" Rose commented aloud. Small, remote villages were tragic but also didn't require that much effort to take.

"From the news I heard this morning, that I'm sure Arie is sharing with you now, I think we can assume the mist plague has a plan. It is moving far too purposefully not to."

She glared at Luc. "When were you going to share that information?"

"You seemed so lost in thought this morning. I didn't want to distract you from whatever you were processing, especially since I knew we'd have a full day of riding to talk about it."

She fought the slight curve of her lips at his attentiveness and consideration. Not fast enough, though. He saw her smile start and responded with a bright, wide one of his own that he rarely showed.

Self-satisfied and amused—a dangerous start for a long ride with the Suden Point.

CHAPTER THIRTY-TWO

It was slow going down the narrow switchbacks that made the path to and from Compass Lake. Exhausted but feeling like she was finally taking action, Rose made camp with Luc for the night at the base of the mountains while Arie had disappeared that afternoon and had yet to return.

They traveled comfortably. She couldn't believe they'd only known each other for a week. They seemed in sync as they unpacked their bedrolls, started a fire, and prepared dinner, each easily accommodating the other in their activity. The conversation flowed, but it wasn't required. The silence was just as companionable. Rose wasn't quite sure how she felt about the entire situation. She stared at Luc as they sat beside each other by the fire, finishing their evening meal.

Remove the Suden Point title, and he had many qualities she had always pictured for her future partner. He was strong, even brutal when required, but also, quietly considerate. He knew how to present the face the world needed to see, but he also knew how to care for those he loved. It was evident in the easy way that he interacted with his family. The fact that he had his family as part of his Suden Point household said it most clearly. Many of the Compass Points left their families out of the power they inherited, except in cases where they were specifically trying to train or coach particular offspring to inherit the next title.

And there she was, thinking about the Compass Point titles again and that he held one. That fact seemed inescapable.

"Do you want to talk about it?"

She gave him the glare that he deserved. "Talk about what?"

"Whatever it is that's getting you all worked up over there. I'd hazard to guess it's the same thing that you were working through this morning, and if it involves me, it might be best to ask me about it."

His eyes were cautious, but the rest of his face was all feigned nonchalance. It was clearly important to him that she trusted him and talked to him about her concerns, but he wouldn't beg her to. He'd done more than was necessary at every turn since they'd made their way to Compass Lake. He at least deserved to know where she was mentally.

"You're the Suden Point," she said flatly.

"Are you just noticing?" His easy charm was back, but the wariness never left his gaze.

"You know what I mean. I understand why you are helping who you believe to be the true Norden Point to reclaim their place, but I can't help but realize that if we succeed with that, we will find ourselves on opposite sides of the Compass table."

"Yes, I am the Suden Point, and you will be the Norden Point." He left no room for argument on the success of their endeavors. "That doesn't mean we have to be enemies after this. The Compass Points preserve the balance on the continent. That is all. I think we can easily do that and remain…friendly." He stumbled over the last word.

"Friendly," she repeated. She wasn't sure if she was relieved or disappointed.

"Whatever word you want to apply," he quickly amended. "Our current and future relationship is our own." He took her hand. "All you need to worry about is what type of relationship you want with me. I assure you that whatever you decide, we can still carry out our duties as Compass Points flawlessly."

She saw nothing but sincerity in his face and a bit of hope in offering her their relationship definition. She wanted to lean into his warmth and offer but knew she had more to consider.

"I'll be sure to add your thoughts to all those already spinning around in my head," she replied. It was the truth but also flippant, so it worked for her.

"Just don't shut me out, Rose." He paused, hesitating slightly. "Can you tell me if you decide to do something drastic?" His voice got quieter as he said the last, and he let go of her hand.

She immediately missed the feel of him—his grounding and calming touch.

"Fine." She didn't like that he thought she would do something drastic, whatever that meant, but he deserved to know whatever she decided. She would give him that.

"I'm exhausted. I think I'm going to get some rest," she managed. Her thoughts kept spinning as she tracked what looked like resignation on Luc's features. How could this all seem so easy for him? For the calculating Suden Point, he didn't seem to consider what a real relationship between them would mean. Didn't he know that this could cause an uprising from the courts?

Maybe that didn't matter.

The secrets between the fae courts, specifically surrounding the Norden power testing, had caused her entire situation in the first place. If more people knew the parts of the test or understood how to interpret the results, would Aiden have been able to do what he did? Those secrets had ruined her life and got her family killed. Were they worth protecting?

She fell asleep late, tossing and turning, and didn't sleep soundly until she found a heat source on the forest floor that she wrapped herself around. Too tired to care, she decided that the problem of why there was a cozy heater on the ground in the middle of the forest was future Rose's problem.

When future Rose opened her eyes, the morning light had invaded the campsite. She decided she hated past Rose and her terrible decision-making. The heater on the forest floor was Luc.

Of course it was Luc.

She'd rolled over to his bedroll and thoroughly entangled their limbs. She couldn't even pretend it was his fault since her bedroll was empty, and she had essentially accosted him on his.

Judging by his continued sleep, he didn't seem to mind. His even breath rose and fell while she considered her options.

"What do we have here, Rose? Are we becoming a bit too good at acting out this fake relationship thing?" Arie crooned as his raven form landed in the camp. *"No one is watching now. I'm sure you didn't have to stay quite so close to him in the night."*

Rose quickly gave up hope of some miracle that her disentanglement would not be awkward and began prying herself out of Luc's arms. He woke as she did so, half-hooded eyes meeting hers and that self-satisfied smile creeping up over his sleep-drenched face.

"Arie's here. I'll start breakfast," she said matter of factly. She refused to discuss why she found herself in Luc's arms with Arie before discussing it with Luc.

Luc looked briefly around the camp, saw the black bird, and let his head fall back to the ground for a few more minutes of sleep.

"I am not having this conversation with you," she said to Arie as she started to move around the camp.

"It doesn't look like a lot of conversation was being had at all," was Arie's smug reply. And then a little softer, *"Do you know what you're doing, Rose?"*

She couldn't help but thank Arie for his concern. He had always been in her corner, no matter how much he teased her. She picked her words carefully, knowing that Luc could hear her side of the conversation.

"I trust him." She found the sentence to feel entirely accurate as the words came out.

The bird nodded at her and let her continue about her work.

After another day and a half of much flatter riding, Rose finally saw the city of Sandrin, and the surrounding bay, glimmering in the distance. Luc had a room in the military quarter, where they opted to stay.

The town itself wasn't huge. It filled the small peninsula, stretching into a bay of water and the sea to the west. The military quarter was the farthest south. It comprised simple structures, buildings no more than three stories high, and each floor was lined with doors leading to their military accommodations.

Luc's room had the same straightforward style as his room at Compass Lake but with even fewer trimmings. A few books were scattered by the bedside table and a single chair, but the room contained no other personal touches. Rose wondered a little at the persona he inhabited while he was here—she remembered that he said he spent quite a bit of time here. She couldn't help but think it had to be lonely. It sure didn't have the warmth she felt in the Suden house.

"I have to check on my people while I'm here. I think I'll take care of it now," Luc noted as they dropped their things on the floor of his room. He left her space to object, but she could tell he didn't expect her to. They had a plan to find both practical and magical tools. While he said he'd take care of the dress she needed, she had ensured that she was left to search for the magical item on her own.

Now, she found that she wanted a partner.

Was she afraid that she would fail, that she was chasing a ghost story and that this trip would all be for nothing more than a stupid dress? Kind of—but she realized she wanted his support to at least try and find the Norden artifact that she sought.

She shrugged as if what she was about to ask meant little to her. "How long will you be? I can wait for you if you want to come with me."

His eyes lit up. "Give me twenty minutes, and I'm all yours."

CHAPTER THIRTY-THREE

Rose and Luc headed north to the Norden quarter of the city. The Norden referred to this part of Sandrin as the historic quarter. It held few residences and many museums, bookshops, and a library. By the time they arrived from the Suden military quarter, it was getting late. Rose hoped they'd have enough time to find where they needed to go.

Rose gave Luc one last glance as she realized she wasn't entirely out of secrets to tell him yet. She lifted the thin gold chain from around her neck, holding the small compass in her hand. Luc assessed her, probably wondering if she needed help with directions.

"You know that old story about Zrak's sacrifice?" she asked.

"The one where the gods decide who should be sacrificed by using a magic compass forged by Aurora herself?" His eyes danced with laughter. He seemed to know already where this was going as he looked back to the compass in her hand. Once he'd decided not to underestimate her, he'd stuck with it. That was clear as he didn't question she held a gods' forged compass in her hand, he just accepted it as fact.

"That's the one."

"And you have it."

"And I have it."

His eyes lifted from the compass in her palm to meet her gaze. "You never cease to amaze me."

Rose felt her cheeks warm.

"So, if I remember the story correctly, the compass was attuned to all four elemental magics. And it was meant to select the god that would sacrifice themselves to right the imbalance."

"That's correct. It directs based on the needs of the wielder."

"Like the continent needed a god to sacrifice themselves?"

"Yes."

"And you've had it this whole time? Why haven't we tried to use it for anything else? Like our need to defeat the mist plague?"

"To be completely honest..." Rose started.

"I love it when you do that," Luc replied, seeming to quite enjoy this new turn in their partnership.

"To be completely honest," she started again, "I never really believed this was the compass."

Arie flew towards them as they stood in the street, compass still in her outstretched palm.

"So you've finally decided to acknowledge what that compass is?"

"You knew?" Rose turned to stare open-mouthed at the bird on her shoulder.

"Knew that you carried Aurora's compass? Yes, of course, Rose. What do you take me for?"

Rose didn't know what to think of that. "I was telling Luc I didn't believe my family's stories. That I wasn't sure of what I had until..."

"Until what, Rose?" Luc asked.

Arie tilted his head and watched her.

"Until...oh fine, until I held it in the ruined workshop at the Lake of the Gods. I was facing west, but the compass pointed south, to where..." She lifted her eyes to Luc.

"To where I stood." His voice was thick.

She nodded.

"Seems like Aurora has still got some tricks up her sleeve."

"What?" Rose turned to Arie, breaking the intimacy of her acknowledgment to Luc.

"Nothing, Rose. So the compass thought you needed to go with him. And that's when you believed you truly held Aurora's compass? Not just a family reproduction?"

"That's right. I mean, how was I to know? Mom, Dad, Grandpa, whenever they told the story of the compass's creation, they'd tug gently on my necklace, but I always thought it was symbolism that I wore a compass like Aurora's since I was Norden."

Luc seemed to have recovered from the compass's feelings about him. "How did your family come across it?"

"I don't know. They never told me." She shrugged. "I think they planned to tell me more about it after the Norden test, but…" Her words drifted off. They'd never discussed it because they'd been killed. She couldn't bring herself to say the words.

"So, are we ready to use it now? What do you need, exactly?"

"I'm ready to use it," Rose repeated for Luc's benefit. "I need something to make my claim that I'm the Norden Point clear. The test isn't enough; the only people who know I passed are Aiden's father, who's dead, and the elder, who I gather is missing."

"You want something to help prove you're the rightful Norden Point. Does such a thing exist?"

"Yes, at least according to Norden legend."

"You're looking for her dagger?"

Rose tilted her head at Arie. His knowledge of Aurora's artifacts seemed deeper than she'd thought. "Yes, we're looking for Aurora's dagger. She forged it herself and gave it to the first Norden Point, with the gift of becoming fae and gaining her water magic."

"It was her promise that she'd always stand by the Norden people. That whoever wielded that dagger had her blessing."

"Yes, Arie." She narrowed her eyes at him. "The dagger represents Aurora's blessing. Which the Norden always took to mean only the Norden Point could wield it. They went so far as to say that only the Norden Point could even get to it."

"What does that mean?" Luc asked.

"Just that it's hidden behind some kind of test of Norden power."

"Well, alright then." He gestured towards the compass, where the point was still spinning in her palm. "Shall we?"

When the compass stopped spinning, it was decisive. Rose, Luc, and Arie set out to follow its directions. It led them to the front doors of the Norden library. They stepped inside the door just as a clerk came towards them.

"I'm sorry, we're closed," he said.

"Can we have just five minutes?" Rose asked, flashing her most approachable smile. "We're visiting from out of town and won't be able to return tomorrow."

"I'm sorry, we really can't," he said, but he hesitated as he moved to usher them back out through the door they'd just come in.

Luc reached in front of Rose, offering his hand to the clerk. "I'm Luc," he said.

The clerk instinctually took Luc's offered hand.

Rose smelled the tell-tale sign of Luc's magic; the scent of cinnamon and pine filled the library.

Before Luc dropped the clerk's hand, he gestured forward with a nod, urging Rose and Arie to move on, to get around a corner where the clerk wouldn't see them. Rose bet that Luc had removed the fact that he saw them come in so they'd have the time they needed in the library.

She and Arie took off, heading around the corner to a central atrium. All around Rose, as far up as she could see, were stacks and books across multiple floors. She wanted to spend days or weeks going through the books themselves. The room was beautiful, with a white marble fountain as the stunning centerpiece. She was unsurprised when the compass pointed them directly to the fountain. At the sound of footsteps, Rose and Arie ducked behind a shelf. After a moment, she peeked around the corner to find Luc, waving them over.

"Where to next?" he asked, a broad smile covering the sharp lines of his face.

"Breaking and entering suits you," she couldn't help but reply.

"No one lets me have fun like this anymore."

"Where'd the clerk end up?"

"Arie wants to know what you did with the clerk."

Luc waved a hand. "He's fine. He continued with whatever his closing ritual required. He looked like he was headed for a hallway with some offices. We should have a few minutes at least. He may not even come back this way."

Rose stood back up. "Let's do this then."

Luc gestured her forward. "After you."

She looked down at the compass again as it continued to point directly to the large central water fountain. Its base had a stone ridge, impossible not to sit on, and it had three tiers of small pools of water. The highest level held Aurora's wave-shaped emblem, water filled it and then fell into the second tier's pool. The fountain's base pool caught the rest of the overflowing water. It was also filled with coins visitors had tossed in to make a wish. As the water streamed down the tiers to the bottom pool, it then filtered back up to the top, cycling through the tiers continuously. The entire fountain was bright white, with one exception—the wave emblem at the top was blue. It was a bright blue, more brilliant than the deep waters of her home in the Lake of the Gods.

She probed around with her magic. It still felt strange to use it freely in front of Luc. She paused momentarily as she felt two similar depths of power behind her. She turned to look where Arie and Luc stood.

She'd always known Arie had magic—he was a shapeshifter of some kind, after all—but she'd never felt his magic next to someone else's. She was surprised to feel that, on the surface, he had as much magic as the most powerful Suden in generations. Maybe he hadn't been kidding when he said he could have killed Luc for her when he offered—a mystery for another day.

She focused her magic around the stone statue and the base of the trickling water until she sensed the presence of Norden magic.

"Got you."

She called her water magic and stepped into the base of the fountain. Luc's eyes held wicked delight as she glanced at him once more. Focusing on her task, she had the water lift her up as she raised her hand to touch the blue wave.

The magic raced up from her feet, to her spine, and finger when she placed her hand on the emblem.

Her magic already coursing through her, a gentle touch was all she needed to slide the emblem back. She gasped quietly as it exposed a circular chamber that seemed to go down into the heart of the fountain.

She raised herself a little higher on the wave she created from the base pool in the fountain. The hole wasn't that deep, just big enough for the prize that she sought. A small dagger lay there. It was well made but plain, except for a stunning blue gem in the hilt. The gem matched the color of the emblem. Anyone who had seen Aurora's emblem would not doubt that this was her artifact.

Rose grabbed her prize just as the chamber started to close.

She turned to Luc and Arie, dagger in her hand, as footsteps echoed in the hall. She let herself back down with her magic and stepped out of the fountain, her wet slippers squishing on the stone. Luc laughed as he stepped up to her and offered his arms. Rose nodded, and Luc swept her off her feet and dashed with them both back behind the nearest bookcase.

Arie had another idea.

"I'll distract him while you two get out of here," he said with delight.

Rose saw him spread his wings and dive toward the clerk as he returned to the atrium.

"What the—"

Rose heard the clerk's exclamation as she nodded at Luc. "Arie says that's our cue."

Luc ran, still carrying Rose, around the outside of the aisles. They were able to slip out the main entrance unnoticed as Arie continued to dive toward the clerk, herding him out of their path.

Luc set Rose down as they stepped onto the street. She couldn't help but laugh wildly at their endeavor.

"We must have looked so ridiculous," she said, wiping the tears from her eyes.

"You might have looked ridiculous. I looked like a hero, sweeping you into my arms to save the day."

"Ah yes, how could I have missed that." She carefully placed the dagger in her bag. "So I guess we call this mission a success?" she asked.

"Most definitely. A little breaking and entering, a bit of magic, and a lot of Norden history. I hope we have a thousand more nights like this." His face sobered as he realized what he'd said, what he'd implied.

Rose took his hand. "There's no one else I'd rather commit petty theft with," she said as she squeezed it.

She didn't question it when she felt a black cat slink around her ankles.

"Alright, Arie?"

"I agree with Luc. That was fun. Do we have any more secret missions?"

"I'd say that was enough for today. Let's go get some food." She couldn't hide her grin as they set off back to the military quarter.

Chapter Thirty-Four

Things went according to plan for the first time in days. The dress they allegedly came for was delivered in short order. She didn't even check the dress as she asked, "Who picked this out?"

"I sent instructions for it before we arrived."

She narrowed her eyes at him as she asked, "You don't think I wanted to pick it out?"

"First, no. It doesn't seem like something you'd want to do. Second, as your current romantic partner, I consider myself highly qualified in understanding your physical attributes and the best way to showcase them in a rather daring statement."

She rolled her eyes and finished packing up for their return journey.

The two days of travel seemed oddly relaxing in contrast to the plans they had when they arrived back at Compass Lake. She couldn't help but enjoy her time with Luc. He was an excellent partner in crime, a strong leader from what she'd heard from his army, and a thoughtful fake romantic partner.

Being honest with herself for once, she acknowledged that he was everything she wanted for herself in an *actual* romantic partner. If the chemistry between them was any indication, she must fit what he was looking for quite nicely too. She just wasn't sure how to come to terms with the fact that he was the Suden Point.

So much had changed for her in such a short time. The mist had taken Tara from her, though only temporarily, she hoped. She'd left the isolation of Bury to come back to the one place she'd run from. She was on the arm of the Suden Point as his fake lover. She knew the weapons she magically forged could stop the mist plague, though not heal those who had fallen to it. She'd also told the Suden Point, of all people, that she was the rightful Norden Point and able to wield the magic of two fae courts.

Unheard-of change and unheard-of claims, but Luc had been there with her through all of it. He'd been a solid and somehow reassuring presence. How did she reconcile that with the idea that if she successfully reclaimed the Norden Point position, she wasn't supposed to be with him? Ignoring it seemed best as they crested the mountain pass, and she could see Compass Lake again.

She'd been away only days after leaving for years but found that her magic missed Compass Lake's power.

"Does your magic miss the lake when you travel?" she asked Luc.

"Definitely," Luc replied. He hesitated momentarily but continued, "I told you that my power is never stronger than when at the Suden house, but it also feels different in other areas filled with their own magic. The Lake of the Gods felt good. I can see why you settled there. The magic was wild but also very soothing."

She nodded. The words probably made no sense to someone listening to their conversation, but they made perfect sense to her. She had picked it for its wild isolation. In that wilderness, she found unbelievable peace. Considering what she'd run from, she'd thought she would never know peace again.

"I'm curious about what my magic is starting to miss exactly. I haven't stepped foot on the Norden property, but I feel the pull of the lake."

He'd been so genuine in his thoughts she wanted to reciprocate, so she let the words flow with little thought. It wasn't until the words were out that she realized they likely gave much more away than she intended. Her magic felt safe…with him. With the Suden Point.

There was no chance he missed the implication as a slow, satisfied smile crept over his face. He didn't have the opportunity to respond as a black bird landed on her shoulder.

Arie's voice dragged her from her thoughts. *"Rose, move faster! The plague of mist is at Compass Lake. I can see the shadows forming to take the village!"*

Almost without thought, she spurred her horse to a run, calling back to Luc, "The mist is attacking Compass Lake." They would never make it in time. They were hours away from the village by way of the switchback trail. She couldn't believe they were not there to defend Compass Lake from the mist. The one thing she could help with! As they started the descent at an unsteady pace, they could see a shadowed mass encroaching on the village entrance.

The mist would not ruin Compass Lake Village as it had Bury. Not on her watch. Her wind magic rose to meet her determination as they descended the single-file mountain trail. For the first time, she opened herself up to Compass Lake, and the seat that was rightfully hers. The Norden Point seat may traditionally be one of water, but the magic of this place would fuel any power within her, including her wind. She spread her arms as if in flight and called her wind. It was alive at her thought, responding freely to her need, sending chills along her spine as she asked for the impossible.

She started slowly because she wasn't suicidal, despite her plan indicating the opposite. The first test of her idea came via her horse. As he trotted down the hill, she pushed the wind, lifting his feet from the ground, allowing him to skip steps while making forward progress. Doing this at speed would be like they were gliding down the mountainside. She wasn't sure she could push them fast enough to make it before the Nebulus formed, but she knew she'd have to try.

"Do you trust me, Luc?" she yelled over her shoulder as they descended.

"It's gotten me this far. Just do what you're going to do, Rose," he yelled back.

She took that as the consent she needed to lift both horses with the wind and move them from the switchback paths to a direct route straight down the mountain.

No longer on a trail, they flew down the mountain toward the village gate. The horses' feet barely touched the ground as her wind swept them forward, not letting them fall. Her unbound hair streamed behind her as she felt the wind rushing past her with a swift motion. The stomach-dropping feeling of plunging to her death never came.

She felt safe and strong as she pushed her and Luc's horses forward on the wind, directing them ever faster to their target—the mass of mist at the trail entrance to Compass Lake Village.

Chapter Thirty-Five

Rose realized she needed to get Luc one of her weapons just before landing. She pulled out the two magical swords she had strapped to her horse. They were hers, forged and infused with her magic, though not from the source. This would have to be another loan for now. Luc's eyes met hers as she drew the swords, and he jerked his head in a motion that could only mean *toss it now*. As she threw one, she sent her wind to help guide it effortlessly into his hand.

Though he had plenty of magic, there was something like awe on his face as he caught the weapon. She admitted that this might not be the time to question his emotions, given that she had just turned their horses into flying beasts to career down a mountain with magically forged blades to beat back the encroaching mist.

She smiled a slightly feral smile as they landed right between the creeping mist and the village entrance. Rose and Luc hopped off their horses in tandem and launched themselves at their faceless opponent.

The mist unfurled to reveal a horde of Nebulus. The first two, unprepared for Rose and Luc's ability to fight back, were quickly overpowered, dissipating as Rose and Luc's swords struck true.

Light on their feet, Rose and Luc moved with confidence in each other. They fought with a unity that spoke of years, not days, of partnership—pairing attacks to keep an eye on each other and take down the enemy.

It wasn't until three more had fallen to their swords that the Nebulus horde realized there were only two of them, though they fought with the strength of many more. No one from the village or other Compass Points had come out to help them.

Realizing their advantage, the Nebulus leveraged their superior numbers to surround Rose and Luc.

Rose wiped the sweat from her brow as she tried to break their formation with her wind magic, but she was too spent after the flight down the mountain. Risking a glance at Luc, she saw him register the beasts working to surround them. She felt the moment he pulled on his earth magic, the ground around them falling away. The beasts plummeted into an open chasm that hadn't existed moments before.

Evidently, Luc had learned from their previous battle. Instead of giving the Nebulus time to sprout wings and stay out of the chasm, he immediately poured dirt over them as they fell into the hole in the earth he'd created. This slowed them down but didn't stop them as, just like before, wings shot from their backs, and they rose back up to fight.

Rose tried to help as she shot more wind magic against the Nebulus's beating wings, trying to send them back and onto the mountain trail. They just had to keep the horde out of the village. They'd start taking down villagers, inflicting the living death plague if they made it in.

Luc, realizing that his earth magic again wouldn't help, filled the chasm so they could press away from the village and toward the Nebulus, now regrouping at the bottom of the mountain.

Paired and ready, they leapt back into the horde as they tried to reassemble. Rose covered Luc as he swung for another Nebulus, his sword striking a killing blow, severing its head from its neck. Not stopping to see the monster dissipate, he turned and used his magic to push himself forward, lunging over Rose's shoulder at a Nebulus trying to sneak up on her. Rose took the safety of him covering her back to stab another opponent in the chest.

Each swing of their swords and connection with another beast lifted the mist creeping toward the village a little more. A horde of a dozen enemies was now down to just two as Rose and Luc made eye contact, wordlessly planning a final charge. Swords held high, they ran forward to take care of the last two beasts, Luc taking the one on the right and Rose the one on the left.

She was tired, so tired. Using so much magic had drained her, and they had been fighting for what felt like hours but was probably minutes. She swung her sword to meet her beast's, the clang of impact jolting down her spine.

Through it all, she kept an eye on Luc to her right. He was still easily attacking and defending, his military training showing through.

She focused her attention back on her battle as the Nebulus's sword swung dangerously close to her shoulder. She rolled out of the way, readying herself for another defensive maneuver as she rose. She needed to end this quickly. Exhaustion was making her sloppy.

As she readied for her next move, a giant brown bear ran into the lingering mist.

What was Arie doing? He didn't have one of her weapons. No matter his magic, he could be taken by the mist if he wasn't careful. She had to get to him quickly. She faked to charge at the Nebulus, and as it moved to defend, she shot slightly right so she could run past it to Arie.

She came upon him in the chaos of battle, only moments before she was sure the beast she'd been fighting would make it to them.

"Arie—" she started to say, but she stopped when she heard his voice speaking aloud. Something she was sure she'd never heard before.

"Zrak, what are you doing?"

Impossibly, a voice replied from the mist. "Exposing our failings."

What? Rose didn't have time to process what she heard as she sensed the mist monster coming up behind her. She turned, knowing what she needed to do but unsure if her magic would cooperate. Meeting her opponent's sword with her own, she dug deep into her wind magic to give the Nebulus a forceful push back. It stumbled backward, and she pressed her advantage, using her wind to create invisible stairs she could step up to get her level for a swing at the beast's neck. It barely had a second to right itself from its stumble as Rose climbed the wind-made stairs and swung her sword, cleanly removing the Nebulus's head.

She fell from the height as the mist creature dissipated, her wind magic giving out as she succeeded in her task. She hit the ground with a thud, knocking the breath from her lungs. She lifted her head to see Luc knock his opponent's sword away and get a successful stab to its chest.

The battle was over. Where had Arie gone? Had he succumbed to the mist? Was he talking to it? She couldn't hold on to thoughts. The only thing she knew, the only important thing right now, was they had stopped the mist from entering Compass Lake Village. She barely had time to see Luc running towards her as she passed out.

Chapter Thirty-Six

She stretched groggily. The cushion of what she was laying on felt familiar as she opened her eyes. She was in Luc's bed. Her eyes met his as he sat in one of the leatherback chairs by the fire, a book in his lap.

"You're awake," he said quietly.

"So observant." She couldn't help the sarcasm in her reply, though her voice was still shaky. Luc relaxed at her quip. He must have taken that to mean that she wasn't seriously injured.

"How are you feeling?"

"I'll be fine." She tested that, stretching her body as he stood to walk over to the bedside.

"I think you overextended yourself with your magic."

"That makes sense since it's unusual for me to battle a mist horde on a daily basis."

A smile cracked his solemn face as he said, "It wasn't just the Nebulus. It was getting us to the village in time. You saved Compass Lake Village, Rose."

Her eyes met his, wondering if anyone else had seen her blatant display of wind magic. While they didn't know she also had water magic, it'd still be news that the Suden Point was with an assumed Osten fae. Yet his face held nothing but relief. If there were any repercussions from her magical display on their fake relationship, he didn't seem to care. He appeared solely focused on the fact that she was awake.

"We should get you cleaned up if you feel up to it."

She nodded, and he walked away to draw her a bath before leaving the bedroom saying he'd give her privacy and find her some food.

If she could have stayed in the bath for the rest of her life, she might have. Her body ached from the battle and magic expenditure. The hot water soothed her muscles and mind in a way she didn't think possible. She kept replaying the last few hours in her mind. She'd used her wind power openly. Though no villagers or other Compass Points had entered the battle, had they been able to see from wherever they hid?

She couldn't be too upset with herself for using her magic. Today her wind magic had saved lives. It had gotten her and Luc to where they needed to go. They wouldn't have made it to the village in time without it. They would have arrived at the village to find mist covering the streets and the villagers in a coma-like state.

Next to her was a pile of clothes she'd hastily dropped on the floor as she got into the bath. She grabbed the bag that sat with them and pulled out Aurora's dagger. Holding the hilt in her hand, she studied the blade. A very different part of her, her water magic, could feel the cool power of water penetrating every aspect of the dagger. It felt like it was forged by water and fire.

Lost in thought, she jumped, splashing water out of the tub, when she heard Arie call her from outside the door.

"Rose!"

"Arie?" She had been worried about him during the battle. She was trying to remember precisely why as he continued speaking.

"Can I come in and talk to you?"

Rose looked down at herself. The bubbles still covered her in the bathwater, so she shrugged, knowing he couldn't see.

"Sure," she called.

A black cat pushed the door open and crossed to the tub's side. It sat on its haunches directly under her hand that was dangling over the edge. Arie always took on the characteristics of the animals he inhabited. As a cat, he placed himself directly in the path of her hand, demanding to be petted. She sighed and absently scratched behind his ears.

"I'm glad you're ok. You did great."

"Arie, were you in the mist? I remember trying to get to you, but you were..." Rose hesitated. She was going to say he was talking to the mist. She thought she'd seen him doing that at Bury too, but she'd convinced herself it was just her imagination. What had he been saying?

"I'm fine, Rose." The cat looked toward the door, and Rose could hear Luc moving around in the bedroom. *"You should worry about how much the Suden Point has been fretting over you. I'd never have believed him capable, given his reputation."*

She glared at the cat. "You and me both. I never could have imagined this when agreeing to be in a fake relationship with him."

The cat looked up at her and blinked its eyes. *"You have a partner in him that could do more for you than I ever could. Someone to be there with you day in and out."*

Rose tilted her head as she maintained eye contact with the cat. She couldn't figure out what he was trying to say.

"Don't look at me like that, Rose. As someone who has had experience having love ripped away from them, I'm telling you not to spend too much time worrying about what the Compass Points or the fae courts will think. If you like him, which I think you do, focus on that, not the mess of what it means for the Norden and Suden Points to be in a relationship." The

black cat's large yellow eyes looked into hers, blinking more than strictly necessary.

She wasn't sure what to say. Arie never spoke of his past. She couldn't even pick which question to ask him when he interrupted her thoughts.

"So, what's next?"

"Next?" Rose pondered aloud. "I think today's events, though taxing, may have been an unexpected boon. Where was the Norden Point when the village was attacked? Where was his strength? Instead, the Suden Point and his magic-wielding partner arrive in style to save the day. I think I can work with that." She smiled to herself. It had worked out better than she could have anticipated.

"Rose?" Luc must have heard her talking to herself. "Is Arie in there? Can I brainstorm too? I'd like to know what we're planning." Rose wasn't quite ready to get out of the bath but wasn't prepared to have this conversation with Luc while she was naked.

"Give me a second. I'm done. We'll come out there." She shooed Arie into the bedroom and gathered herself to leave the comforting waters.

She emerged from the bathroom feeling different from when she had gone in. Wrapped in the coziest robe she'd ever worn, she wandered over to the fire to find a plate of food sitting between the two high-back leather chairs. Arie had already placed himself directly in front of the fireplace. She grabbed some of the food and sat down.

"The Norden Point has called an emergency Compass Point meeting tonight. Better late than never, I guess." Luc sat down in the accompanying chair.

"What is the guest policy at these types of meetings?" Rose asked as a sly smile crept across her lips.

"Usually frowned upon," Luc said. "I'm sure an exception could be made for the savior of Compass Lake Village. I'm surprised that the Norden didn't ask to speak with us directly. The meeting seems as good a place as any to ambush him if you're up for it."

Rose's smile was all teeth. "I thought you'd never ask."

CHAPTER THIRTY-SEVEN

The Compass Points were expected to be at the Solstice Ceremony ball that evening, so the meeting was scheduled for just before. If the situation weren't so serious, Rose would wonder if this were a ploy by the Compass Points to force Luc to show up for the festivities. The attack today made the social responsibilities of the Suden Point irrelevant. The meeting would make for a tense beginning to the evening's events, but when all was said and done, they'd know where they stood.

Rose held the ball gown that Luc had picked out for her in front of herself in the mirror in the bathroom. She had told Luc that she wanted to make a statement. It seemed that he took that to heart.

The dress was stunning, even more so when she slipped it on. It was a floor-length gown the color of the darkest storm. Its light grey pattern was barely visible on the dark fabric, with swirls that suggested movement. She couldn't decide if they were meant to represent a windstorm or waves but decided that maybe the point was that it could be either or both. The dress had a form-fitting bodice with a plunging neckline, and the silky skirt pooled at her feet. She couldn't remember ever wearing something so beautiful.

It was perfect, giving her confidence and a layer of armor to face her past. She spun a few more times for herself in the mirror before finishing twisting her hair up and walking out into the bedroom. She stopped, catching her breath as she glimpsed Luc stepping out of the closet. He looked perfect in his formal wear: well-tailored black pants with a black shirt and jacket, as would be expected of the villainous story that he sold of himself. Her eyes took in the way the clothes showed off his trim and powerful body. After staring longer than what was socially acceptable, her eyes found his, and she realized that he'd been doing the same.

He stepped towards her. "You look exquisite."

He held out his hand, and she took it. Not sure what he was getting at, her body understood before her mind as he effortlessly signaled a spin with his hand as if they were already on a ballroom dance floor.

"You chose well. Keep this up, and you'll have to pick out an entire wardrobe for me," she teased.

His face held too much emotion when she glanced at it, like he thought doing something so mundane together might be fun, but he wasn't sure if that was something for which he dared to hope. The thought crossed his face as quickly as it had come, and she recognized his version of a cool mask as he offered his arm to her.

"Ready for this?" he asked.

"Of course not, but we're doing it anyway."

The Solstice Ceremony ball and the Compass Points meeting were both to be held at Norden house. The appropriate conveyance for such a formal evening was by boat. Rose hated herself just a bit at the excitement she got from such a traditional journey around the lake. Like their first promenade when she arrived.

Night descended on the lake, candle-lit lanterns at the front and back of the boat ensured people could see the Suden Point and his presumed lover as they made their way.

Luc paddled them stoically, and they talked little as they traveled. They were both more than aware that they had plenty of onlookers, and conversation on the lake could carry for all to hear. Rose was glad no one but Luc was close enough to see her slight shudder as Norden house came into view.

She had never realized before how well the house was guarded against sight. From nearly every other point on the lake, one couldn't tell where Norden house stood. Only when you were right on top of the structure could you see the path leading up to the house and the lights alive within. As a young girl, she had thought it was such a spectacular view. It was a power of its own to feel that you could see the goings-on of the lake but that no one could see you.

As they reached shore, Luc jumped out and offered his hand to help her. She leaned on his strength to make her graceful exit from the boat, and without his offer, she went ahead and slid her hand from his to wrap around his arm. The way she casually made the move without his request seemed to please him. She caught his self-satisfied smile as she peeked at him while they walked side by side on the beach and started the ascent up to Norden house.

Her spine straightened with every step she took. A feeling of power rolled up her body from her feet. She almost stumbled at the unexpected onslaught. She'd forgotten she was stepping into the Norden seat of power.

Her seat of power.

They were greeted at the door, and though receiving dubious looks from the caretaker, Rose and Luc were shown into the library. It was just as she pictured it, though she'd never been allowed in this room as a child—all rich wood bookcases and furniture with a fire already roaring in the fireplace. The table was circular and held four chairs.

Though none were currently occupied, the presumed occupants were already in the room. Juliette was at the bar getting her drink. Her smile grew wicked when she saw Rose on Luc's arm, and she quickly finished her drink preparations and made her way over to the fireside, where the Norden and Vesten Points were having a heated discussion.

"Where were you, Aiden? Our people were in danger, and you didn't even show your face!"

"I think that's what we'd all like to know," Luc purred as he took Rose's hand from his arm and positioned her slightly in front and to the left of him, his arm resting on her lower back.

"What's this, Luc? This is a Compass Point meeting. Guests aren't welcome," Aiden snapped without even a cursory glance at Rose. "We all know you have a new infatuation, but you can't bring her here."

"She did more for Compass Lake today than you have in your entire tenure, Aiden," Juliette chimed in from the sidelines of the conversation.

Aiden's glare at her was immediate, but he still had yet to turn his attention to Rose.

"Yes, yes, thank you, what was your name…." His gaze finally lifted to her as he attempted the bare minimum of acknowledgment for her protection of the people under his care. His eyes snapped to hers, and he froze.

"Rose," he breathed.

"Hi, Aiden," her voice was even.

"You two know each other?" Juliette helpfully chirped. It was as if she knew this was the evening's entertainment, and she never wanted it to end.

Rose watched Aiden work to choose his words carefully. Instead of "How are you alive?" or "Didn't I kill you?" he schooled his features.

"What are you doing here? With him?" He sneered the last part as his blue eyes shot in Luc's general direction.

"That," she said, pausing to turn her head and give Luc an appreciative once over, "is none of your business." She could hear Juliette's barely disguised laugh and readied herself to continue.

"Excuse me, sorry, Rose, was it?" The Vesten Point interrupted what was sure to be a delightful reunion. "We are forever indebted for your actions today. Your arrival was nothing short of miraculous. I hesitate to even think about what would have happened had you and Luc not arrived when you did. You have our deepest thanks. Though…" He stuttered a bit. "I'm not sure what that has to do with you being at this meeting or how you seem to know Aiden. Do you have business for the Compass Points, or should I have the caretaker assist you to the ballroom? I hope it goes without saying that we want to celebrate you as the guest of honor at tonight's ball."

"Carter, I think we're just about done with the discussion," Aiden said from behind him.

"Done?" Carter repeated, dumbfounded. "Luc just got here. We haven't even begun."

"I said we're done," Aiden said flatly.

Rose felt the magic in the room shift. She expected the smell of sweet nectar, which had always been the smell of Aiden's magic when they were kids. Aiden's eyes flashed from their usual piercing blue to a dark grey, and the smell of magic was old—moss and oak. Rose remembered this. She'd experienced it more and more in their childhood. She could never figure out what it meant, but she knew that grey-eyed Aiden was very different than blue-eyed Aiden.

"Rose, I'd be honored if I could escort you downstairs to open the ball as the Compass Points' honored guest," Aiden said.

Luc stepped forward, moving between Aiden and Rose as Aiden offered his hand to escort her.

As tempted as she was to take the opportunity of time with Aiden, she was known to all of Compass Lake as Luc's lover. Walking into the ball on Aiden's arm would be a major slight.

She wrapped her hand around Luc's arm as she replied, "I already have an escort downstairs if the meeting is over. I'll save you a dance."

Aiden balled his fists at his side as he seemed to decide how to proceed. He pushed his shoulders back as he replied, "Very good," and walked out of the room.

"What just happened?" the Vesten Point asked.

"Don't worry about it, Carter," Juliette replied. "I assure you that wasn't the last of whatever this was."

Chapter Thirty-Eight

"Are we on track?" Luc asked as he carried his plate of food to one of the standing tables dispersed throughout the room. The ballroom of Norden house was grand, specifically for these types of occasions. Everyone at Compass Lake was invited to the ball before the Summer Solstice Ceremony. It was one of the only times all fae courts were welcomed into the Norden house.

Before Rose could respond, Juliette sauntered over to their table.

"Are you going to tell us what is going on, Luc?" She said Luc's name, but her gaze was locked on Rose.

"What are you asking, Juliette?" Luc's words were clipped and formal. "You've never seen fit to question Aiden before."

Juliette pushed her long hair back off her shoulder. "Don't act childish, Luc. We all had different ways of dealing with Aiden as the Norden Point. Your way was simply more confrontational than mine."

"More confrontational?"

Rose could see Luc's anger rising in the narrowing of his eyes, moments away from red-rimmed irises.

"You let him walk all over you in those meetings. You ignored me whenever I tried to discuss the poor decisions he was leading us to make."

"I think," Rose said, placing her hand gently on Luc's arm, "that Juliette is listening now, and maybe that is more important than what has happened in the past."

Juliette's eyes lit up with amusement at Rose's intercession.

"I have a question for you." Rose considered her words as she asked Juliette, "Do you…" She fumbled, unsure how to ask. "Do the Osten still worship the Lost God?"

Luc's attention moved quickly from Juliette to Rose. She had shared her suspicions with him about Zrak being related to the mist, but they'd never discussed approaching Juliette about her patron god. No matter Luc's distrust, Rose believed Juliette had the same goals they did.

Juliette tilted her head as she appraised Rose. "Of course we honor Zrak and his sacrifice. Just as any fae court worships their patron."

Rose thought briefly before formulating her next question. "The other fae courts' patrons aren't lost. How do you commune with Zrak if he sacrificed himself?"

Juliette chuckled at that. "What an interesting line of questioning. I'd say you don't know any better than to ask a fae about their magic, but I've heard multiple accounts of a great deal of magic used to defend the village. We all know that the Suden Point is powerful, but I'm willing to bet some of that magic was yours, and you do know better."

This didn't faze Rose. She didn't regret using her magic to save the village. She'd pick revealing her magic ten times out of ten to stop others from suffering Tara's fate.

Juliette smoothed out her dress as she continued. "Did you make the magical weapons, Rose? Are you part fae?"

Evidently Juliette couldn't help but search for the most straightforward answer, as Luc had. Rose was thankful once again that she was easy to underestimate.

"Well, that's quite a rude question, too, isn't it," Rose replied.

Appraising each other, Rose and Juliette remained locked in a staring contest. Luc couldn't seem to decide how to help. Before anyone could press further, Rose heard the trampling of little feet running across the dance floor.

Luc's nephews sprinted through the ballroom, David in the lead. They had been heading toward the food when they saw Uncle Luc and made a beeline for him instead. Aaron and Andrew walked more casually around the dance floor behind them. Though coming from behind in the sprint, Thomas threw himself at his uncle, feet lifting off the floor. He had so much blind trust. There seemed to be no doubt in his mind that his uncle would catch him. Luc didn't disappoint as he plucked Thomas out of the air, the other two boys' hands outstretched towards him.

"Was it a race to see who could get to me first?" Luc asked as Juliette and Rose's standoff was well and truly interrupted.

"Enjoy your evening." Juliette waved away the tension of their stare as she walked away.

"Hi, Rose, welcome back. Glad to see you're up and about." Andrew greeted them as they arrived behind the boys. Luc nodded at Andrew and Aaron. He'd said they had come to check on her when she was still passed out.

The boys jumped and tugged on Luc, demanding his attention, while Aaron and Andrew turned to Rose and spoke more quietly.

"We can't thank you enough for what you did," Aaron said, looking a little sheepish. He'd continued to be a little standoffish to her after the incident in the library.

"You protected us, the boys, and all of the residents at the lake," Andrew continued.

"Luc was really worried about you when we stopped by. We haven't seen him like that in a long time," Aaron noted.

"I was just trying to help," Rose said, deciding to respond to their first point instead of the commentary on Luc's affections. She knew Luc cared for her, that she cared for him more than was good for either of them. Yet it wasn't her place to explain the situation to Andrew and Aaron.

"Rose, we don't quite know what is going on with you and Luc. He hasn't been particularly forthcoming about your relationship, but, whatever it might be, he certainly cares deeply for you. We hope you know that," Andrew finished.

Rose nodded, not quite finding the words to respond. Thankfully she didn't have to as Luc extricated himself from his nephews and reached out a hand to Rose.

"Dance with me, Rose?"

The music had been playing softly in the background, but the dance floor was empty at this particular moment. She laughed a little. "No one is dancing, Luc."

"Then there is plenty of room for us."

She couldn't help herself. His smile was infectious, and in the chaos of the evening, she wanted to be surrounded by his warmth for just a few moments. He swept her into his arms as they moved across the floor.

If having his hand on her back sent fire dancing through her veins, dancing with him was a shock to her senses. She'd thought she'd become desensitized to him with all the time they'd been spending together, but she was acutely aware of every point at which their bodies touched. He pulled her closer as they toured the dance floor.

"What are you thinking about?" he asked.

"Who knew that the fearsome Suden Point could move so gracefully."

"They say dance lessons help prepare one for sword fighting."

"Who says that?" she wondered aloud.

"Well"—he laughed—"maybe it was just what my mom told Aaron and me to try and stop us from fussing too much about the dance lessons she forced us into."

The revelation caught her off guard, and she couldn't help the laugh that escaped her.

"I love hearing your laugh," he whispered, pulling her body closer to his as they continued their movement.

The fire of their connection was more than she could take. Ignoring any worries of Norden and Suden Points and the uncertainty of their future, she leaned forward, intent on pressing her lips to his. She'd been dying to feel that connection to him again since their kiss in the market. Luc's eyes went from surprised to devious delight within seconds.

She couldn't mask her dissatisfaction as she heard an assertive cough next to them, interrupting her progress.

"May I cut in?" Aiden stood before them.

Rose was surprised to see how much the dance floor had filled out. When they'd started, they had been the only couple, and now dozens of pairs whirled around them. While she'd been able to ignore Aiden's offer to escort her into the ballroom, declining his public request for a dance now would look rude.

She took a deep breath, leaning in to kiss Luc's cheek. "Hold that thought," she said.

"I will remember this." A teasing smile lit his face while she was still close enough that they shared breath—a delicious tension hanging there, unfortunately, and completely doused as they separated. Luc's cool mask was in place as his hand slipped from her waist and he walked towards the crowd's edge.

She took Aiden's offered hand, her gaze going straight to his eyes. The bright blue gave her little comfort as she stepped into a formal position with the man who had killed her family. The man who had tried to kill her. The man who had stolen her rightful place as Norden Point.

"You surprise me, Rose," Aiden said, a smile plastered on his face as he made eye contact with guests over her shoulder.

"What? That I'm alive? Yes, I guess that would be a surprise to you after trying to kill me."

"Such a wild accusation," he replied too calmly for her liking. "I believe the caretaker and his family perished in a tragic fire on the property."

She turned her face to meet his, anger rushing through her. When she saw his face, a cold rush ran down her spine. His eyes had turned an ageless grey.

"Who are you?" she whispered.

"What an astute question. I always knew you were too smart for your own good." He shook his head slightly. "Aiden always tried to say you weren't a threat, but I knew better. It was one of the many reasons you needed to go." His fingers on her waist gripped her body tighter, caging them together for this conversation.

She fought to remain calm. He couldn't try to kill her so publicly, could he?

"That doesn't answer my question," she said, letting her anger at the man who killed her family fuel her words. She wouldn't succumb to the fear of not knowing what monster inhabited Aiden's body. "Are you Zrak?"

He chuckled at her question as one laughed at a small child's antics. "I see I don't have to worry about your friend telling you too much. How very like him."

Rose couldn't hide the confusion from her face. She glanced at Luc on the edge of the dancefloor, watching their every move.

"Not your beloved Suden Point," he replied.

Her mind raced, but she couldn't search for the meaning of his words as she felt his grip tighten again, trying to lock her in place. She felt his finger fumbling as if trying to line something up on his hand.

Instinct told her she had to get away from him. She couldn't just run off the dance floor, though. They were playing a dangerous game of showmanship, and if she wanted to claim the Norden Point seat, she couldn't run away from him now.

She stepped out of his hold into a spin, giving herself distance. What kind of being could inhabit another's body?

A god seemed to be the only answer.

What had Aiden done? She remembered even a glimpse of the grey eyes the day she met him. He had to have done something reckless as a child.

Shaking herself free of a confusing mix of sadness and regret, she focused on her anger. It was always easier for her to wield. It was too much of a coincidence that a godlike being was controlling Aiden. They had to be connected to the plague of mists. She needed to find out what he was and how to end him.

She felt the familiar warmth of Aurora's dagger strapped to her thigh. She briefly wondered how connected Aiden and the being were. How responsible was he for his actions when the grey eyes were present? Was there any way for him to survive a separation? The weight of the dagger against her leg gave her comfort, though a last resort with so many unknowns.

"I think that's about enough from you, Rose," the grey-eyed Aiden said as she spun back towards him. The hand that was around her waist was outstretched, ready to catch her. Rose caught a glimpse of a large, triangle-shaped ring on his finger with an onyx rock center. It looked like a dark mountain. The point of the triangle facing toward her had a needle point that stretched above the tip of his finger. It hadn't been there before. She didn't know what it held, but she was sure she'd regret it if she let him catch her with it. She tried to slow down her return to his hold, but short of ending the dance, she didn't know how to avoid it.

In her moment of indecision, Luc stepped in between her and Aiden, catching her waist. His eyes flashed red as he said, "I can take it from here," not bothering to turn to face Aiden.

"Wha…" Aiden hissed in quiet outrage at the interruption.

Worse, Rose saw that he hadn't slowed the movement of the triangle's point. Instead of connecting with her waist, it had punctured Luc's as he forced himself between Rose and Aiden.

She looked down as Aiden pulled the point out of Luc's side and flicked the needle back into the large ring.

"You," Aiden whispered in outrage.

Luc shook his head as if to shake off his red-rimmed irises. He was almost successful until he stepped forward to move Rose away from Aiden, and his leg wasn't entirely steady.

"Poison?" Luc hissed, his voice barely above a whisper. He didn't want to draw more attention to their partner swap than necessary. "I didn't think you could be that stupid."

But Aiden was already walking away, removing himself from whatever scene may ensue. Rose looked at Luc, attempting to school the emotion on her face. She couldn't believe he'd stepped in. She couldn't believe he'd taken whatever Aiden had been trying to stab her with.

"Luc, what was it?"

"We need to get somewhere private. I can feel it moving quickly."

Rose didn't need to be told twice. She knew this house and knew exactly where to take him. She led him off the dance floor and down one of the many hallways. A hallway she was sure would be unused during the solstice celebration as it held only a classroom. She got him through the door before his legs gave out.

She couldn't hide her relief when a black cat slinked in through the door before she closed it.

Chapter Thirty-Nine

R ose closed the door behind Arie's cat form as she turned to Luc. He'd sprawled across the top of a desk in the front of the room.

"Why did you step in!" She couldn't decide if anger or fear for him would be the winning emotion.

"You know why, Rose," he replied in a voice much more exhausted than his usual confident manner.

"Not the time for this, Rose. What happened to him? I didn't see it all."

"Aiden—well, not Aiden—stabbed him with the tip of his big triangle ring."

Arie's tail flicked wildly as Rose spoke.

"We have to move fast if we're going to save him."

"What do we do? I can't heal poison!" She tried to keep her voice down, but panic was rising within her, flooding her body as she thought about losing Luc.

Losing Luc before she ever really had him.

She couldn't believe she'd wasted so much time worrying about what the fae courts and other Compass Points would think about a relationship between them. Since when did she care at all about that kind of thing? Her parents had taught her better. Her parents had taught her that mixed fae lines didn't matter. Yet, their insistence on the secrecy of hers had stuck with her.

Her mind returned to the present as Arie hopped onto Luc's

stomach where he lay on the desk. His efforts at breathing became more and more labored.

"What are you doing, Arie?"

He kneaded his front paws into Luc's chest. *"I'm trying to see how much time we have, or if we're too late."*

"We are not too late, Arie." She meant to reassure herself, but her words came out with far more emotion than she was prepared for.

"Don't worry, Rose," Luc said, reaching for her hand. She moved close enough to him to let him take it. His hand was hot, like some internal battle waged within his body, though his grip was weak. "I wouldn't have this any other way."

"I would!" she raged. "I would have it another way! That poison was meant for me. You shouldn't have stepped in. I can't..." She choked on her words. She couldn't lose anyone else. She'd already lost so much.

She'd lost her family, Tara, to this terrible mist, and she was about to lose the first man she could see herself being with. Someone who challenged her but also understood her. A man who comprehended her strengths and power and was unafraid of them. A man she could...

She shook her head. She couldn't think about that now.

This was not going to happen without a fight.

"Arie." She held back the impotent tears as she tried to figure out what to do next. "Arie, I have Aurora's dagger." She dropped Luc's hand momentarily and reached under her dress to pull it out. "Do you think this will help? I can't remember if it has any healing properties, but the goddess surely had healing powers."

The cat shook his head.

Rose was ready to start yelling, to run back into the ballroom, appearances be damned, and scream for a physician. But before she could move, she began to smell a scent she hadn't encountered in a long time—ten years, to be precise.

The scent of the forest floor, of trees and grass, hit her nose as she looked at the black cat continuing to knead Luc's chest with his paws.

"Arie, what are you…"

The cat shook its head again and swished its tail, indicating it was not to be disturbed.

Slowly, Luc's breathing leveled back out as the forest smell permeated the room. She remembered it from the first time she'd met Arie. When he'd first spoken to her mind. When he'd first caught up with her in the forest. She'd just associated it with his voice, not taking the time to register the scent of his magic.

What kind of magic did he have? Would it heal Luc? He must be if Luc's breathing was any indication. The labored breaths retreated, leaving behind a slow, even cadence, as if he were asleep.

Arie's tail twitched again as he hopped off Luc's stomach and onto one of the other, smaller desks in the classroom.

"He'll be alright, Rose."

She took a choked breath, feeling so much tension leave her body at these words. She didn't know what Arie had done, where he got his magic from, or what it meant, but she knew he'd never harm her.

"Arie…what did you…?"

"Another time. He should wake shortly. Thankfully, he had his own natural defenses to that attack, or not even I could have helped him. It should speed his recovery. You two should be seen at the fireworks and get out of here. Don't give Aiden another opportunity to strike tonight."

"Okay."

"I have to go."

His words caught up with her, along with the questions that had been building in her mind. Questions about the mist, questions about the being that inhabited Aiden.

"Do you know the thing inside of Aiden?"

"*I do,*" Arie replied. "*Your words this evening about how the attack was delivered confirmed it. That wasn't poison.*"

"Arie…" She wasn't even sure what to ask. "Where do you have to go?"

"*I have to check on one more thing. There is even more at stake here than you realize.*"

"More than the plague taking over the continent? More than the wrong Norden Point in the Compass?"

"*Yes.*"

"But you won't tell me."

"*I will tell you, but not tonight. I'll be back before the Ceremony tomorrow morning.*"

Rose's shoulders slumped. She trusted Arie, even if he wasn't ready to tell her everything. He'd saved Luc. He saved her. He continued to show up for her. She'd give him the benefit of the doubt here.

"Okay. See you in the morning."

The cat dipped its head slightly.

"And, Arie," she said quietly as he approached the door. "Thank you."

"*Of course, Rose. But do me a favor. Don't wait too much longer to tell him, alright? You don't want to live with that kind of regret.*"

Rose tilted her head, trying to parse what Arie was and wasn't saying.

Loved. The thought she'd pushed away before. She wasn't sure she was ready for that. But she knew she wanted a chance to see what she and Luc could be together. She didn't have time to respond to Arie as his tail swished again, and he disappeared.

JILLIAN WITT

Rose didn't have to wait long. She perched next to Luc as he lay there, still sprawled on the desktop. His breathing even. She pushed his hair back, running her fingers through it in a way she hadn't been able to do freely since their market kiss.

"If this is the treatment I get for being…whatever that was, I should try it more often," came Luc's groggy quip.

She couldn't help but smile. She'd trusted Arie when he said that Luc would be okay, but there was just something about Luc saying it himself that made her warm inside.

"I'm sure I can be persuaded to keep up the treatment without an attack on your person," she said as her fingers curled deeper into his hair.

"I'll keep that in mind." Luc sat up. She didn't even try to stop him. She was sure he wouldn't listen. Flirting may have helped him ease back into the situation, but he was likely still angry that Aiden had managed to stab him with some kind of poison.

Luc rubbed his hand over his chest where Arie had pawed at him. "What did Arie do to me?"

"You'll have to ask him yourself when he gets back. Though I suspect it'll have to wait until tomorrow."

Luc seemed to wrestle with his next thought. "I felt my magic fighting whatever that was, but I don't think it would have won on its own. Whatever Arie did wasn't pleasant either, it felt like flames cooking my body from the inside."

"He said it wasn't poison, but didn't give me more than that," Rose said.

"You didn't know he could heal, did you?"

Rose shook her head. "No, but to be fair, that was kind of our thing. He never asked about what I was running from and what magic I had, and I never thought too hard about what he was. We just enjoyed each other's company." She shrugged. "Though I'm starting to think he knew more about me than he let on. I guess the time for ignoring those kinds of questions is at an end."

She stood up from the desk and turned towards the door. She wasn't quite sure what her face would reveal. Her confusion over Arie? More likely, the overwhelming relief that Luc was okay. He grabbed her hand as he sat on the edge of the desk. He gently tugged, wordlessly asking if she'd face him, if she'd talk to him.

She knew she would before her body turned. She rolled back toward him, fitting into the space between his sprawled legs. He squeezed her hand.

"Are you okay?" he asked.

"Shouldn't I be asking you that?"

"I think the fact that I'm breathing answers the question for you. You, on the other hand, seem like you've been through something."

She pushed his shoulder back. "Yes, you idiot, I went through almost losing you!" The force of her own words surprised her. She knew she'd been ignoring this for too long, but she hadn't expected it to erupt now of all times.

Luc's lip curved up at the corner. "Well, I'm sorry about that. I'll work to ensure it doesn't happen again."

She shook her head. She knew she sounded ridiculous. They were about to try and replace the Norden Point. They needed to figure out what the being inhabiting Aiden was and what it had planned. And on top of that, they needed to stop the mist from spreading farther. The danger was undoubtedly piling up. She knew that neither she nor Luc could guarantee their safety. But she also knew they could ensure that they could stand together to fight whatever they were up against.

Rose leaned in. Her intentions must have been evident because

Luc's lips met hers midway. She barely felt the warmth of his lips before slipping her tongue into his mouth, deepening the kiss. Luc's breath caught and then his hand slid up her waist, tugging her closer as she stood between his legs. She felt a thrill of excitement as his hand cupped the back of her neck. His long fingers stretched, wanting to tangle in her hair, then sliding up her nape when he realized it was tied up in a twist.

With an effort, their mouths parted, breath still mingling, and eyes locked. His smile was bright and promised much more if she only said the word. And yet…she seemed to remember that they had something else to do.

They had to make sure everyone saw them together before they left. They couldn't let Aiden's sly attack on them make them appear weak. She kissed his lips again, pulling herself out of the haze.

"Hold that thought," she said.

"You say the most frustrating things." He smiled ruefully as he let his hand drop, freeing her to put a little distance between them while she laid out their next steps.

"We have to make sure we're seen at the fireworks display before we can get away. We can't let Aiden chase us out of this public event. Not if we want to challenge him tomorrow."

"You're right, of course," he replied as he jumped off the desk.

She was happy to see how quickly his strength rebounded. No one would suspect he'd been attacked this evening.

"Let's get this over with," he said with a wicked smile as he moved toward her, passing her to open the door. "I've got a held thought waiting to be explored further at Suden house tonight."

Chapter Forty

The lake was so perfect at night. It held a quiet calm that she had yet to see anywhere else.

The fireworks were just starting when they made it to the small sandy beach before Norden house. The Norden Point was out on the dock with a few others, clearly in charge of the show. Rose held Luc's arm and leaned her head on his shoulder as she watched the display. He smoothly disentangled his arm to slip it around her waist and pull her closer.

Explosions of color and sound filled the sky. Each crack and burst across the quiet lake was a surprise and delight. Rose enjoyed the display while fondly remembering the few balls she had experienced as a young girl. Even when she hadn't gone, she and Grandpa still tried to stay awake late enough to watch the fireworks.

From the corner of her eye, she saw a dark shadow dash by the familiar shed on the beach. She peered closer. It looked like a black cat dashing away from the lake's edge and the noise of the fireworks. She'd assume it was Arie if he hadn't said he'd be gone the rest of the night. Just as she was about to dismiss it, she heard a shout from the beach.

One of the fireworks had slipped before takeoff. It shot off in the wrong direction, back toward the lawn instead of safely out over the lake. All the fae stood in stunned silence and apparent inaction as it rocketed toward the shed. The way the firework perfectly hit the roof and exploded on impact was uncanny.

JILLIAN WITT

She wouldn't have thought a firework could cause so much damage quickly, but she didn't have time to process it as the shed erupted in flames. The familiarity of the fire froze her. The echo of her childhood home going up in flames was too much to bear.

She stared at Aiden, who looked on, seemingly unconcerned, at the shed. Rose knew no one was inside but could not let its burning stand. A glance told her no one else was doing anything about it, so she decided to handle it herself.

She pulled her water magic up through her body. She could feel it instinctively reaching toward Compass Lake. It rushed through her, faster than expected, as she pulled a cresting wave from the lake and guided it toward the burning structure. She crashed wave after wave from the lake over the shed until the flames were thoroughly doused. She had no sense of how long she worked or how much magic she spent. Caught up in the rightness of the ground beneath her feet and the water magic she called, she still felt Luc's strength at her back as he protectively caged her vulnerability while she worked. She wasn't even close to spending all of her strength when she finished—the power from the Norden Point seat flowed into her as she called.

Her display seemed to have distracted and stalled the fireworks. She could feel Aiden and the rest of the fae courts' eyes on her as she returned to herself.

"My apologies for the interruption. Care to continue?" she called out toward the other Compass Points congregated at the lake's edge.

"I think we've had just about enough excitement for one night," was Aiden's terse response. It was too dark to see, but she'd bet money his eyes were flashing grey.

"Oh, that won't do, not on the Summer Solstice," she nearly sang, her confidence building by the minute. "Carter," she called to the

Vesten Point, standing slightly to the side. "Can you give me some light? I've got another display for us to enjoy."

Carter scanned the crowd, the people eager to see what Rose would do. Carter shrugged, not making eye contact with the Norden Point behind him as he did what Rose asked. He may not be the loudest, but Rose suspected there was a depth to him that many missed.

The Vesten Point looked at Juliette, who nodded. He threw multiple balls of fire into the air, and Juliette's wind magic kept them floating out over the water so that the lake's edge was visible to the audience on the beach.

Rose pulled the water magic back to her as she started her second display. This one was much more enjoyable than the first as she started small, with a burst of water shooting straight into the sky in front of Norden house. Then she made a row of spouts, one shooting after the other as they chased each other across the lake. The audience gasped and cheered as she built up steam, joining the spouts with bursts and eruptions of water in time. She had created her own fireworks display out of the lakewater, and even the lake seemed to enjoy it.

As she built up toward a finale of waterworks, she couldn't help but relish the feel of the Norden magic. Her water rushed through her, stronger than ever, and she loved every minute. She was the rightful Norden Point, standing on the beach of her seat of power.

"So about that held thought," Rose said to Luc when they made it to his room.

Luc's gaze set a crash of sensation through her body as their eyes locked.

"It's ready and waiting for further exploration," he replied, his voice rough.

Her lips curved as she turned her back towards him, a silent request for his expertise in removing her dress.

Luc's deft fingers made quick work of the ties. She could feel the moment the cool air hit her back, his fingers dancing over her bare skin. She let the dress fall to the floor as she turned to face him.

"Beautiful," he said. His scorching gaze traced down to the dagger holster on her thigh. "And so well prepared." Wicked promise in his voice.

Rose took careful steps backward toward the bed. The exhaustion that had plagued her the entire way home was nowhere to be seen as she crooked her finger at him, encouraging his progress to her, watching each flick of her finger pull Luc another step.

He removed his jacket with the first step, untucked his shirt from his pants at the second, and then she pulled him to her.

She wanted him. She knew that the Norden Point and Suden Point being together would cause problems, but they would handle it, just like they'd handled every other obstacle they'd faced thus far.

She was ready to take Arie's advice and not let the opportunity slip away.

"Let me help you with that," she said as she pulled his shirt over his head, running her hands over his strong shoulders, down the length of his taut stomach.

"Rose," he breathed.

"We have unfinished business, you and I." She stared at him evenly, although the warmth pooling in her stomach at her words told a different story.

"That we do," he started, but she cut him off as she slid her hands back up his bare chest, wrapping her hands around his neck.

She didn't know who moved first. Their lips crashed together.

She opened to him as their tongues tangled with all the words Rose never found the right way to say. She wanted to say that she trusted him, was glad he was here with her, and wanted him as her partner, not just as an act.

In response to her unspoken declarations, Luc's mouth found its way to her neck as he nipped and kissed the point just behind her ear.

"Allow me," Luc said, and he slid to his knees before her, kissing his way down her body as he went. He sucked at her thigh, teasing around her most sensitive spots, while his fingers moved to unlace her dagger holster.

"This could be dangerous for the next part." His smile was sinful. His teasing sent chills across her body as she stood bare before him.

Then his tongue started a different kind of teasing. Tentative at first, each lick and suck wholly igniting the flame that he fueled in her.

She couldn't urge him on fast enough as he built her pleasure. He responded to her body's unspoken request as he brought her to the edge, driving her mad with need until she unraveled around him.

Before she'd recovered, Luc stood and closed the distance between them again faster than she thought possible. As he picked her up, she wrapped her legs around his torso and he moved them greedily to the bed behind her. She wanted desperately to feel his weight shifting over her as they moved together. As if sensing her desire, he lifted her farther, shifting her to the center of the bed. He wasn't far behind as he crawled toward her, shedding the rest of his clothes in the process, his mouth moving to her breast as he caged her body. She wrapped her legs around him again, pulling his body down to hers.

"Ah ah, I'm not done yet," he teased, as he caught her nipple between his teeth.

She couldn't catch her breath.

She didn't want to.

She ran her hands down his back, scratching lightly, as their lips came back together, exploring and teasing in kind.

She unwrapped her legs, and as with most of their relationship so far, he seemed to know exactly what she was asking for, moving his knee to part her thighs, his delicious weight settling on top of her. Opening her eyes, she met his.

"This is real," she whispered. It wasn't a question. It was finally a statement. She saw lust, yes, but also adoration as he looked reverently at her.

"It's been real for a while, Rose. I've just been waiting for you to catch up." His lips quirked up in a smile as her eyes widened at his confession.

His lips found hers again, coaxing, demanding. She was only too willing to offer everything he asked and more.

Their eyes locked again as he pulled back from the kiss, a final question in his gaze. She pulled him to her as he pushed inside of her, meeting her demands. She felt like the earth shook beneath her as their bodies connected and began to move together.

She didn't care that soon she could be the Norden Point, and he'd still be the Suden Point. She didn't care that they weren't supposed to be together.

She only cared about the rhythm they created that was all their own. Their pleasure built together this time. His head fell to the crook of her neck, his lips breathing out a prayer that sounded like her name as they both found their release.

CHAPTER FORTY-ONE

S he woke with her limbs entangled with Luc's. Though it was very intentional this time, there was still no possible way to get up without alerting him. Even as she considered it, his eyes popped open and found hers.

"Good morning," he said.

"Good morning," she replied, evaluating his sleepy but self-satisfied smirk. There was no way to wipe it off, not after last night. As she stretched out languidly, she decided that he had earned it.

"Do we need to have an awkward regret conversation?"

She couldn't hold back the laugh. "Coffee first might be nice."

His face closed off as he started to get himself up to fulfill her request.

"Luc." She pulled him back to her. "It was a joke. No regret conversations to be had. Although, it is traditional to ease a new partner into these types of conversations, not just attack them first thing in the morning with it."

His smile was back, the one that was all teeth. The one that she wasn't sure she would ever tire of. "I have heard that before, but I've never been great at relationships."

"First…" She put up a finger. "We've allegedly been in a relationship for a week, so…you should be better. Second…" She lifted the second finger on her hand. "It's also frowned upon to jump right into relationship discussion after bedding someone." She paused thoughtfully. "Though the rules may not apply if you were already in a fake relationship with them."

"I'll take that under advisement for any future relationships."

She playfully pushed him away. "Okay, that's about enough of that. You can go get me that coffee now."

"Not a chance," he said as his arm snaked out to pull her to him. He kissed her lazily. This wasn't the fierce passion of last night but the slow, deliberate exploration from one who is confident he has all the time in the world. Her body responded immediately, arching into him as he pulled her closer.

"We really should get up," he breathed when their lips parted. "We don't want to be late for the Ceremony."

She sighed. She'd been trying to forget that they had to return to Norden house this morning. The summer solstice was a two-part endeavor. First the evening ball, and then the following day, the Compass Points and the elders from each fae court met at the Norden beach to perform a ceremony on the lake, replenishing their power as part of the Covenant with the gods at the fae's creation.

Today would be the day. She'd been seen as the savior of Compass Lake Village. She'd been seen to have the Suden Point's support. She'd gone toe to toe with Aiden last night, though she wouldn't say she'd won precisely.

She needed to find Arie. To understand what he knew about Aiden and, she suspected, about the mist plague.

Luc's lips trailed down her neck, interrupting her to-do list and leaving her wondering why they had to get out of bed. Images from last night flooded her mind, and she shivered in delight as her body started to warm again in want.

"Rose, are you decent?" came the coy question from just outside the window. Rose rolled her eyes, pushing herself up and ending their activities that had just been getting started.

"Arie's here," she said to Luc as she pulled on some clothes and went to open the window. Luc headed to the closet to do the same.

"I see you took my advice," Arie said as he flew into the room in bird form.

"How could you possibly know that?"

"I've been sitting outside the window for a long time just waiting for the least awkward moment to interrupt."

"And you thought listening at the window was less awkward than interrupting?" Her eyes rolled again inadvertently.

"Your eyes will get stuck that way if you keep this up," he replied.

"Where did you go last night? Did you figure out whatever you needed to confirm?" she asked. She needed to know what she was working with before she moved against Aiden.

"You're going to pretend you didn't see me on the beach?"

She remembered the fire and the black cat she'd sworn she'd seen fleeing from the shed last night.

"Arie." She glared at him. "You said you had to leave! What did you do?"

"Oh, nothing you won't forgive me for. I ensured no one was in the shed or close enough to get hurt. We just needed to remind the Norden Point who they were messing with. I think it went perfectly."

She held in another eye roll, but just barely. "That was rather reckless. What if I hadn't stepped in?"

"Oh, there was no chance of that. You are quite predictable in that regard. Less so when it comes to sticking to a 'fake dating' plan, emphasis on fake,*"* he said dryly as his black eyes turned toward Luc, stepping out of the closet, dressed for the day.

Rose knew he was joking since he'd encouraged her just last night, but she enjoyed watching Luc squirm as Arie's piercing glare remained directed at him.

"Keep in mind, I can only hear half the conversation," Luc said, raising his hands. "But let's remember I am not the bad guy here."

"He always thinks it's about him." Arie probably would have rolled his eyes, but it was hard to accomplish as a bird.

"Well, we are staring at him. And honestly, Arie, you look menacing." She couldn't help but smile. They still had a lot to do, but she was happy. She walked over to Luc and let him wrap his arms around her, a rather affectionate move, but she wanted him to know there was no real question about him.

"Arie is just being overprotective while also being a troublemaker. Did you catch that he directed the firework that started the fire last night?"

Luc nodded. "A risk, but it paid off. Most of Compass Lake witnessed your water magic on display. It was protecting them from the fire and delighting them with the continued water show. That, plus the wild tales about you singlehandedly fighting off dozens of Nebulus. I think it's safe to say that everyone knows you are a powerful Norden."

She nodded in agreement.

"At least he gets it," chimed in Arie.

"I didn't say I didn't get it, Arie. I just said it was dangerous, and it might have been helpful to talk to me first before manipulating me into a position!"

"Noted."

She looked at Arie, ready to press him further on what he had needed to confirm before the fireworks and why it was so quick, but Luc interrupted her thoughts.

"Let's get going," Luc said. "We don't want to be late."

"I'll meet you over there," Arie said as he flew out the window he'd come in.

Chapter Forty-Two

Sooner than she cared to, Rose and Luc stepped from their boat and on to Norden house beach. Rose took Luc's hand and felt the Norden seat's power fill her. He squeezed back as they made their way through the crowd.

Their moment of happiness didn't last long as the other Compass Points met them on the beach. Carter gave Rose a bashful smile. Juliette nodded, though she raised her brow when only Rose was looking.

Rose turned to face Aiden. For a moment, it was just the two of them. His blue eyes shone brightly in the morning sun. He looked so much like her childhood friend today. Her stomach roiled; Rose wished she knew more. She wished she'd had time to press Arie on what she was dealing with. She needed to know if her friend was still in there at all. If there was a chance he wasn't wholly responsible for her family's brutal deaths. Some part of her, she suspected, wanted to know her friend hadn't destroyed her life on his own.

"I doubt it will help if I point out that guests aren't allowed at the Ceremony?" The moment over, Aiden directed his words to Luc.

"It's on the beach, Aiden. Everyone comes to the lake's edge to watch. If it makes you feel better, Rose can stand a few steps away from us to preserve the exclusivity of your Ceremony."

"Now, now, boys," Juliette tsked. "The Compass Points remain indebted to Rose, don't you agree, Aiden?" She ran her fingers carelessly through her long hair as she said, "We can't make a hero, a returning Norden, watch from the sidelines."

Rose stiffened imperceptibly at Juliette's words. "A returning Norden." Rose knew she'd exposed herself as more than half-fae last night. The wielding of water could only be done by a Norden fae. No, the word that caught Rose off guard was Juliette's use of *returning*.

Aiden glared at Juliette, knowing she had painted him into a corner. He couldn't make Rose leave now.

"Fine." He pointed to the beach. "Stand over there. Don't get in the way."

Rose walked over to the water's edge and sank to her knees, the proper observance of the ceremony to honor balance with the gods. She tried to get a handle on the Norden magic she was feeling. She assumed it had something to do with this morning's ceremony.

She felt her magic dance with the lake water as the Compass Points began.

"Let's get this over with," was Aiden's inspirational speech. While it was mostly the Compass Points in hearing distance, Rose's gaze skimmed the Norden elders farther up the hill, whispered amongst themselves at the Norden's disrespect.

Aiden began the ceremony, walking up to the lake's edge before them so that his bare feet touched the water. Rose could feel his magic spiral into the lake as he stood in the shallows. It wasn't so much an offering as a command for the lake to do his bidding. He wanted the lake water to move away from his toes and towards the lake's center. The Norden Point's job in this ceremony was to control the lake water, such that it erupted like a geyser in the very center of the lake, and the rest of the lake bed was exposed to the elements.

Aiden pushed with what Rose considered to be a surprising

amount of raw power. His magic carried that older, darker scent. She was sure his Norden magic was corrupted by whatever force he partnered with.

The lake started to recede from the shoreline on which Aiden stood. As she watched, it began to retreat into the center of the circular lake, leaving only the muddy earth behind.

This part of the ceremony was usually the quickest. The Norden Point moved the lake water while the others poured their earth, fire, and wind magic into the exposed lake bed. Their magic burned and turned the land below the water. No piece of the lake bed was left untouched, so the land would start new and refreshed, when the water crashed back over it. The combination of fire, wind, and earth magic usually took a while to work through all that was left without the water.

From her vantage point, sweat dripped down Aiden's brow. The water was giving him trouble. He continued to exert his magic, but it came at a high physical cost. She was just close enough to hear parts of his mumbling.

"Help me," she heard him say, but he certainly wasn't looking at her.

"What good are you .... can't .... complete this simple task."

The words drifted on the wind to where she knelt in the sand. It sounded tense. Aiden wiped the sweat off his brow before balling his hands into fists at his sides as he tried to control the water.

Rose quickly made eye contact with Luc. She hadn't seen this ceremony in years. But she was sure that this wasn't normal. Luc responded with a shrug.

Despite his efforts, Aiden had only managed to push the water a few yards from the shore. He had much more to do to create and hold the traditional lake geyser the ceremony required. Minutes ticked by. The crowd of Norden elders grew restless and murmurs passed among the attendees.

"What is he waiting for?"

"He's been acting so strange."

"I don't know if he can do it."

At the last comment, Aiden's legs shook. He was pushing too hard, but the water was giving nothing.

Rose looked back at the Compass Points again. Aiden was not going to complete his task, their faces agreed, but no one seemed sure what to do.

Rose, already on her knees at what used to be the edge of the lake, closed her eyes. She offered thanks to the gods, no matter how distant they'd been, for bringing her back to her home, introducing Luc into her life, and for Arie, her inconstant companion.

Things weren't great on the continent, but they were good enough for individuals to find pockets of joy and thrive. Rose imagined dozens of scenarios of simple joy, from the villagers she'd met, to the Compass Point elders to Tara and her constant faith. She gave thanks on behalf of them to the gods as she called on her Norden magic.

The water rolled through her body like a mighty wave crashing. By helping Aiden with the ceremony, she discovered that she had access to more power than she realized. She focused her attention on the barely receding water and gently coaxed it to the center of the lake. It moved quickly, just like her water show last night. The water bent to her will with little effort as it rolled to the lake's center and crashed into a powerful jet stream shooting up into the sky.

For all his facade as the Norden Point, Aiden was utterly at a loss as to what had just happened, and it showed. He had given up all pretense of attempting to use water magic and was staring around in bewilderment.

"What is going on?!" he whisper-yelled, knowing there was no way to hide his lack of involvement from the others but not wanting to proclaim his confusion to anyone watching from the shore.

Though Luc's gaze immediately snapped to Rose when the water receded, he was unwilling to point her out to Aiden.

Juliette, it turned out, had no such qualms. "It seems you've been replaced," she cooed, pointing toward Rose's bent body. It was held in a pose of gratitude to the gods, not the position of exhaustion that Aiden had been in only moments ago.

"Unbelievable. She can't lead the ceremony."

"It seems she can, and she is." Juliette flicked her hand palm up, wind rushing around her. "If you'll excuse me, I must complete my part of the ceremony now. Though she doesn't look too stressed, I don't want Rose to hold the water longer than necessary."

Juliette walked to the shoreline, pushing her wind over the exposed lakebed. Luc glanced at Aiden as though making sure he wouldn't do anything rash while Rose was in a somewhat helpless position on the ground. Once he seemed sure Aiden wouldn't lunge for her, he headed to the newly uncovered lakebed and used his earth magic to turn it over. Lastly, the Vesten Point called on his fire magic to scorch all that remained. The Compass Points worked as a unit, quickly and efficiently to complete their task.

When they were finished, they turned to Rose.

She felt something like a sigh of relief from the water as she released the erupting spout and let the water pour back over the lakebed. She knew, without opening her eyes, that the lake had already stretched back out to its shores.

Just like the wave that had rolled through her body when she'd taken over the ceremony, a reverse flow cascaded through her as she completed it, moving her body back up to sit on her knees. She opened her eyes to find the four Compass Points staring at her with looks varying from awe to anger.

Meeting Luc's eye, she winked at him as he made his way up the beach. The wink, though not for him, proved too much for Aiden.

"What the hell do you think you're doing, Rose?"

Chapter Forty-Three

A iden charged toward her, anger in every one of his long strides as he approached her spot on the beach. She got to her feet, not wanting to be talked down to, literally or figuratively.

"I guess I was doing what you couldn't, Aiden. You're welcome, by the way." She gestured out to the lake behind them. "Do we know what would have happened if the ceremony hadn't been completed?" She looked around at the Compass Points who had joined them. "I think you were about to find out."

Barely contained rage crept into every feature on his face. "You can't just show up here and take over the Norden Point's sacred ceremony."

It was her turn for the rage to flit across her face. More than anyone, he knew she could and should show up at Compass Lake and take over the Norden ceremonies. Now and forever.

She was the true Norden Point. If this didn't prove it, she wasn't sure what would.

"I think Juliette said it best. I can, and I did." Her spine straightened. "What were you even doing at the lake's edge? Were you talking to yourself?"

"That's none of your gods' damn business, Rose."

Luc echoed, "I'd love to know as well." The Osten and Vesten Points nodded from the sideline.

"Who were you talking to? And what would you have done if Rose didn't step in?" Carter piped in nervously. "It's not like we had multiple chances at the Ceremony, Aiden. We're all just concerned at the chaos and destruction the gods would have unfurled had we been unable even to complete our part of the Covenant." Carter, at least, seemed genuinely concerned though it appeared he was the only one.

Aiden took a moment to glare at Carter before turning back to Luc and Rose.

"We would have figured it out." He spat out each word. "We had it under control."

"Who is 'we,' Aiden? This was your job. It's already a time of crisis for the continent with the mist plague. Messing this up was not an option, and you did not have it under control," Rose shot back.

She saw the change the moment it happened. The ageless grey color descended over Aiden's bright blue eyes.

"Aiden?" she questioned, knowing it was no longer him.

"While it seems the rest of the Compass Points thank you for participating in today's ceremony, I do not. Do not trespass at Norden house again."

Her mind spun at the audacity. This was her home. He was in her place. Whatever, *who*ever this was, they needed to go. She'd had just about enough of them.

"Aiden." She steeled her voice as he walked away from her and back to the house. "I may be a guest of the Suden Point, but let's be clear, I am the rightful Norden Point."

That dangerous rage was back as Aiden turned to face her. "I'm not sure what you mean by that," he said coolly.

"I am the most powerful Norden, and I've proved it with my magic twice in as many days. I passed the Norden Point test," she said loud enough for the elders to hear. Though she was sure they'd been listening to every word said on the beach. "You know it. It's why you tried to kill me ten years ago." She lifted her arms in a challenge. "But I'm still here, and where is your magic, Aiden?"

She barely had time to react as a dark funnel erupted from Aiden's outstretched hand. A tornado of sand, dirt, and rocks wrapped around the two of them, pulling them together on the beachfront of the Norden house.

"Don't you worry about my magic," Aiden bit out as his magic continued to surround them, making it difficult for Rose to move. "My magic is fine, and quite powerful, more so than any Norden's."

"What are you? Aiden, are you in there?" she asked, feeling foolish but having to try. "What have you done?" She pushed her magic against the wall of earth debris that wrapped around her.

"Are you responsible for the mist plague?" she asked.

"Always with the wild accusations, Rose. I'm surprised you didn't figure it out last night from your friend."

"Arie," she whispered mostly to herself. What did Arie have to do with this being? She pushed against the swirls of deadly dirt and rocks with her wind enough to give herself space to breathe. She no longer felt like the debris would suffocate her. With her circle of wind like a cloak wrapped around her, she stared down at Aiden.

"Is that what he's going by? He always was one for stupid nicknames."

As if their discussion of Arie called him to them, a black bird flew through the thick barrier of smoke, fighting against the deadly debris and wind. It reached Rose's shoulder.

Aiden glared at the bird. "We were just talking about you."

The familiar voice spoke aloud for her and Aiden to hear.

"What are you doing, Aterra? Interfering with the Compass Points is forbidden."

"A fun loophole," he said. "Turns out this one"—he pointed to himself in Aiden's form—"isn't actually the rightful Norden Point. So I didn't break any rules." He casually shrugged as the sandstorm spun around them. "You should talk. You've all but made that one your pet." He gestured to Rose.

"Point of fact, Aterra. Thanks to your schemes, she's not currently a Compass Point," Arie replied.

"Arie, what is going on?" Rose whisper-yelled. Her volume was irrelevant since they were all still confined within the swirling storm of earth, but she thought it would be nice to know why Arie was calling Aiden *Aterra*, the name of one of the gods, and not the lost god, Zrak.

"That's exactly what I'd like to know, Rose, but let me help with some introductions. Rose, meet Aterra, god of earth. He seems to have some agreement with the current Norden Point."

"Always sticking your nose where it doesn't belong, Arctos." Anger dripped from every one of Aterra's words.

"Aterra, Aurora, Zrak...Arctos..." Rose was whispering the names of the gods as she paused. She laughed. An inappropriate time, sure, but what choice did she have when she got to the last god, Arctos?

"Arie, short for Arctos, self-proclaimed Lord of Fire." Aterra laughed as he made what he seemed to suspect was Rose's first introduction to the Vesten god.

The bird transformed into a bear, putting himself between Rose and Aterra. He looked back at her, unable to smile in this form but showing off his teeth as he tilted his head at Rose.

"You're a god?" she asked. Shocked, but not. She fell back on sarcasm, her old standby, saying, "We need to talk about what's appropriate information to obscure in the future."

"Sure, sure, add it to the list." He laughed as he turned back to face the present threat. "Let's focus on your friend here and the unwelcome god inhabiting his body."

Rose's attention snapped back to Aiden. She might have a god on her side, but Aterra was still a threat. Arie hadn't moved against him, and she was beginning to suspect he knew what they'd been up against.

"What have you done with Aurora?" Arie growled. "Let her go."

"I'm afraid we can't do that," came Aterra's calm reply. "She has an important role to play in this game."

"So, what's your plan here?" Rose asked. "You pulled me into this tornado to what? Kill me again? You seem to have failed twice at that already."

"Enough!" Aterra yelled. "I don't need you two trying to understand something beyond your comprehension."

Arie snorted.

"Rose, you stand in my way again, this time I won't miss." Aterra lifted Aiden's hand and pulled the swirling storm of debris tighter around them closer. Rose flexed her shield of wind, expanding it to cover Arie. It continued to hold a slim layer between their bodies and the tornado of rocks and dirt, leaving it unable to bind them fully. The shield was thin enough, and Rose was sure that Aterra expected her to be Norden, not Norden and Osten. She hoped to hide this small protection from him. Let him think that he was suffocating them. Arie looked at her as if realizing that she was also protecting him. He switched back to the communication she knew and loved.

"I know I owe you some answers, but I wonder if you'll trust me enough to do something reckless to get us out of here."

She laughed inappropriately again. She wasn't sure how close Aiden was—the debris surrounding them blocking her vision—so she just nodded.

"Good. I'm going to give you a little boost. When you feel it, I need you to stretch this shield for all it's worth."

Rose nodded again at the too-simple instruction.

Before she could blink, the bear at her side melted away. Was he leaving? She didn't have to wait long for an answer as Arie's magic unmistakably merged with hers. He'd inhabited her, likely much the same way Aterra had with Aiden.

That *was* particularly reckless.

It seemed though, that she was in control of how to direct their combined magic. The power of the Lord of Fire surged through her. It straightened her spine and poured through her limbs, waiting for her command. There was no room to hesitate. Instead, she focused on Arie's words, *stretch the shield for all it's worth*, and she did.

She pushed her wind, no longer creating a thin barrier of protection but her own swirling cyclone that stretched and sent Aterra's tornado backwards. It circled him like he had been circling her and Arie. She pushed his cyclone closer to his skin, magically trapping him in his stolen body.

She wasn't sure what Arie had in mind for an endgame, but she had Aiden caged with no intention of letting him go. She did not have a sword with her for the Ceremony, but she had Aurora's dagger hidden in her high boots. She had kept it with her at all times since finding it. She pulled it out and took steps toward the captured god in Aiden's body.

Could she do this? She'd killed in battle when needed and in defense, but not someone disarmed. Not her childhood friend who made a deal with a god. Was Aiden in there? Did he bear responsibility for what he'd done?

She knew she needed to end this before Aterra found a way out. He was a god. He wouldn't stay trapped for long. Her steps quickened as she tried to close the gap between them.

The earth cracked around Aterra as Rose realized it was already too late. Her indecision had cost her. The ground shook and separated, creating a pit between her and the swirls of wind in which she'd tried to trap him.

She stopped running forward as the cracks in the earth expanded like shattering glass.

The sandstorm stopped as Aterra focused his magic on splintering the ground before them. Visible again on the beach, Rose glimpsed Luc running toward her just as the earth split around Aterra and pulled Aiden's body down into the giant chasm.

Chapter Forty-Four

Luc and Rose both moved in stilted steps forward to the hole that had swallowed Aterra. They both knew it was too late. He was gone. He was not dead, of that Rose was sure, but Aterra's power had opened up the ground and swallowed him whole.

Rose was sure she would see Aiden and Aterra again, likely too soon.

She leaned over the crack in the earth as she and Luc reached its edge. Luc gently took her hand as she surveyed its unknown depths, lacing their fingers together, anchoring her. She smiled at him even as guilt gnawed on her for not moving faster to strike when she had the chance.

He was still out there.

And if she understood Arie correctly, Aterra was holding Aurora hostage somewhere. With so much unbalance between the gods, she knew the Compass Points needed to act. She still wasn't sure how it was connected, but she knew the plague of mists was a part of this. She knew that to remove the blight from the continent, she would need to rein in Aterra. She just felt like she was missing some connecting dots.

She looked around, her eyes searching for her own mischievous god.

Arctos, Lord of Fire.

Arie, her family.

"I know you missed a lot, but one thing I have to take care of before we plan our next steps." She pointed at the raven sitting on a low tree branch. "That is Arctos, Lord of the Flame, and he owes me some answers."

Luc's mouth opened and closed before he shook his head. "Figures," he replied. He squeezed her hand. "I'll hold off the others then wait by the lake."

She watched him go, then turned to stare at the bird. She knew he wouldn't force their conversation but would not leave without talking to her, either. He'd give her the space she needed to decide what his being a god meant. She walked over to his perch.

"Why don't you come down here, Arctos." She drew out the syllables of his full name. "So we can talk."

"Are you going to yell at me?"

"You are an ageless god, Arctos. Why don't you grow up and come down here to find out." She sat down, back to the tree in which he sat. He flew down, turning into a black cat before reaching the ground. He padded up next to her seat, sitting back on his haunches.

"Ok, I'm ready."

"Ready for what?" she asked.

"For you to yell at me."

"And why should I do that, Arctos?"

"Arie, please. You should do that because I…because…are you really going to make me explain it?" The cat tilted its head to the side, seeming to evaluate her sanity.

"Yes, Arie, why don't you tell me why I should yell at you."

He sighed deeply. So heavily she thought she could see the ageless god for once instead of the entertaining companion.

"I didn't tell you who I was. We were family, but I didn't share things with you and revealed the truth inconveniently."

"Very," she hmphed, crossing her arms over her chest. "I'm not mad at you, Arie. You were always honest enough for me to know that you played by your own rules. You didn't ask about my magic, though now I'm sure you were well aware of it, and I didn't ask about yours. I just had no idea the scale of what you were hiding." She looked into the cat's piercing yellow eyes as she finished the thought. "Why didn't we talk about it? You knew what I was, right? Was that why you were with me?"

The cat blinked a few times. *"I did know who and what you were—all of it. At first, I was just focused on keeping you alive. You were too important of a player to leave to chance."*

"But then you and I had so much fun together. Even in your grief. Even in mine. We have a natural rapport, you and me. I'm not sure if you've noticed."

It struck her then. His grief. His regret. His lost love.

"Is it Aurora?" she asked quietly.

He nodded. *"I'm sure you realize I have more to lose in this game than I let on. And if I told you who I was…"* He paused, his tail flicking as he thought about his next words. *"If I told you what was at stake and what I needed you to do, it would have changed everything. I didn't want that."*

Rose let a soft smile cross her lips. "I like our relationship too, Arie."

"Destiny was always going to come for you. Whether in the form of the dangerous Suden Point or something else. I knew someday we'd have to face that I was Arctos and you were the rightful Norden Point. I just found myself not wanting to be the one to force that upon us." If a cat could shrug, he did.

"I can't pretend to understand what you're up to, but I love you, Arie, and I am happy for our time together. I'm here if you need me, no matter what kind of godly games you play."

The cat straightened, as if realizing he'd been acting far too human. *"Glad to hear it, because we've got some work to do."*

"Let's go get Luc. He's probably going to need to hear this."

CHAPTER FORTY-FIVE

Luc waited down by the water. Though they'd started first thing in the morning, the day had slipped away. He'd briefly spoken to those gathered on the beach before he sat on the shore. Even while speaking to Arie, Rose caught his gaze intermittently falling to various Norden elders as they seemed to get enough courage to confront her. Even with his shoes off, pants rolled up, and toes dipping in the lake, a glare from the Suden Point held anyone who tried to interrupt her in their place. Luc's shirt sleeves were rolled back. He was trying too hard to look relaxed. He'd placed himself far enough away that he couldn't see or hear Arie and Rose's conversation.

While it was thoughtful of him to give them their time alone, Rose knew she needed Luc for whatever was next. Whatever Arie, or Arctos, would unveil about how to fix their world, she knew Luc would face it with her. She suspected they'd need all the Compass Points.

She padded down to the beach and plopped down next to him, her shoeless feet splashing into the water. Arie's cat form followed.

"So I'm assuming you can talk to both of us simultaneously, Arie. Don't make me play your translator for Luc just because you're lazy."

Luc choked on a laugh next to her. "Doesn't the Lord of Fire demand your respect?" he joked as he gently knocked Rose's shoulder with his own.

"*You two are going to be a problem, aren't you?*" came Arie's voice, clearly into both of their minds. Luc looked at her and then back at the cat.

"That is unnerving. You like it when he does that?" Luc said, looking at Rose pointedly.

"I never said it was pleasant, but it's better than me having to repeat everything for you." She shrugged.

"So let's start with how much you could hear, Luc."

"Not much. The dust storm kept us away, and the conversation isolated to those in the cyclone."

"In summary, Aiden is Aterra, Aterra is holding Aurora hostage, and..." She let the sentence hang, unfinished. "Well, I think Arie's going to need to fill in the last part. How is this connected to the plague of mist?"

"This can't be headed anywhere good," Luc muttered as he pulled his feet out of the water and half-turned himself to look back at Arie, who refused to get closer to the water in his cat form.

"*Well. That part is interesting. You were definitely on to something with the mist's connection to the Lost God. I'm still unsure how Zrak is doing it, but he does control the mist.*"

"So put Zrak on the enemy list. Check," Rose noted.

"*I wouldn't be so sure,*" Arie replied. "*His methods certainly call forth questions, but I think he used the plague of mists to expose Aterra's interference with the Compass Points. After the creation of the fae and the Compass Points, part of the Covenant was that the gods vowed not to interfere with them. They were to hold us in check, keep us in balance. Manipulating one of them inherently disregards that promise.*"

"You're saying Zrak was trying to make Aterra's control over Aiden known?" Luc questioned.

"*I think so. I did try to speak with him at multiple locations where the plague spread, but he was either silent or too vague with his words. I* can feel his power clearly, though. It's unmistakable. I assume that's how you could guess it was his as well, Rose. Your Osten line couldn't help but recognize its creator even if you didn't understand it."

Rose pursed her lips, thinking over what Arie was saying. "But the attacks. Why leave the Suden people alone when it was the Norden Point that was rotten? And why were Luc and I unaffected by the mist?"

"Aterra is the god of the Suden people," Luc reminded. "It may have been a backward attempt to try and point to the problem, but the mist left Aterra's villages alone."

"Zrak needs to work on his pointers. That is murky at best."

Luc chuckled. "Make sure you tell him that."

"If you two are done..." Arie cut back in. *"I agree. Not Zrak's most obvious sign, but he is a god. He would point to the god he wanted to be exposed first; the fae Aterra took hold of would be secondary."*

"Why didn't he tell you that when you tried speaking to the mist?"

"No one, not even the gods, knows what happened to Zrak when he sacrificed himself. I don't know where he resides or what power is available to him, but you were right on the beach—a sacrificed god is likely not really dead."

Rose took the win but there was no joy in it. Zrak's involvement only complicated matters further.

"What about why the mist didn't impact Rose or me?" Luc brought them back to the question at hand.

"I think, again, we can thank Rose's lineage. My belief is that it had to do with your weapons. Though you tailor your magical blades to the power of the user, you can't help but put some of yourself into them," Arie explained. *"I've seen it while you worked. Those blades bore the Osten wind. I think that that kept the mist at bay. It would have been like fighting itself."*

"I didn't realize," Rose said, looking at her fingers as she rubbed her hands together. "But Osten fae fell to the mist...."

They did, but we have no idea the strength of their magic. The Osten magic you mold into your weapons is quite concentrated, Rose. Almost as powerful as your Norden line.

"And so, what, you two confronted Aterra on the beach, and he took an escape hatch through the earth?"

"Basically."

I'm sure he just transported himself to safety, wherever he thinks that is.

"So what next?" Luc asked, and Rose put her hand on his knee.

Our first goal is to install Rose as Norden Point, Arie replied.

"Arie, that's so five problems ago. Does it mean anything now?"

First, it is yours. It was always yours. Second, it is a current problem and will remain a problem. A false Norden Point still means that the Compass Points themselves aren't balanced. It breaks the strength of the entire system. How can an unbalanced Compass keep the gods in check?

"You'd think the gods might have put rules in place to prevent this from happening," Rose said dryly.

"You're pushing your luck here, Rose," Luc said, though he couldn't conceal his laugh.

I'm going to ignore that comment.

"So, what, I tell the elders it's me? That I'm the rightful Norden Point?"

"I think they already heard you say that, along with the other Compass Points," Luc pointed out.

Rose looked around. The Norden elders were still clustered on the hill. Juliette and Carter stood slightly apart but in the same area. They must have moved up there when the sandstorm started. She was sure they had a lot of questions. She was sure many of them had opinions about what should happen next. Likely some that she would disagree with.

"You think I should become the Norden Point?" Rose asked as she turned back to Luc. Her eyes searched for something in his. She wasn't quite sure what she hoped to find.

"The better question is, why wouldn't you?" he replied.

"If it was so easily stolen and corrupted, is it something I want to be a part of?" she asked. "And I just found you. What if they try and make me give you up," she added in an even softer voice.

"The seat is what you make it. You know that." Luc tilted her chin upwards, forcing her to meet his eyes. "And you and I get to decide what happens between us." His voice was that of the commanding Suden Point. "No one else does."

"I hoped you'd say that," she said, looking back at Arie, who was staring out over the water, tail flicking as the only indication that he was listening.

"I agree with Luc. About both points. Of course, the elders will fight you on the latter, but change is always a struggle for the fae courts."

"Fine, I'll do it. And after that?"

"With the Compass Points' strength returned, we'll have to go after Aterra. I'm sure the mist won't stop until he's taken care of."

With a deep sigh, Rose asked, "Is that all? Do you think we can go home now?" She noticed the word as soon as it had slipped out. She'd been thinking of Suden house and had said *home*. She looked at Luc and found his warm brown eyes waiting for hers. They brought their own light to the beach as the sun set, casting a dusting of reds, blues, and purples cascading through the clouds.

He'd caught her phrasing too.

"I think you've had enough for one day," Arie replied. *"We start early tomorrow. Though you two should go clear things up with the others. They look antsy."*

She got up from her seat on the beach and walked with Luc to give a brief explanation to the elders and remaining Compass Points. They were not thrilled with Rose and Luc's assertion that there was nothing more to be done tonight. But with a promise to begin work early tomorrow morning, they reluctantly let them return to Suden house.

Rose dropped herself into the boat she and Luc had used to get across this morning. Luc joined her with much more grace. Arie leaped off the shore in cat form, but before he could hit the water, he turned into a raven and soared.

"I'll catch up with you two later," he said as he flew away.

Luc paddled them across the lake in the setting sun. It was even more peaceful than usual. Given the day's events, no one else was on the water. They were all probably hiding. The reds and pinks in the sky faded into a deep blue as the sun went down behind the trees.

"Red sky at night, sailor's delight," Rose whispered as they were about to hit the shore at the Suden house.

"I don't think there are any sailors on this lake," Luc teased.

"I think it's just a good omen."

"Oh, we're looking for omens now?"

"I'd say we're looking for any indicators that we can stop Aterra and the mist."

Luc shook his head as he hopped out of the boat. He offered a hand to Rose to help her out.

"We've thought about Aterra just about enough for today."

"He did try to kill me. A third time."

"Acknowledged," Luc chuckled. "I'd rather think about what we can do to forget that, at least until tomorrow." He ran his hands up and down her arms, spreading warmth with every inch he touched.

"If I'm to be the Norden Point, Luc, it's quite inappropriate for you to touch me like this." She couldn't keep the smile from her lips. And Luc couldn't help but move closer with her words.

"I think this lake is ready for a scandal."

"Like the Norden Point and Suden Point sharing a bed?" Her voice was low and mischievous.

"That sounds exactly like the scandal we're looking for." Kissing her slowly, he wrapped his arms around her waist and pulled her closer to him like he couldn't get enough. Her response was automatic, wrapping her arms around his neck and running her fingers through his hair.

She knew tomorrow would bring more problems. Like fighting with the elders about becoming the Norden Point while sharing the Suden Point's bed. Or rallying the Osten and Vesten Points to fight Aterra, figuring out what Zrak was up to, and stopping the mist.

With more problems than she could process, Rose sank herself into Luc's kiss. Tomorrow's problems would greet her with the sun, but tonight, tonight she'd enjoy one more night without the responsibility of a Compass Point.

ACKNOWLEDGMENTS

As Bridgerton's Lady Whistledown would start, Dear, Gentle Reader, THANK YOU. Ok, that diverged quickly…Anyway, thank you for taking the time to read about Rose and Luc and the magical world of the Compass Points. I hope you enjoyed reading it as much as I enjoyed writing it.

To Ian and Loki for listening to me talk at them for months, maybe years. To Josh, my intern at Myth and Magic Book Club, I see you. I appreciate you. Like. From Jill. To Katie, my partner in crime, I wouldn't have done it without you. To my mom, who doesn't even like fantasy but is my biggest fan. To Rebecca, you break me, but you make me better. To all the friends and family who supported me along the way---I'm thankful for each of you.